CW01091327

STA

SECRETS

A CALVERT NOVEL

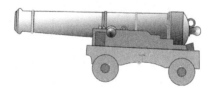

By
LEIGHTON
HARDING

STATE SECRETS

This Novel is written in British English and the spelling reflects that fact!

Cover design by the Author

To my Wife and Editor, with much thanks.

STATE SECRETS

STATE SECRETS

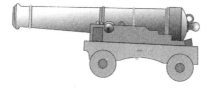

Commander William Calvert sat on an upturned wine box. He was desultorily picking weeds from a small raised area of dried earth which showed no sign of any plants. The Commander was 25 years old, with a strong face dominated by a pair of bright blue eyes over a broken nose. His black hair was tied back in a sailors queue, but a lock kept falling over one eye. The year was 1801 and he was a prisoner of war. The British were at war with the French Revolutionary Government. It was a war that could drag on for years, and there was no sign of a peaceful settlement. William and his crew had been prisoners for twenty-two months. His schooner *Snipe* had sprung its timbers off the north coast of France whilst trying to deliver an agent. They had carried out many of these trips before, but the schooner had long needed a refit. She had been damaged in one of the many engagements with the enemy. At the last refit, the new timbers had not been properly seasoned so had sprung. William had sent many messages to the Admiralty pleading for the suspect timbers to be replaced.

Despite having been patched with canvas and tar, the waves had finally won the battle. Will had been forced to beach the schooner to save lives. Now he sat trying to pass the time in the fortress of Verdun.

The fortress was really a large gun emplacement shaped like a multi faceted star. The accommodation was a series of buildings that had originally housed the Garrison. The rations were meagre to say the least. The fortress housed only the officers of the ships of the Royal Navy, that had been captured by the French. William had found himself virtually the senior officer, when a captain had been taken off by the French as being insane.

There were a string of buildings where the officers were accommodated according to rank. William as a commander was now the most senior officer amongst those held there. His square chin and broken nose gave him a pugilistic look relieved by the laughter lines at the corners of his eyes. He had a ready smile and an infectious laugh that endeared him to his colleagues. He had achieved his rank early as a result of having been the Sailing Master of a frigate where he had taken over when his captain had been knocked out at the start of an engagement. Whilst he was in charge of the quarter deck he had managed to sink two French frigates at the same time. He had fought at the Battle of Cape St. Vincent as a young Lieutenant and been noticed by Admiral Lord St. Vincent. As a result he had been promoted early to the rank of Commander and been given the American built schooner *Snipe* to attack the French invasion craft being assembled along the north coast of France and the Low Countries. Again he had excelled and then been given the task of landing secret agents on the coast of France. After two and a half years of success the

2

schooner had finally paid the price of inferior workmanship.

Will was trying to start a garden using potato peel and off cuts from any vegetables that he could glean from the cookhouse. The weather had been particularly dry for April and therefore his little vegetable bed was virtually dust. He had tried to instigate all kinds of games, competitions, and sporting events to try and occupy the inmates time. He was lucky that his first Lieutenant - James Craddock and Lieutenant Kemp were housed in the same block as himself. The midshipman and the warrant officers were in another building. The French paid little attention to the prisoners other than providing the terrible food once a day. If there had been any means of escape William would only have taken it if he had been able to do so with all of his crew from HMS *Snipe*. It might have been possible to have made up ropes from the sparse blankets, but once one was able to get to the bottom of the high walls, there was the town, the guards and then over 100 miles to the coast. The coast was swarming with soldiers that made up the French invasion force preparing to invade England. The Seamen and the Marines from *Snipe* were not in the same prison. William had no idea where they were incarcerated.

When their ship had floundered, the secret agent had managed to escape along with the surgeon who was a French royalist, and William's servant Thomas Tucker. William had no idea why Thomas had gone with the surgeon. Not that he would have been any use as a servant in the prison.

William's mind was miles away when he suddenly realised that somebody was approaching him. He looked up to find it was the Camp Commandant. Unusually the Commandant had a broad smile on his face. He was a wizened little man with a pockmarked, fox like face, but today he was beaming. Will stood up to show respect; he had found it helped in his dealings with the man.

"My friend, my friend." Said the Commandant; in guttural French, advancing towards him.

Will was extremely surprised; the Commandant had never spoken to him like this before. The Commandant came up and put out his hand to be shaken. Will automatically took it and they shook hands.

"We are at peace." The Commandant said.

"I beg your pardon." Said Will.

"We are at peace!" The Commandant said slowly to make it very clear.

"How do you know?" Asked Will.

"Today they agree to a cessation of war."

There had been no indications that a peace was in the offing. If it was true, it was wonderful news; if it wasn't it would depress the junior members of camp.

Normally the Commandant was always complaining that being a commandant of a prison camp was like being a prisoner oneself. Today he was in joyful mood.

"We'll go home!" He said.

"When?" Asked Will.

"Oh! I don't know." He said vaguely, waving his hands in his usual Gallic manner.

"But soon!"

"If we really are at peace at long last, will you do me a favour?"

"My friend, of course!" Replied the Commandant.

"Will you keep asking about transport to get us to the coast?"

"Oh!" Said the Commandant. "I will see what I can do."

With that he turned on his heel and walked away, waving one hand in the air.

The curiosity got the better of the Lieutenants, lounging outside their hut. One of them detached himself from the group and strolled over.

He was a tall angular man, considerably older than Will. He had been a prisoner long before Will and the crew of *Snipe* had arrived. At first he seemed to resent the fact that Will was much younger, but senior to him. Craddock had taken him aside and explained the reason why Will had been promoted at so early an age. His records said it all.

After that the man had been friendlier, though still reserved in his dealings with Will. He never used the correct form of address "Sir" when speaking to Will, but Will ignored it for a quiet life.

"What was all that about?" The Lieutenant asked, leaving off the Sir as usual.

"Says that a peace has been agreed today, and that we are all going home."

"Good God!"

"I suggest we don't mention it to the junior mess, just in case it is a rumour."

The Lieutenant eyed him for a moment and then nodded his head.

"When are we likely to know for certain?"

"I suppose when we are back in England!"

"May I tell the other members of our mess?"

"I suggest you say it is a rumour, for now."

"Very good, if you say so." And with that he wandered away, hands behind his back as if to the quarterdeck born.

Confirmation came in an unexpected manner. That evening the church bells began to ring out, discordantly, but they were still being rung for a reason. The republic had abolished the church. The clergy had been forced out of their offices. It had to be members of the public celebrating.

When the members of the other mess huts came over for an explanation, Will had to admit that the Commandant had indicated that a peace treaty was being signed.

Will regarded the assembled officers and warrant officers. They were a sorry sight. Their uniforms were worn and in some cases virtually thread-bare. Any gold braid was tarnished. Their foot-ware was in a terrible state after being forced to march for days from wherever they had been captured to Verdun.

There was no way of celebrating; they had no hidden supply of wine or any other drink. They were all dangerously thin, as they had to survive on one meal a day, and that was virtually inedible.

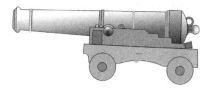

It took ten days for the French military to get their act together. An assortment of carriages was drawn up outside the main gate to the fortress. Most of them appeared to have been commandeered by the Army from aristocrats, because you could see under the badly painted sides, hints of coats of arms. Instead of the usual two horses; the coaches were designed for, there was one sorry looking apology for a horse. The Midshipmen and Warrant officers had to travel in long wheel base farm carts drawn by braces of oxen. The carts had canvas covers over rickety wooden hoops. Their drivers were soldiers, with a sergeant in charge.

Will was led to the lead coach as befitted his position as the most senior British officer present. The Commandant and a couple of his junior officers stood around to see them off.

What would have normally taken a day, took three days, because of the slow moving ox carts. At each stop, the sergeant tried to get them food, but the natives were so poor themselves, they were loath to provide anything. The French Army had taken most of the produce. It was only when they stopped at places that had garrisons, that they were able to get sufficient food, though it was hardly edible.

"You would think that the French would behave to officers in the same way as we do to their fellows." Commented one Lieutenant.

"It's because they have loped off the heads of the aristocrats, so they don't know any better." Came the reply.

French naval officers who were prisoners of the English were given the chance of giving their word of honour, and then free to be accommodated in private homes, and allowed to walk the streets.

It did not get any better when they finally arrived at Calais. There were no English vessels awaiting them. There were no English boats of any description in the harbour. The Sergeant was forced to keep them in their coaches and carriages or carts, whilst he sought the help of the garrison commander. Finally they were deposited outside a warehouse and told to dismount. The warehouse was damp and smelly. Fish had obviously been stored here, along with things that's odour could not be identified precisely. Later in the day a cart arrived with some soldiers, who dished out what was described as a stew, but certainly contained no meat of any type. There was the consolation, that they also provided freshly baked bread.

They were no longer prisoners of war, so there were no guards. They were free to wander around the town, in between the rain squalls. Will and Craddock strolled down to the port where the landing craft were moored. Will asked one of the French sailors who were wandering about to name the different types of vessel, which he did. It was information that Will stored away in case it would be useful.

It wasn't until two days had passed, with the rain coming through the roof, and nowhere to lie down in any comfort, and no covering, that finally a Packet boat put into harbour. Will accompanied by the sergeant and Boatswain Tarrant, went to the quayside to arrange passage. The captain of the packet told him to "Bugger off!"

Tarrant's massive frame shoved past Will and lifted the packet captain up in the air by his lapels.

"Don't you ever talk to my Captain like that! We are prisoners of war; we stopped them Frenchies from crossing that bit of sea behind you and raping

9

your women, whilst you had a cosy fire to return to. And I imagine you made a healthy living smuggling, didn't you? You are going to take these fine officers, or I am going to throw you over your pretty little ship into the 'hogging' behind you. If you try and get out, I will make it my business to see that I throw you further each time. Now do I make myself clear? Or do I make myself clear?"

The unfortunate captain had been trying to kick Tarrant, but the boatswain was so strong he could hold the man out of reach. The man nodded. Tarrant placed him carefully on the quay, brushed him down and said.

"I thought you would be reasonable under the circumstances."

It was not going to be possible to transport all the prisoners on the one ship, but luckily another packet arrived, so they were able to divide the number between the two.

All the prisoners filed down and onto the boats, making rude remarks to the sergeant, who didn't understand a word, so just grinned.

When the last of the prisoners was aboard, the sergeant waved good-bye and disappeared towards the town.

There were so many men crowded on the packet's deck, that the crew had difficulty in hoisting the sails, until the warrant officers came to their aid. As it was, the Channel was not kind to them, not only was there a short choppy sea, but it decided to rain on them, and there was nowhere to shelter. It was a very damp group of men who at last saw the white cliffs through the squalls.

When they entered Dover harbour, there was no sign of any Navy ship. Once they had disembarked, with shouted thanks to the bemused packet crew, Will suggested that they waited where they were, whilst he tried to sort something out. He asked the locals if anybody knew of any Naval Officers about, but met with shaking heads. He resorted to seeking out the town hall and asking to speak to the Mayor. This portly being, was shocked to discover that there was a group of British Naval Officers, wet through, just released from prison in France, and that nothing had been arranged for their arrival. He asked Will to wait whilst he went off to consult. An hour later he returned, with what Will took to be the entire town council. It had been decided that the officers should be given accommodation amongst the townsfolk, until the Admiralty could be contacted to sort out the mess. Will found himself lodging with the Mayor, a portly fellow, with a bustling air of self importance. The Mayor was persuaded to write a letter to the Board of Admiralty for immediate dispatch, by fast rider. Will was allowed to write his own letter, suggesting that it could be disastrous if the ordinary seamen arrived back and there was no organisation to send them on their way. The town would definitely suffer, and questions would be asked.

For the first time in months, Will and his fellow officers had edible food, and beer or wine. Even spirits were provided at some of the homes. The good people of Dover were extremely kind to the British Officers who made a sorry sight in their faded and darned uniforms. There was entertainment in the form of buffets with the young ladies vying with each other to sing the most popular ditty.

Three days later a clerk arrived, with two beefy bodyguards in a coach from London. This gentleman sought out Will and a room in the town hall was provided for him to issue travel warrants and a limited amount of money to each officer, so they could get to their homes.

Knowing that Tarrant had no home to go to, Will suggested he got a warrant to Totnes, and then he could make his way to Calvert House, near Totnes.

Will also left a note with the clerk for Allwood, his faithful coxswain, if he arrived at Dover, suggesting the same thing. He, himself once he had made sure things were running smoothly, got himself a warrant for London, together with a enough money (signed for) to provide sustenance for the journey.

Once in London he made his way straight to the Admiralty, where the doorman refused him entry at first. Patiently Will explained that he had been a prisoner of the French, and was not impersonating a naval Officer, as the doorman hinted. He had to promise a tip when he had funds, before he finally got through the doors. Once inside he had the same problem, before being shown into the hated waiting room. The room was full of Captains and other ranks waiting in the hope of an audience and a commission, as otherwise they would be on half-pay.

Will was shunned by the Captains, who looked askance at the scruffy Commander who joined them. Even the Lieutenants kept their distance. Will was forced to stand leaning against a wall waiting for a seat to become free. The trouble was other Captains seemed to join the swelling group. At the end of the first day, Will was forced to give up and return to his lodgings. The extra night meant he ran out of money completely; so he was forced to walk all the way to the Admiralty. A different pair of gate keepers gave him repeated grief, so he had to wait until a servant was sent to find out if there was such a person as Commander Calvert. Finally he was allowed in and returned to the crowded waiting room to undergo the ordeal once again. It wasn't until late in the afternoon of the second day, when Will had just about given up hope and was wondering where he could stay without money, that he was shown through to the Secretary to the Board.

Sir Evan Nepean, the distinguished Secretary to the Board of Admiralty, looked up as Will was announced, and then stood up to meet him.

"Sorry about the fiasco at Dover. Somebody here didn't do their job: probably my fault for not checking. You look terrible; if you don't mind my saying so. Was it very tough?"

"Mostly boring, and the food left a lot to be desired."

13

"Sit down, do." Nepean said indicating a chair. "Is it all being sorted at Dover now?"

"Yes Sir, the clerk is there, and the town folk know where sailors returning are to report. The Mayor and Council of Dover were very kind and helpful."

"I shall ask his Lordship to drop them a note. Of course you would not know, the Earl St Vincent, Lord Jervis is the new First Lord. You served in *Victory* under his command I believe."

"I had that honour, Sir!"

"I suppose you are after a ship?"

"Well, no Sir, actually I want to return to Devon and see if my fiancée will still marry me after all this time!"

Nepean smiled. "A very good idea, and get your health back, eh?"

"Yes Sir."

"Anything else?"

"Yes Sir, I was wondering about the Court Martial."

Nepean stared at him for a moment, and then laughed. "Of course, I suppose tradition has it that you should be Court Martialed for losing your ship, but I hardly think you should worry about that at the moment. Get married and wait and see what happens. Earl St. Vincent knows all about it. He has read all the signals. Anything else?"

"Is it possible to get some back pay, or at the very least a travel warrant."

"My dear fellow, of course, you won't have a farthing on you, will you?" He rang a bell and a servant arrived immediately. Nepean signed a note, handed it to the fellow and muttered something, Will didn't catch.

"By the way, had your Surgeon in here, together with your servant. Wanted to make sure we knew the stranding of *Snipe* was not your fault. They both wrote depositions to that effect. I was surprised at how well your servant wrote, very intelligent young man that."

"Yes, I intend to make him a Midshipman; if I ever get another command."

The Admiralty servant returned with a bulging leather bag, which chinked as he placed in front of Nepean. Nepean shoved it across to Will. "There you are, should keep you going for a bit!"

Will thanked the Secretary and stood up to leave, when the door to one side opened and in walked the older, but still imposing figure of Earl St. Vincent, victor of the battle of the same name, and now First Lord.

"Eh Nepean..." He stopped as he realised that Will was in the room.

"Good God, young Calvert isn't it?"

"Yes Sir!"

"Welcome back to mother England. Not had a good time by the looks of you! Improperly dressed I see!" Then he turned to Nepean. "Got anything for this young commander?"

"He hopes to be allowed to return to Devon to get married."

"Good for you Calvert; nothing better than a good wife to keep you on the straight and narrow –

what? Mark you. You can well afford to with all your prize money due. Pop in when you are free Nepean, will you?" The great man said to the Secretary, before turning back to Will.

"If we ever go to war again, and I think that is highly likely, I shall not forget you. We need young Nelsons like you."

"Thank you My Lord, and thank you Sir." Will said and he made for the door. As he went out he heard the Earl say. "Keep tabs on him Nepean, we....." and the door shut behind him.

He walked as fast as he could to the 'Swan with two necks', the coaching Inn from where the mail coaches to Exeter and Plymouth departed. For once his luck was in, there was a cancellation. He had to ride on the outside, and rain was in the air.

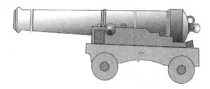

It was a very damp William who arrived in Exeter next morning soaked to the skin, and feeling very depressed. There were very few people about at that hour of the morning. He managed to find a coffee house that was open and ordered a coffee and buns. He had the feeling that he was steaming gently as he ate the buns and sipped the coffee. Feeling better he managed to buttonhole a likely looking fellow who was dressed as a clerk. He asked the fellow if he knew where he could find Kenton's bank. At first the clerk looked extremely apprehensive. Then he relented and indicated that the bank was two streets away on the left. Will strolled to where he had been told he could find the bank. Sure enough there was a Brass plate with the words 'Kenton's Bank' inscribed on it. The troubled was that the doors were firmly locked. At least it wasn't raining, so Will was able to loiter about until he saw a dark suited gentlemen arrive and unlock the doors. However, when William tried to gain access he found that the inner doors were firmly locked. He discovered a bell to one side and pulled the handle. He could hear the bell sounding faintly in the distance.

"We're not open!" Came a faint voice from inside.

Will had nothing for it but to wait until the bank opened its doors to the public. A good hour later, other clerks began to arrive. Will stopped an elderly looking Clerk who he judged might hold a responsible position.

The man recoiled in fright when William asked if the bank was open. The man looked him up and down, and Will realize that he must look like a vagabond.

"Excuse me; will Mr. Kenton be in today?"

17

"I don't know. You had better speak to the manager."

Will thanked the man and followed him through the inner doors. Here he was stopped by a burly doorman.

"You can't come in here - who do you think you are?"

"I am Commander Calvert of His Majesty's Britannic Navy. I have come to see Mr. Kenton." Replied Will,

The doorman hesitated, he was on dangerous ground. He put up a hand and said. "Stay there, I shall have to have a word with the Manager."

A few minutes later, the gentleman Will had first seen opening up the bank came through from a door at the back accompanied by the doorman.

"Can I help you?" Asked the Manager.

"I hope so. I wish to speak to Mr. Kenton."

"I am afraid that you will have to come back tomorrow, Mr. Kenton will not be in today. Shall I make an appointment?"

"No thank you, I shill ride over to his house."

"I don't think that Mr. Kenton will see you there!"

"Why not, I am engaged to his daughter. I would have thought at least she might be pleased to see me after over a year as a prisoner of the French."

The Manager's demeanour changed perceptibly.

"I am sorry Sir. I didn't recognise the uniform."

"Not your fault. I have lived in it for far too long. Could you show me where I can find stables, where I can rent a horse?"

The Manager led him out of the bank and showed him with exaggerated arm gestures the way to a recommended stable.

Will thanked the man. He couldn't raise his hat, as he hadn't had one since *Snipe* had been wrecked.

The first horse he was offered didn't look as if it would make it to the bridge over the Exe. Will demanded a better mount and the haggling began. When asked where he was going, the Kenton name immediately had an effect. The price was lowered considerably and a much better animal was led out.

It was a long time since Will had sat in a saddle, and he hadn't ridden much before. He hoped his nerves didn't show. It was a good thirty miles to the Kenton Estate and it took him four hours to make the journey. Luckily the horse seemed a tolerant sort, and put up with Will's incompetence. The fact that he seemed to be able to eat as much snatched snacks as he wanted to on the journey, probably made up for the inexpert use of reins and legs.

When Will finally found the gates to the Kenton Estate; knowledge gleaned from various yokels on the way, the gate-keeper was slow to respond, and came out munching on something. "Yer?"

"Kindly open the gates, will you?"

"Go round to the tradesman's entrance, half-a–mile down that away."

"You don't recognise me, do you?"

"Nope!"

"I am Commander Calvert. I am the engaged to

Miss Isabella!"

The man came right up to the horse's side and peered short-sightedly up at Will.

"By God, I recognise you now – sorry Sir, but you don't seem dressed proper, somehow."

"No I agree with you. It's what months in a foreign prison camp can do to you!"

"You been interred then Sir?"

"You could say that!" Replied Will; as the man opened one of the gates to let him through.

The horse seemed to sense that there might be more sustenance at the end of the drive, because he trotted down to the front steps to the house.

A footman came down the steps as a groom appeared from nowhere to take the bridle. Will threw his leg over the horse's neck and slid gratefully to the ground. He could hardly walk.

The footman gratifyingly recognised him and accompanied him to the open front door.

Humphreys the Kenton's butler came out from the back of the house adjusting his coat.

"Commander!" He exclaimed and came forward.

At that moment a well remembered voice came from the stairs.

"Who is that, Humphreys?" It was Isabella. Directly she saw Will, she raced down the remaining steps and threw herself at him. She kissed him firmly on the mouth. His arms went out and enfolded her in his arms as their kiss intensified. After a minute she stepped back, somewhat red in the face, but with a sublime smile. Will found himself grinning inanely back at her.

"It's been a long time! I've missed you so much!"Breathed Will; his heart pumping.

"So have I! I've missed you more than words can say!" Isabella said quietly; still gazing into his eyes.

Will had written many letters from his prison, but had not had a reply. He had written saying that since there was no end in sight to the war, he could not possibly expect her to remain tied to him. He would understand if she wanted to break off the engagement.

He held her two hands and gazed into her face. Was it his imagination, or was she even more beautiful than he had remembered. They stood studying each other. She had lost weight, a certain youthful roundness to the face had been replaced by high cheek-bones that off-set those amazing eyes.

"You're awfully thin Will!" She exclaimed. "And what has happened to your uniform? It is all worn; your breeches are torn and your boots look as if they are about to fall to pieces."

Will was about to reply, when Mrs Kenton hove into view.

"William? Is that really you?"

"Isn't it wonderful Mother, he is restored to us!"

Mrs Kenton came forward and kissed Will on the cheek, something she had never done before. Isabella had let go of one hand, but firmly retained the other.

"You look exhausted; and you must be hungry. Humphreys, make sure that cook finds something for the Commander. William, come through to the family dining room."

Isabella, still holding tightly to Will; fell in behind her mother and through to the more intimate dining room, that the family used when they did not have guests.

They sat round the table and Isabella moved her chair to be closer to Will.

"Now you must tell us exactly what happened to you." Said Mrs Kenton.

Will felt Isabella's hand take his under the table and give it a reassuring squeeze, so he outlined what had happened to *Snipe* on that fateful night and what had happened afterwards.

He had only got as far as the blowing up of the ship, when Humphreys entered carrying a small silver tray, followed by two footmen with larger wooden ones. A cold collation was set out before him that almost turned his stomach; he was so used to meagre rations. Humphreys set a cut-glass wine goblet in front of him and poured red wine from a cut-glass decanter. The ladies waved away any food or drink.

It was only Mrs Kenton who prompted him to continue, or suggested he ate more. The wine was delicious, but he dared not drink very much as he felt he would fall asleep.

He picked at the food, using the excuse of talking to hide the fact that he had not eaten much.

It was Isabella who came to his aid.

"I think Mamma that Will is very tired. I think we should let him have a rest."

"Oh, of course, silly me, and it was getting so

interesting!"

Isabella rose from the table and led Will out of the room and up the stairs to an upstairs bedroom. Here she gently pushed him to sit on the bed and then pulled off his boots, placing his feet on the bed. She then lent over him and tenderly kissed him on the lips, lifting one of his hands to her breasts.

She stepped back smiling at him and walked around the bed to draw the curtains, then in the darkness he heard "Sleep well my love, you are safe now!" And the door shut with a click.

Will eased his cravat and before he knew it he was fast asleep.

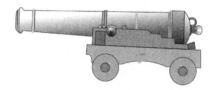

Will awoke with a start. He sat up trying to adjust to his surroundings. Gradually he could begin to make out the dim shape of the room.

"You awake Sir?" Thomas Tucker's voice came from by the window, and Will could vaguely make out the shape of somebody sitting in a chair by one of the two windows.

"That you Thomas?"

"Aye Sir!"

"How long have you been sitting there?"

"Not long Sir. Miss Isabella asked me to come and sit with you in case you needed anything."

"How did you get here?"

"Miss Isabella sent a rider to get me from your house Sir."

"What time is it?"

"Nearly dinner time Sir."

"Good God, I must have been asleep for hours!"

"Probably needed it, Sir: shall I open the curtains?"

"Yes – yes do that."

As he pulled back the hangings, Thomas said. "I have looked out some of Mr. Kenton's clothes that I thought might fit you Sir."

"Does he know?"

"It was his idea, Sir. Miss Isabella told him your uniform was in tatters."

"So it is; but still very decent of him to lend me his clothes."

"They are a wonderfully kind family!" Thomas said as he helped Will off with his coat.

"Stay like that for a moment Sir, if you will."

Thomas walked over to a bell pull by the fireplace and pulled it.

"Thought you might like a bath Sir."

"Am I that bad Thomas?"

"Well to be honest, I wouldn't let you sit down to dinner in your state!"

Will laughed. He had always got on well with his young servant. They had been together ever since Will had been promoted to the wardroom. Will had found the young lad to be very bright, so had taught him to read, write and do mathematics. He had even got to the stage just before they had both been

24

wrecked of teaching him navigation, including star and sun sights. Will was going to make him a midshipman, the next command he had, if ever he had one again.

There was a knock at the door and two footmen came in carrying a copper bath, followed by a string of maids carrying large jugs of steaming water. A Lady in starched black with keys hanging from her waist came in carrying a huge pile of towels. She nodded to Will, with a smile and then organised the maids into spreading some of the towels on the carpet and the bath was placed on them. Then the maids poured the water into the bath, and disappeared to re-appear with more.

One arrived with soap and a back brush. The spare towels were placed near the bath, and the woman in black tested the temperature. She had some cold water added, then indicated to the maids and footmen that they should retire.

"There is more hot water in those jugs, and cold in those Sir. Enjoy your bath." And she too left the room.

Thomas helped Will out of his clothes that he had worn continuously ever since the *Snipe* had been beached.

Thomas put them in a corner of the room. "Shall I get rid?" He asked.

"I rather think so!" Replied Will as he stepped into the blissful warmth of the bath.

"So what happened to you?" Asked Will; lathering himself with the soap.

"Well, when we beached, I went to get your

25

instruments and pistols. I put the pistols in your leather bag, together with your sextant, but there wasn't room for the Celestial-globe, compass or clock. I got a blanket and bundled them up in that. The Surgeon found me as I was climbing out onto the deck. He asked me what I was doing so I told him. He said that they wouldn't last a minute and that I better come with him. Then he joined up with the Agent. Nice fellow, he took the blanket so I had only to carry the bag. He made us walk along the beach in the water so that we didn't leave any prints. Then he found what he was looking for, or rather feeling for, because it was very dark, as you will remember. It was a rocky spur that ran down into the sea. He turned onto this and this led up to a narrow crack in the cliff. We had to feel our way, but he seemed to know what he was doing. We had to climb up this very narrow fault. It was damned hard going – pardon me for saying so – but it was. We was all cut and bruised when we finally got to the top. This Agent fellow, he just led off and we followed. How he knew where he was going, I haven't a clue, but we arrived at a quite large house. He knocked a kind of code on the door and then we was let it."

"We <u>were</u> let in – Thomas – we were let in – carry on."

"Sorry Sir. We were let in and shown into a kitchen where we were given food and wine. The fellow who had let us in, he was given orders and left. It was a woman that set out the food and drink. We ate and then the Agent told us to follow him.

26

We went out the back and there was a farm cart. Your stuff was hidden under the hay, Henri, the Surgeon was told to take off his outer clothes and given a smock thingy. I was forced to take off my uniform and given very itchy trousers and a short smock, with an old hat to put on my head. All the time the Agent was rabbitting away in French to Henri. Then the Agent said goodbye and good luck and off we went on the cart. Henri beside the driver and I sat on the backboard."

Will was busy washing every part of his body, scrubbing away months of grim. Thomas was well into his story and went on. "We must have gone on for hours; or it seemed like it. Then the dawn came up and we continued. We was – were stopped once by some soldiers, but they didn't bother to search the hay. Then we got to a little port. We stopped on the hill above it and Henri went off. I stayed with the cart. Couldn't have a conversation with the driver, I don't speak the lingo. Anyway, Henri comes back after a long time and saying something to the driver. We set off again to another place, but this time it is a small farm. Henri goes off again. I get given some bread and wine and we settles down to wait again. This time Henri comes back all smiles. We uncover your things and say goodbye to the driver and set off down a narrow path. Suddenly we come round a bend and there is a beach with a number of fishing boats pulled up on it. By this time it is getting dark. Henri leads the way down to one of the boats. We puts your things in the boat and then we heave. God don't we heave. Thought it would never move, but Henri gets this bloody big stick and leavers the bows up and off she slides into the water. We hop aboard, pole off, then row like you have never seen anybody row.

After a bit Henri messes about and finally we gets the sail up. I get out your compass and Henri strikes a light. Enough to see North, so that's where we head.

Thomas used the brush on Will's back, as he continued his story.

"When the sun comes up, we couldn't see no land, so we just continued heading north. I pointed out to Henri that we didn't have a tidal atlas. He laughed and told me I would make a sailor one day. So we kept going and that evening we see land. Disappointing though, because we could then tell what the tide was doing to us. Then of course it got dark. Henri suggested we dropped the sail for the night. We took turns on watch, but by first light we could see what I took to be the Isle of Wight to Larboard and some low lying land straight ahead. So we upped the sail and made for the sandy bit. We beached the boat – you would have been proud of us! We then walked inland for a bit until we came to a shack. The fellow there didn't want to know, so we continued heading north. Finally we gets to a farm. And our luck was in. The Farmer was going to market in Chichester. He thought we were spies at first, but when I spoke he seemed to change his mind. He let us have a ride."

Will stood up and Thomas passed him a towel; then busied himself with laying out the borrowed clothes on the bed.

"Luckily Henri had a little money, so we were able to take the stage to London. Where we went to the Admiralty and made our reports. A Sir Evan Nepean gave us some money, so we could get to Devon. We came here, told Miss Isabella what had happened. The Kenton's put us up for a couple of nights, but Henri said we should go to your place. Mr. Kenton put a coach at our disposal."

Will had started to dress, when Thomas said. "Wasn't too sure about shoes - I hate to say so, but I think your feet are rather bigger than Mr. Kenton's feet. He has rather small feet for his height. I think I better check with the footmen."

Will was left to complete his dressing, except for the shoes. The clothes fitted moderately well, although Will felt rather constrained, because his shoulders were broader than the owners. Finally Thomas came back with two pairs of shoes for Will to try. One pair fitted reasonably well.

"Have to do something with your cravat Sir. That will never do. We are not at sea now." With that he untied Will's effort and retied the cravat. Looking in the mirror Will was forced to ask where he had learnt that skill.

"Henri!" Was the brief reply; as Thomas used a brush to make sure the final result came up to his high standards.

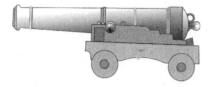

Will wandered down the stairs to find Humphreys waiting for him.

"This way Sir." He said leading the way to a pair of double doors that Will knew well led to the formal sitting room.

"Commander Calvert!" Humphreys announced, with a broad grin afterwards for Will's sake,

Will discovered the ladies sitting side-by-side on one sofa; whilst Mr. Kenton sat alone in an armchair. He rose, placing the paper to one side.

"My dear William, welcome home!" He said advancing hand out stretched.

Will took the proffered hand and shook it.

Will was shown to the sofa opposite Isabella and her mother. Humphreys appeared at his shoulder with a glass of wine.

"We have been telling Mr. Kenton all about your troubles." Said Mrs Kenton. "So you won't have to repeat it all again."

Kenton laughed. "I am sure it was much embellished in your favour!" He said grinning.

"How could you imply such a thing, my husband?" Replied Mrs Kenton.

Will, not used to family familiarity was relieved to find that they all thought it funny. It hit him that he was surrounded by a warmth that he had missed so greatly. Isabella just sat there smiling at him.

"We shall dine presently. How was your well earned rest?" Asked Mrs Kenton.

"A blessing indeed; I dropped off immediately."

Isabella spoke for the first time.

"I hope Thomas didn't disturb you. He was so keen to be there when you woke up; I didn't have the heart to stop him."

"No not at all, I woke to find him guarding my flank, so to speak. And I must thank you Sir for lending me something to wear."

"I hate to say so, but it looks better on you than me!" Kenton said, smiling broadly.

Humphreys entered and announced that dinner was ready..

"Let us go through?" Said Mrs Kenton.

Mr. Kenton stood up and offered an arm to Mrs Kenton, so Will offered his to Isabella who blew him a kiss behind the backs of her parents. They went through to the small Dining Room where Will had eaten his last meal. This time it was set with a damask cloth surmounted by a many branched candelabra. Their chairs were held for them by the footmen, who then shook out the table napkins and handed them to them. A large white lidded bowl was brought in with an equally large ladle and soup was ladled out in front of them. Then they were offered freshly baked rolls from a silver basket, before the servants departed. Only then did Mrs

Kenton start the conversation after her first sipped mouthful.

"I had a word with the Bishop the other day, when we read that a treaty had been signed. He suggested that a 'Special Licence' was the ideal thing – whatever that is. What do you think?

Will had his mouth full so could not reply immediately. Isabella came to his rescue. "I hardly think that Will would have even thought about it Mother."

"On the contrary, I thought of nothing else the whole time I was locked up. Only trouble was I thought that you would have given up on me and found a more suitable spouse."

"Good God Will, I am not that fickle! One doesn't fall in and out of love just like that!"

"I am sorry. It was just that there seemed no end to the war. I thought I might be an old man by the time I was set free."

"Then I would have been an old spinster!"

Will looking up realised that there was no animosity in her words, she was smiling at him through tears.

"Thank you for being so loyal!"

"So what do you think Will?" Asked Mrs Kenton.

"I am for marrying this woman as soon as possible, but I shall have to get some clothes, or I shall be standing at the altar in borrowed clothes, and I thought that applied to the bride only."

"I'd forgotten about 'something borrowed'. I wonder where that started?" Laughed Isabella.

"Well am sure that we can find a tailor very quickly. You don't have to get married in uniform do you?" Asked Mrs Kenton.

"I don't really know. I've never got married before!" Joked Will..

"Actually, I think that Thomas has already set things in motion." Declared Mr. Kenton. "He came to me when he first arrived today and asked if it was possible for me to send a messenger to Plymouth to get a Naval tailor to come over to measure you for new uniforms. He thought that you might have changed slightly since you last had a uniform made by them."

"You know, that young man of mine never ceases to amaze me. I am definitely going to have him as a Midshipman, if I ever have to go to sea again."

"Well let us hope it isn't for a long time!" Said Isabella. "I want to get to know my husband, really get to know him!"

"Might not like what you find!" Reposted Will with a grin.

"Then I shall whip you into submission!" She said challengingly.

"God, you'd think you two were married already!" Laughed Mr. Kenton.

And so the evening went on, with pleasant banter between them, that Will found very comforting. He remembered that the gentle art of teasing was part of their everyday life.

After dinner, rather than the ladies leaving them, they all stayed around the table talking animatedly.

The question of the marriage was raised once again by Mrs Kenton, and this time they were all in agreement that they should have a very quiet wedding. Will's mother and step-father would be invited; Craddock would be summoned as best man, but otherwise only very close friends and relatives would be invited. Of course Will would have to have a uniform to get married in.

"I shall have to get a new sword as well." Said Will.

Isabella abruptly got up and left the table as he said it. He didn't think anything about it assuming she needed to go to the toilet or as he thought of it the 'Heads'. She was only gone for a very short time before she returned with a naval sword with a belt attached.

"Thomas was devastated that he had to leave your sword behind, so I bought you one as a present." She said handing it to him.

Will didn't know what to say. He stood up, went round to Isabella and kissed her on the cheek. Finally he managed. "I don't know what to say, except thank you, my love. Now I shall be properly dressed for our wedding. She didn't move, she sat there gazing into his eyes oblivious of her parents. "I can't wait!" She breathed and lent forward to repay the complement, but this time she kissed him on the lips.

Kenton broke the mood by declaiming. "I think a celebratory drink is in order." And he turned to ring the bell pull.

A footman entered.

"Tell Mr. Humphreys that I want the best Brandy and five goblets." The footman retreated.

"Five glasses?" Queried Mrs Kenton.

"I thought Humphreys should join us."

"Why?"

"To keep him sweet! He will have a lot to organise."

"What about Thomas?" Asked Isabella.

"He went back to Calvert House. He wanted to tell Tarrant and Co all about Will's return."

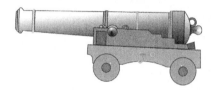

The next day Isabella organised one of the Kenton coaches to take them round to Calvert House, as their future home was now called. It was a lovely day so the coach's folding top was down. Isabella wore a light weight coat over her dress, which Will couldn't help noticing showed off her figure to perfection. She really was a stunningly beautiful creature now. On her head a bonnet with flowers in the band framed her face. He knew it wasn't really correct, but he kissed her on the lips in the hall when she appeared ready to leave. She showed no sign of objecting, but just kissed him back. Humphreys must think it very bad form, but Will couldn't have cared less. In the coach Isabella took his hand and held it the whole journey.

As they passed through the various villages, bystanders smiled and some even clapped. A couple of youths shouted out something they didn't catch, but nothing could dent Will's happiness.

The gates to the drive were open as they turned towards the house. The gate-keeper touched his forelock in traditional salute. And there was the house, much as he remembered it, except for the wisteria on the front. The coach came to a halt in front of the house, and as the footmen unfolded the steps, Henri de Cornes *Snipe's* Surgeon came out of the front door, followed by Thomas, and then two other characters that Will did not know. Finally Will remembered to hand down Isabella, before he began to introduce her to the assembly.

"Will, there is no need I know them all well." She said with a wide smile for the group in front of her, who all had smiles on their faces.

"I have been coming here virtually every day, to get the house ready for you."

"Really!" Will shook his head, but turned to greet his crew who he considered also to be his friends.

There were newcomers to the household he had not met as they had been taken on by Isabella. He was introduced to his Butler, Mr. Clarkson and his Housekeeper Mrs Merridew. Then it was indoors to meet another line-up, this time the household staff. There was the Cook, Mrs Price, two footmen, then a row of maids of various stations, that he lost count of.

"I shall get to know you and try to remember your names as we go along." He said.

Then Isabella said. "Now I am going to show you what I have done. I hope you like it, because I shall be devastated if you don't!"

"I am sure I shall like everything, if you have had a hand in it!" He replied gallantly.

She had re-organised the place completely. The rooms had been repainted or re-wallpapered. The paintings that they had bought with the house had been re-hung in a completely different manner. The rooms that had seemed slightly impersonal now had a friendly welcoming feel to them. Upstairs she showed him where she had changed a bedroom into a private sitting room off their bedroom. What had once been a dressing room off the sitting room had been converted into a private pantry, with china, a spirit stove and other changes, so she could prepare hot drinks for them herself. The Sitting Room was on the corner of the house so had windows to the south-east overlooking the river Dart, and to the East where it got the midday sun.

Will wandered around behind his bride-to-be, poking into every nook and corner, marvelling at the changes she had made. Isabella led him through to the servants' stairs and showed him how the rooms at the top of the house had been altered to make them far more comfortable. Then it was back down the servants' back stairs and out to the Coach-house and stables. Here there were no longer weeds growing between the cobbles. The doors to the stables were freshly painted dark blue. There was a rush as the grooms realised that their Master had entered the yard. A stout man with bandy legs was very obviously in charge. Isabella introduced him as the Coachman, Jeffreys. He was dressed like the others in a dark blue coat with gold buttons. Then there was the head groom, a little man with no teeth but a broad grin and the rest of the stable lads and grooms, all smartly dressed.

Laughing Isabella took Will over to one stable where a horse eyed him speculatively.

"This is my present to you, so you can ride with me and also round your estates." Said Isabella; fondling the horse's nose. "He is called Homer, as we both wanted you to come home."

Will couldn't help himself, he felt choked. To cover his emotions he went up to the horse and scratched him under the chin.

"Hello Homer, you going to teach me to ride properly?"

The horse seemed to look him straight in the eye.

"He has a lovely temperament, and he goes like the wind."

"Have you ridden him?"

"Of course. I had to make sure he wasn't going to buck or play silly with you."

Will took Isabella's arm and said quietly. "Thank you from the bottom of my heart."

She wriggled her nose at him.

"You have done so much for me, and I haven't even brought you anything!" He said with a frog in his throat.

"Will don't be silly; I've had months to plan things and hope you would come back to me very soon. You've only been free a few days, and do you know what? The best present you brought was yourself and the fact that you hadn't even stopped to get a new uniform or clothes. That showed me how much you wanted to get back to me. All my prayers are answered!"

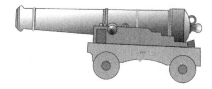

They returned that evening to Kenton House, as Isabella insisted that he spend a bit more time with her parents as they discussed the wedding arrangements. That evening details were put down on paper and lists of what had to done made to jog memories.

Kenton, because he would be in Exeter the next day was given the task of seeing the Bishop, an old friend. Mrs Kenton would visit the vicar of their local church, who owed his living to the good offices of the Kentons. Will and Isabella would return to Will's place in the hope that the tailor would show up. Isabella couldn't wait to get Will up on his horse, so they could ride around the estate. She had visited all the farms and got to know the tenant farmers and their wives.

On the trip to the house the next day, Will discussed the idea of having a boat so they could reach Dartmouth easily and not have to drive the long way round.

"Would it be a sailing boat?" Asked Isabella.

"Of course, though it would have to have oars as well, the wind isn't that reliable."

"So what do you do at sea?"

"Wait!"

"What just sit there for days?"

"If needs must."

"Really?"

"Happens in the Atlantic, there is an area where it is known to happen a lot. Also you get very light winds in the Med. And then just as suddenly it can blow a gale."

"Won't blow gales in the Dart will it?"

"No!"

"Good, so will you teach me to sail?"

"Really?"

"Absolutely!"

"Of course."

"So who are you going see about it, then?"

"I'm not. I thought it would be a project for Tarrant and Allwood, when he gets here, to get their teeth into. Keep them out of mischief."

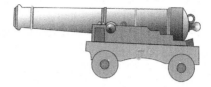

The next few weeks for Will were rather strange. He had moved into his house and was sleeping in a spare bedroom, so that the master bedroom would be a new experience for them both when they got married. Isabella came over to Calvert House every few days. The first day that Isabella would be absent, Will had his coach take him into Totnes. Here he sought out a tailor and was measured for both a civilian day jacket, but also a riding coat and breeches. A visit to the nearby boot maker meant an order for two pairs of shoes, riding boots and a pair of hessians. The bootmaker measured every part of his foot as well as drawing around each foot. He explained he would make 'lasts' of both feet. Clothes for use in town were ordered from tailors in Exeter.

Isabella had brought her horse, Commander, over from the Kenton residence, so they could ride out together, accompanied for forms sake, by two grooms. Having virtually lived on the estate whilst Will was imprisoned, she was able to introduce Will to his tenant farmers, their wives, families, and workers. When she wasn't with Will she was arranging the wedding with her mother. Will had no input into the arrangements other than to make sure that there were sufficient carriages for the guests coming from his side of the family and his friends. His mother had already written to Mrs Kenton accepting the invitation to stay at the Kentons on the night of the wedding, but apologising for the fact that her husband would not be able to attend due to necessary work on the farm. Will was of the belief that he really didn't want to be faced with 'society', as he, unlike his wife, had never mixed in any other group than fellow farmers. Will's mother had been used to meeting all types of people as the wife of a wealthy ship owner.

The Bishop of Exeter had been buttonholed by Mrs Kenton and agreed to a 'special licence', but only so long as he could perform the ceremony. Will had written to his First Lieutenant James Craddock, asking him to be his best-man. Isabella insisted that Will be married in his uniform, so the Naval Tailors had been ordered to make new uniforms to replace the ones lost.

There would be a full-dress uniform of dark blue with a stand-up collar in the same material, with gold lace at the edges. The gold lace edged the rest of the coat around the edges and down round the tails. The lapels were edged with wider gold lace and had nine gold buttons down each. There was one line of lace on each cuff with a three pointed flap edged in gold lace with an inner matching lace. There were three gold buttons on the flap of each cuff. There was a white waistcoat, white breeches and stockings. Black shoes with gold buckles, and a gold epaulette on the left shoulder finished the full-dress uniform off. The undress uniform was of the same dark blue, but with no gold lace, just the buttons, but those at the cuff were parallel to the bottom of the cuff. Blue breeches were worn, and often hessian boots when required. No epaulettes were normally worn.

It felt very strange to be on dry land, but free to come and go as he pleased. He had the impending Court-Martial to trouble him, but Isabella made light of it, saying that the worst they could do was to release him from naval service. What Will feared was that he might be reduced back to a Lieutenant and loose seniority. He had a feeling that whilst she supported him, Isabella might privately prefer that he was dismissed the service. He assiduously prepared himself; going over every minute of the final moments of *Snipe's* break-up and his beaching her.

Tarrant and Allwood, who had finally made it to Calvert House; when not supervising the construction of Will's 'yacht', as they termed her, spent the rest of their time preparing a proper landing stage. Will had a lot of time on his hands, so raided the library and read widely. Henri de Cornes, *Snipe's* surgeon, would occasionally join him for dinner when Will was alone, but spent most of his time travelling about the district assisting the sick. Will provided him with a bed to sleep in and food, as well as a horse for him to get about. Henri only charged those he thought could well afford to pay for his services. The poor were treated for free, with Henri letting the patients know that it was courtesy of Commander Calvert of Calvert House. Will had no idea that he was being credited with the free medical service, but it did no harm to his reputation.

Two days before the date set for the wedding, Craddock finally showed up. Will was mighty relieved and was proud to reintroduce his friend to Isabella. On the wedding day, the weather was in two minds as to how it would proceed. It dawned with an all over covering of grey cloud. Will accompanied by Craddock, Tarrant and Allwood, rode in the repainted coach that had come with the house. Thomas Tucker, smartly dressed in Midshipman's uniform accompanied Mrs Merridew, the House keeper, Midshipman Gardner and Lieutenant Kemp, late of HMS *Snipe*; in a hired coach. A series of farm vehicles followed with Will's tenants.

The Church had been dressed in an amazing display of hot house flowers. There was even an arch over the church door of winter roses, specially grown in the Kenton greenhouses. Will stood for sometime outside greeting the guests and the sun began to edge through the clouds. Tarrant and Allwood, dressed in smart dark blue coats with brass buttons, helped Tucker as ushers. As Will made to go inside, Henri arrived on his horse, complete with his two medical saddle-bags, hitched the horse to the lynch gate and strode up the path to Will, giving him a slap on the back as he passed, muttering he was sorry to be a bit late. Inside the church a small group of musicians played suitable music, as the guests took their seats. Will sat in the front right-hand pew feeling more nervous than he could remember. Craddock sat beside him telling him jokes to relieve the tension. Then the music changed and the Bishop appeared indicating to Will that it was time he stood. Then down the centre of the small church came a vision in white. When Isabella took her place beside Will, she put out a hand and squeezed his to reassure him. Then she threw back the veil and Will gazed once again at her loveliness. He had to swallow hard to regain his composure, as she gave him a radiant smile.

After the signing of the register Will and Isabella emerged from the church into brilliant sunshine, and had to pass under an aisle of naval swords crossed above their heads. Then through the lynch gate to discover a brand new light weight coach waiting for them, complete with four matched bay horses. Proudly on the coachman's seat sat Will's Coachman Jeffreys and waiting by the door and steps, the two footmen who had ridden behind Will to the church. Will handed Isabella into the coach, noticing as he did that the coach was painted in the same dark blue as his own.

"A wedding present from my parents!" Whispered Isabella as Will sat down beside her.

Will was not looking forward to the reception, or the speeches. He was surprised to find that with Isabella at his side it was not as bad as he had imagined. The formal dining room and drawing rooms of Kenton House had been made over for the reception. There were flowers everywhere. Will had to stand with Isabella and her parents, together with his mother to receive the guests. He was gratified to see that his mother was as smartly dressed as the Kentons in the latest fashion. When all the guests had arrived the wine and food were served by flunkeys carrying round trays laden with choice morsels. Will had never been a great drinker, and with a speech to give he nursed his glass. He was gratified to find that his old skipper from *Artful* had made the effort to attend. Captain Crick had been an inspiration to Will, and had promoted him to acting Lieutenant which had changed his life. By the time the Bishop had made his speech in praise of Isabella; Mr. Kenton had made his addition and it was Will's turn he found it difficult to remember what he had prepared. He made a very short one, praising Isabella for remaining true to him whilst he had been a prisoner and thanking the Kentons for their kindness towards a mere Commander.

Craddock, who always had had a an amusing way with him, made a very funny speech in praise of Isabella's attendants, that brought blushes to the cheeks of the bridesmaids, and scowls from the two pages.

After the reception, Isabella and Will went out to their new coach, followed by the younger members at the reception, who tried to tie things to the coach, which were immediately confiscated by two irate footmen. Finally leaving to cries of good luck they were driven to Calvert House where they were to spend their honeymoon. Isabella dropped all form of decorum, once she was inside their home. She danced round the hall laughing with joy. Then she led Will up to their bedroom. This was a moment Will had been dreaming of, but dreading as he had never been with a woman. Isabella shut the door to the room, turned the key in the lock and then came to Will and put her arms round his neck and kissed him.

"Hello, my husband. Don't look so afraid, I won't eat you, although mightily tempted. And don't worry, I asked an old friend who is married to explain all the intimate details, as neither of us have ever done this before, I hope!" She arched her brows.

Will laughed and promised her he was as much a virgin as she was.

"Good then we can experiment together!"

Will found that Isabella was as good as her word. Gently they explored each other until aroused they finally made love. Will was surprised at how much Isabella seemed to enjoy the experience. Isabella was an enthusiastic lover.

Then days into their blissful life together, the bomb-shell arrived. Will was given a date for his impending Court-Martial. There was Christmas to partake in and then three months before the dreaded date. He was also required to go to London before the hearing for an interview with the Judge

Advocate. The missive said that sooner would be better, but that if he liked to give a date when he would be available, the Advocate's office would see that it was accommodated. Although January would be a bad time to travel, February could be worse, so he wrote to say he would be in London during the last week in January. Isabella asked her parents if they could make use of Kenton House in London, so she could accompany Will. This was instantly given and their plans were laid.

Christmas was spent at Kenton House, followed on Boxing Day by a reception at Calvert House, for their new neighbours.

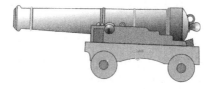

The last week in January was as expected not the best time to travel. It took them twice as long as normal, due to fords being too deep and the road so muddy, speed was down to walking pace in places.

When they finally arrived at the Kenton's London House, Will was surprised to find that it was just outside town to the West. The house was beautifully symmetric in red brick behind a red brick wall. A sweeping drive led up to the front door, with a garden between the drive and the road. The place was smaller than Will had expected, with windows on either side of the front door. Inside they were greeted by the Housekeeper. The hall had a black and white tiled floor with an elegant staircase curving up to the first floor. To the left Isabella threw open the double doors to reveal a pleasant sitting room with a window to the front and two further windows to the side. Two couches faced each other on either side of a white marble fireplace with a classical mirror over it. Isabella showed him through the door at the far end of the room which turned out to be a small study with a desk and bookcases on all the walls not taken up with the windows, door or fireplace. On the opposite side of the hall was a matching sized room to the sitting room which was the dining room, with a table which could seat about twenty people. Beyond it apparently was the butler's pantry and the domestic offices, such as the kitchen and staff quarters. Upstairs Isabella showed Will her parent's room and then went round the landing to another room which was over the sitting room. This was the main guest bedroom where they would sleep. Her bedroom had been next to her parent's room, when she had stayed before. Behind the house was a small walled garden and then the stables and coach house with the accommodation for the extra servants that the Kentons brought with them and whom Will and Isabella had following on. That night they had a cold collation, as the cook, butler, Isabella's maid and Thomas had not yet arrived, travelling as they were in the older coach.

When Will attended the Judge Advocate's office he was surprised at how friendly the staff seemed to be. He was immediately shown into an airy office and joined by a tall dark haired gentleman with a ready smile, who introduced himself as the Judge Advocate himself. A clerk sat at a side table poised to note down everything that was said.

"Before we begin – there is no need to note this Briers – I want you to know that all we are trying to solicit is exactly what happened to your ship. I already have the ship's log. Your servant brought it to the Admiralty when he escaped. Sir Nepean has kindly sent over copies of the correspondence between you and the Board of Admiralty prior to the beaching of your vessel and its ultimate loss. I am however required to interview you before any Court- Martial takes place."

Will nodded his understanding.

"If you wouldn't mind speaking in sentences with pauses in between, to aid the scribe."

The Clerk nodded his thanks and indicated he was ready. Will then told his story, concentrating on the last hours before the crew had been captured. When he had finished he offered his Journal, which Tucker had also saved. This was deemed not necessary, as they already had the ship's log. The Judge Advocate asked though that he be allowed to keep it so he could read it, but that it would be returned before the Court-Martial.

To Will's surprise, the whole interview only took an hour, and he was back out onto the rainy streets of London with all their bustle and noise. He had arrived by sedan chair, but there appeared to be a shortage of such conveniences due to the inclement weather. Will was forced to walk the two miles to the Kenton Residence. He was soaked when he finally arrived, despite his boat cloak.

Now that the older coach had arrived, a hot lunch was the order of the day, with a hot toddy to warm up the inner man. Isabella listened in close attention as Will recounted his experiences.

"So now we have time on our hands! What would you like to do?" Isabella asked after he had finished.

Will admitted he had no idea what one did in London, as he had only ever passed through.

"Well it isn't the season, but there are still plays to be seen and places to go. It rather depends on the weather. "

"Can I leave that side of things to you?"

So for the next few days Will was introduced to the theatre, the circus. And on one fine day they strolled through Vauxhall Gardens, though it was not the season for it really.

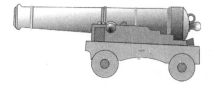

Back at Calvert House in Devon, for Will the waiting continued. The weather was its usual uncertain self, and it was only occasionally that the weather permitted a long ride out. The 'Yacht' was completed and in a small amusing ceremony, Isabella christened it the *Lady Isabella.* It would be used to carry produce from the tenant farmers to Totnes and Dartmouth. It also, on a couple of days, gave them the opportunity to teach Isabella the rudiments of sail. During the wet days, a lot of the time was spent reading; in Will's case books on agriculture. Isabella managed to persuade her mother to come over once a week to play the piano, so that Isabella could teach Will to dance. He had protested that he had two left feet, but discovered that he had a sense of rhythm which helped him a lot. It wasn't taken very seriously so there were a lot of laughs. Occasionally they were invited to lunch with neighbours, and quite often joined the Kentons for meals and sometimes stayed over.

Isabella insisted that she should accompany Will to Plymouth for the Court-Martial, to give him moral support. Nobody had any idea how long the proceedings would take, so Thomas Tucker was dispatched to Plymouth to find suitable accommodation.

Thomas was back within a week having arranged for a house which he thought would be ideal. It had a view over the harbour, so that Isabella would have something to watch, whilst her husband stood before his peers. Tarrant, as *Snipe's* boatswain had been summoned to attend, along with Allwood the Captain's Coxswain and Tucker the Captain's servant cum ship's clerk.

Two days before the Court-Martial was due to start, the Calverts travelled in convoy to Plymouth and took possession of the rented house. Will was able to take Isabella on a tour next day of the sights of the town and over to the Tamar to see the ships of the fleet moored and at anchor. He showed her the exterior of his old home, which was now sold, and she enthused about its position and character.

Court-Martials always took place in the fore-noon, so it was a difficult morning for Will as he prepared himself for his ordeal. Isabella did not try to accompany Will to the steps, where he would have to find a boat to take him out to the flagship. For this he was extremely grateful, as it would only have added to the pressure. She hugged him to her, kissed him hard on the lips, and told him she loved him, before he stepped out to mount up into his coach. At least he would arrive in style.

When the coach stopped at the head of the steps; where years before he had been accepted into the navy; a smartly dressed Coxswain asked Will if he was Commander Calvert. Will said he was, and the Coxswain told him that Captain Crick had instructed him to take the Commander over to the Flagship. It meant a lot to Will to have the moral support of his previous Captain. He was given all the normal courtesies of a captain as he climbed through the entry port to the flagship. A flag-lieutenant greeted him, and suggested he might like to take a turn about the deck with him as the Court was not quite ready. There was no hint of disrespect in the young officer's demeanour. He was polite and amusing which lifted Will's black mood slightly.

A lieutenant approached them and said that the Court was ready to start. Will accompanied by the flag-lieutenant followed the Lieutenant to the doors of the Admiral's quarters. The Court would be presided over by the Rear-Admiral, the flag-Lieutenant had told Will, as the Fleet Admiral had called for the Court-Martial as per Admiralty instructions.

It was difficult to make out the faces of the Board who sat at a table with their backs to the windows. It was a bright May day so they were in silhouette as far as Will was concerned. The Lieutenant who had summoned them asked for Will's sword, which was placed on a table in front of the Rear Admiral who presided.

"Good afternoon Commander Calvert, I shall first read the warrant, so to speak, and then you may sit down over there. I know normally everybody should stand, but in this ship the deck-head is so low it would be ridiculous." Said the Rear Admiral; in a pleasant voice. Then he took a sip of water or may be something stronger and read.

"The Court, pursuant to an order from the Right Honourable Lords Commissioners of the Admiralty, dated the 2nd day of May Instant and directed to the President will proceed to inquire into the Cause and Circumstances of the grounding and subsequent seizure of His Majesty's Armed Vessel the *Snipe* commanded by Commander William Calvert."

Then a legal gentleman stood up on the opposite side to Will and cleared his throat. "Do you plead guilty or not guilty to the grounding and loss of His Majesty's Sloop *Snipe*?"

Will composed himself and then said in a firm voice. "*Snipe* was not grounded, she was beached!"

"Really Sir, you must get your facts right! You will amend the charge to beaching!" Said the Rear Admiral; addressing the legal gentleman.

The Legal man stood frozen, shocked at the Rear Admiral's out-burst.

"Well Sir, it goes on to say the loss of the sloop *Snipe*."

"I know you fellows have no idea about ships, and I know that technically *Snipe* comes under the generic group known as sloops, but for accuracy in this Court-Martial, I insist that His Majesty's ship *Snipe* is correctly referred to as the schooner *Snipe*, is that clear?"

"Yes My Lord!"

Will heard chuckles from the line of Captains at the table. He had counted them and was surprised to find, it being peace time, that there was the bare minimum of nine sitting in judgement.

The Legal gentleman now looked flustered.

"Do you plead guilty to the loss of your ship?" He asked glancing at the Rear Admiral.

Will had gone over this over and over again. "Not guilty!" He replied again in a firm voice.

To Will's surprise the Judge Advocate stood up, bowed to the Rear Admiral and Captains, then lifted a single piece of paper.

"If it please this Court, I should like to take Commander Calvert over the lead up to the unfortunate loss of the ..er... schooner *Snipe*." He turned to Will, and the light being strongly on the face of the Judge Advocate, Will was sure he smiled slightly before he went on.

"I know that this Court will understand that you are not at liberty to say exactly where or why you were, where you were; as you were under direct orders from the Board of Admiralty. So unusually in this case I shall only concentrate on the condition of the ship in question. I have here My Lord President, copies of the signals sent by Commander Calvert to the Board and edited parts, apposite to the case, of those sent in return by the Board. This is on the direct orders of the First Lord of The Admiralty, Earl St. Vincent." He put down his paper and picked up a sheaf of papers.

"September 12th at Sea. Commander Calvert to Board of Admiralty....

I shall in future for brevity leave these openings and closing out, if that is all right by My Lord President?"

The Rear Admiral as President of the Court

nodded his agreement.

"I have to report to the Board that it appears that the timbers replaced as a result of enemy action, have not in the opinion of our Carpenter been sufficiently seasoned, in that the said timbers are springing, to allow an un-acceptable amount of water to ingress, which the pumps are unable to cope with, whenever this ship is on a starboard tack. We have had to put men over the side to try to place a canvas and tar patch over the offending area. I ask that His Majesty's Schooner *Snipe* be allowed to return to the dockyard to have the problem rectified."

He placed the sheet of paper he had been reading from on the table in front of him

"The reply! Much edited I am afraid, but the answer was NO, carry on, deal with it yourselves." He put down the paper.

"24th Sept at sea.

Once again I must ask permission to place His Majesty's schooner *Snipe* back in the hands of Portsmouth Dockyard to replace the timbers that are springing to the danger of the ship. Ingeniously the Carpenter has drilled holes in the offending timbers and by means of Turks heads and tackle held the timbers in position. However the warping, despite the corking and another patch, means that we are unable to sail on the Starboard tack for any length of time, as the ingress is more than the pumps can cope with. Further more in any seaway, the patches do not last.

He continues, but I cannot reveal the rest of the

contents. Now the reply, again edited.....

It is imperative that you continue with.........
There is no mention of there being any thought to
when the problem might be repaired."

He put down that paper.

"13th October 1799. At Sea.

Sirs, I must most urgently implore you to allow
His Majesty's schooner *Snipe* to be allowed into a
dockyard to have the timbers afore mentioned
replaced. The leakage is so severe that we are
unable to sail on the Starboard tack for more than a
few minutes, making manoeuvring very difficult,
and impairing our fighting ability.

The patches need to be replaced every time after
the sea has been able to reach them, and it now
being that time of year, the seas are very
unforgiving. We have tried nailing the patches into
place, but they only last a few minutes longer. I am
afeared that if the timbers spring any further, we
could lose the ship and there could be a
considerable loss of life."

The Judge Advocate turned to look at the
President. "They go on in this vein with stone
walling replies. I can read the rest, but I think that
by now the board will have realised the position the
Schooner was placed in, and that of her
Commanding Officer. I should just like to read part
of the last signal from the Admiralty, which was
never received by the ship.

" 12th January 1800

Their lordships have considered your request and
have passed orders to the Superintendent

Portsmouth Dockyard that he should be ready to receive His Majesty's Schooner *Snipe* directly she is able to make it into port, to have the hull surveyed and any necessary repairs carried out as quickly and as proficiently as possible."

The Judge Advocate placed the papers very deliberately on the table in front of him.

"On the 12th January 1800, just after midnight, the timbers sprung! I can call the carpenter if the Court so desires, but this Court-Martial is about blame! It is about whether Commander Calvert was to blame for the subsequent ... I put it to the Court....... necessary, beaching of the Schooner. Unfortunately I am not allowed to say where the Schooner was or why, but she was fairly close inshore. The Commander beached the Schooner in the hope of being able to affect a temporary repair at first light. Unfortunately the French were already aware of the presence of the Schooner, so moved in and captured the crew."

The Judge Advocate paused for effect and turned his head to make a point of looking at each of the Board one at a time. "Does my Lord President require any more witnesses?"

The sun went behind a cloud, and Will was able to see clearly for the first time the assembled Captains. He recognised his old Captain, Captain Crick and a couple of others. One at the far end of the table was scowling at him, his face bright red. Will thought he must be a drinker.

"Should have let the bloody ship sink, rather than let her fall into the hands of those damned

Frenchies!" The red faced Captain said.

"You are out of order Captain Ballantyne. You will kindly keep your thoughts to yourself. As it happens, the Commander, managed to elude his captors to blow the schooner to pieces, so denying them the use of the ship! Judge Advocate, I think that the Board has heard enough. We shall adjourn to consider." The Rear Admiral stood up followed by all the other Captains, Ballantyne, being the last to rise; Will had the sudden realisation that the man was drunk.

The Court was cleared, everybody streaming out onto the deck.

Craddock came over to speak to Will, as he had been summoned to attend. Tarrant, Allwood, the Carpenter and both of the midshipmen, came over to join them. Will had not noticed Henri, the Surgeon, but he joined them after speaking to the Judge Advocate. Tucker stayed to one side, but ready to undertake anything Will might require.

Five minutes later they were all called back into the Admiral's day cabin. Will the last to enter was relieved to see that his sword had been placed with the hilt facing him.

Will stood in front of the President to hear the verdict.

"This Courts-Martial unanimously acquits Commander William Calvert and exonerates him of any charges against his person. I should just like to add my personal admiration for the secret work undertaken by the Commander, under what we have seen from these proceedings to be the most difficult conditions.

I have had the privilege of being privy to the remarkable number of enemy vessels captured by the Commander and his crew."

There was a round of applause, and then the proceedings broke up. The Rear Admiral insisted that drinks be served, but Will noticed that Captain Ballantyne was not present. The Rear Admiral came over to Will, slapped him on the back and said quietly in his ear. " Don't worry you'll get another ship very soon, mark my words!"

Captain Crick insisted that Will join him in his barge for the journey back to shore. Will invited him to join Isabella and himself for dinner, but Crick thanked him, saying that he had to get back to his ship as they were sailing on the first Tide in the morning.

When Will arrived back to their rented house, Isabella came forward a worried expression clouding her lovely face.

"Exonerated completely!" Cried Will and she flew into his arms, oblivious to the servants.

Isabella led him through to the sitting room, and made him go through the proceedings in detail.

Next day they departed for home to spend the summer enjoying each other's company and exploring the river Dart and its creeks.

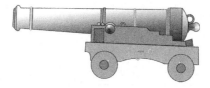

Summer gave way to autumn, and then to winter and Christmas, but this time there was no Court-Martial proceedings hanging over Will's head. His Agent had paid the Prize Money that was due to him, so there were no money worries. Will had been extremely surprised to find that he had control of Isabella's considerable fortune. He immediately went to his father-in-law and protested. He was told that it was the law. Will then asked Mr. Kenton to look after the money on their behalf. He also made a will, leaving everything to Isabella. Christmas was a great festival, due to Isabella's organisational skills, with parties, a ball and a separate party for all the staff and tenants.

In April 1803 a riding messenger arrived from the Admiralty with orders for Will to attend at the earliest possible date. War had not been declared and there had been little to suggest that the Government was willing to expand the Navy. As a result the household was thrown into confusion.

Isabella insisted she accompany Will, so a messenger was sent to the Kentons to ask if they could use the London House, and if so to continue on to London to warn the housekeeper of the London House. This time the old coach was sent off first with, what Will called the Van. This was an enclosed grocery type wagon, with no sign that it was other than a small businesses delivery cart. In this were loaded Will's sea-chest (just in case), Isabella's clothes, extra domestic utensils and the staff's clothes.

Tarrant wanted to accompany Will, but he had to submit to being left in Devon, until he might be needed. He volunteered to be Will's clerk if necessary, so long as he sailed with Will, if the Commander was to be given a ship. What mystified Will was that the signal had been addressed to 'Captain' Calvert, rather than his correct rank of Commander.

Just in case, Will made a rapid circuit of his tenants to check all was well with them, before he and Isabella set off in the light coach. It had been hoped by Isabella that the old coach and the van would arrive first, so that the house would be ready for them. The light coach with just Will and Isabella aboard passed the two other vehicles on the outskirts of London. However after Will had been dropped off at the Admiralty, everybody else arrived at the house at about the same time.

It was early evening and the lanterns either side of the front entrance arch to the Admiralty were being lit, when Will made his way through the yard, up the steps and through the doors. As usual he was met by one of the Admiralty servants, who expected a tip, dependant on one's rank. Will recognised the man who greeted him, because he had been forced to promise to tip him later when he first returned from imprisonment in France. Will had honoured his word.

"Captain Calvert, Sir, you are improperly dressed, if I may make so bold!" Said the Admiralty Porter; advancing on Will.

Will stood and raised an eyebrow questioningly.

"We wus told to expect Captain Calvert and to show him up to the First Lord's corridor immediately he arrived. Now I knowst only one Calvert of distinction, and that be you Sir. Captain Calvert it says on the form... see here."

"Well thank you for advising me of my supposed promotion, I only hope you are right, but if I am incorrectly dressed, I am sure I shall be given a dressing down by the Admiral..eh?"

"Yus Sir!" The Porter grinned at Will. "This way Sir."

Will was led up the main stairs, past the waiting room for officers and others, to a corridor, where a single chair was set to the side.

"If you wait here Sir, I shallst inform the Admiral's clerk that you have arrived." He leant down and spoke confidentially in a whisper to Will. "Actually we was told to expect you tomorrow or the day after!" He straightened up and gave Will a friendly nod.

Will was left there as the light faded and the corridor grew dark. He thought he had been forgotten until suddenly a door at the end of the corridor opened and a clerk, holding a candle stick, shuffled forward.

"Captain Calvert?"

"I think that is I, but I haven't been given a

commission as such, so I am still a lowly Commander."

By the candle light it was hard to tell if there was any reaction.

"Follow me Sir, if you please."

Will was led to an imposingly large door, which the clerk knocked on, then entered halfway. "Captain Calvert, My Lord." He then stepped back to allow Will to enter.

It was a large room, lit by many candles. In the centre was an imposing desk from behind which the noble Earl rose to greet Will.

"Calvert, come in, come in. Made it in much better time than I expected. I am sorry to call you in so suddenly, but that is the nature of things, What?" His Lordship pointed to a chair set beside the desk and sat down again.

"We have a Commission for you. Not quite what I was preparing for, but that's life, isn't it?"

Will nodded.

"Right, we have a vacancy for a Captain of a frigate at the moment moored in Portsmouth Harbour. Her Captain has disappeared! He either fell overboard, committed suicide, or was murdered. Since they have found no body, we are none the wiser. However, it is never ever that simple. The ship's First Lieutenant reported the loss to the Port Admiral. When questioned, the Lieutenant revealed that the ship was in a state near of mutiny! The late Captain, never allowed anybody ashore, including his officers. According to the Port Admiral there are rumours that he indulged himself in obscene practices. The Admiral considers it extremely likely that the Captain was murdered - by whom, or how nobody knows... or they are not telling! I want you to go straight to Portsmouth, take command of the ship and sort things out. But...and it is very great but! There was another reason why the Board were going to give you a command of a frigate, and that is a State Secret; so as before you are working directly to the Board."

Admiral Lord Jervis lent forward lowering his voice.

"We have intelligence that the Spanish are shipping gold from the Americas, and passing it on to the French. It is, between ourselves, almost certain that we shall be at war with the French again before the year is out. We want to stop at least some of that gold, but we don't want the Spanish to realise that it is the Royal Navy that is stopping it. So, what I want you to do is go away and think about... as well as taking command of His Majesty's Frigate *Optimist*... how we can achieve that aim. Immediately you think you have control over your ship, you are to return here and we will discuss your ideas, and compare them with our own. Of course this is strictly secret, but you have already proved yourself in that area of trust."

The First Lord rang a little bell that was on his desk and a clerk appeared immediately.

"Captain Calvert's Commission... and er a copy of the Port Admiral's report on *Optimist*." The clerk disappeared.

"I think a drink is in order, don't you? Bye the

66

way, do change your epaulette to the correct shoulder, before leaving." But it was said with a smile.

The Earl poured out two glasses of Claret and handed one to Will, who by now was standing.

"Here's a curse on both the French and the crawling Spanish!" The Admiral raised his glass and drank. Will sipped his. He wanted to keep all his faculties about him.

"I understood, Sir, that you considered that the Navy had too many Commanders and Captains and therefore were not promoting anybody."

"Ah! Good point Calvert, but I see that you are not infallible! You were promoted in 1801, when you got back from internment. Because of the nature of your previous commission, we didn't publish it; it just appeared in the Navy List. I am very surprised that you didn't receive notice of the fact."

"Yet during my Courts Martial, I was always referred to and spoken to as Commander!" Replied Will; intrigued.

"Well, you were a Commander at the time of the loss, and I knew the outcome of the Court-Martial; that's why we furnished the Judge Advocate with all the relevant documents. There are those who get where they are through patronage – something that weakens our Navy, in my opinion, or time served in the rank, or – just occasionally, because they show themselves to be brilliant officers. I promoted Nelson before his time because he was an outstanding leader – courageous as well. Both Lord

Spencer and myself considered you to be just the type of person we needed in our Navy. I gave you that chance because I recognised you were a thinker as well as a brilliant seaman. You have shown yourself to be able to tackle difficult assignments, using your own methods. I consulted Lord Spencer and he agreed it was right to put you in a pigeon hole for future objectives, if they were required. It was to our benefit that you were already a Captain on the Navy List, so we could slot you in where necessary without causing too much attention."

"Thank, My Lord, I understand it all now, thank you, and thank you for your trust in me. I promise I shall do my utmost not to let you or this Country down."

Back at Kenton House, London, Will found that the well oiled machine was back up and running. Isabella was sitting in the drawing room by the fire, doing her needle point. He crossed over, kissed her and sat down opposite her. Isabella was not slow to notice the change of sides for the epaulette.

"Oh God, your back in harness. What do they want you to do this time?"

Will explained about the fortunes of the late Captain, he didn't touch on any future plans.

"Well at least we are not at war, so I shan't be praying all day, every day!"

"I shall have to leave tomorrow first thing. I suggest that I take Thomas with me to find a place for us to rent, so that we can at least see each other as much as possible. It is likely that the ship will have to go into dry-dock for a time, so that means I could be with you more than normal."

"Well I suppose it had to happen. I married a Naval Officer after all. Anyway, congratulations on your promotion. What are you now?"

"A confirmed Post-Captain. The first foot on the ladder to Admiral, if I live long enough, there being so many ahead of me."

"Well Lord Nelson made it to Admiral very early."

"Yes, my love, but his uncle had influence at the Admiralty which gave him a head start, and then his ability did help. Trouble is you have to really put yourself on the line to get noticed. Frankly I am quite happy to remain a Captain, if it means I am able to come back to you!"

Isabella jumped up and crossed to kiss him. "I'll ring for a celebratory drink!" She said, tears in her eyes.

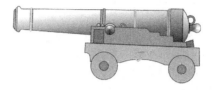

Will left at first light with Thomas Tucker on hired mounts. It would be quicker to ride, and it meant that Isabella had the use of the light coach around town. They arrived at the quay in Portsmouth dockyard at about six bells of the afternoon watch, three PM in laymen's terms. Having secured a waterman to take him out to *Optimist,* Will sent Tucker to stable the horses, and to start looking for rented premises the next day.

Optimist lay anchored about half-a-mile up-stream from the landing quay. She was hidden from view by other bigger and grander ships that were anchored or moored nearer the dockyard. The waterman was a stringy individual with disproportionately developed biceps due to his calling. He had an infectious grin, which revealed but a single tooth jutting down from his upper lip. Every few strokes he would spit tobacco juice over the side, but always well away from the passenger, so down wind. He knew however exactly where *Optimist* was anchored.

"Strange goings on, on that ship, it be told." He said and then a few minutes later. "Her Captain disappeared – talk of the town. Some says he was murdered, others he fell overboard drunk! Always drunk he was! I've seen him myself, trying to get into his gig. Had to be helped every time."

He rowed on for a few more minutes.

"Ballantyne, that was the name... that's what it was.... Captain Ballantyne. Always had a red face and cursed like you never wanted to hear a gentleman curse......Even offended my ears, and I hear things that would make your toes curl!" He grinned even wider.

Will realised he was talking about the Captain who had criticised him at the Court-Martial. He remembered he had thought he was drunk at the time.

Will had stayed up after Isabella had gone to bed to read the Port Admiral's confidential report on the incident and on the ship itself. The Port Admiral had dismissed the man as a drunken sot, a sodomite, and pervert of the worst order. It had also transpired in the report that the Boatswain had been the Captain's confidante and was the scourge of the lower deck. According to the testimony of the First Lieutenant, Lieutenant Derwent, the boatswain was always accompanied by two 'minders' to protect his back. He was often drunk, very abusive, and thought nothing of using his starter[1] for no good reason, than his own perverted pleasure.

As the waterman's boat neared *Optimist* a lookout called out "Who goes there?"

---

[1] Starter – a ropes end or cane, used to 'encourage' laggards.

"Optimist!" Called Will, as the Captain arriving at his ship.

"That's it, we is *Optimist* !" The fellow called back.

Will was stunned, he was at a loss as to what to say, when the Waterman took over.

"It's a Captain, you raving idiot, your new Captain!"

"Oh My God.!" Could be heard muttered over the water, then. "Captain coming aboard!"

Even a half a cable off you would have heard the scramble of feet and the sounds of the boatswain's pipes. The waterman brought his craft neatly alongside the Frigate and Will paid him, before scrambling up the side and in through the Starboard entry port. He was greeted by a line of Lieutenants and beyond them Midshipmen, all leaning forward to get their first glimpse of their new Captain.

A tall stooped Lieutenant with a forlorn expression and deeply set eyes stepped forward. "Welcome aboard Sir. I'm Lieutenant Derwent, I take it you are come aboard to take command?"

"I am Lieutenant, and I shall read myself in immediately."

"Aye Sir! Excuse me....Call all hands on deck for Commissioning!" Shouted the Lieutenant, before turning back to Will and politely asking his name.

"Calvert!" Replied Will.

"Thank you Sir, but we had no notification that we had a new Captain. May I introduce the Officers?"

Will nodded curtly. He had to feel his way with

this ship and crew.

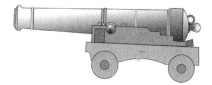

Derwent stepped forward and round to stand beside Calvert. He then proceeded to introduce the two other Lieutenants. The second Lieutenant he introduced as Oscar Cranfield. The third was called James Formby. Each knuckled their brow and did a formal little bow. Standing just slightly apart was a Lieutenant of Marines, which surprised Will.

"Unusual to have a Lieutenant of Marines aboard a frigate." Commented Will.

"Oliver Jackson, at your command Sir. Only just been assigned. They changed the marines aboard only two days ago."

Will took out a folder of papers and handed his father's leather bag to the third Lieutenant,. These were his commissioning letter and the articles of war. He then walked to the stern ladderway, and mounted to the quarterdeck. The crew had already taken their places, where ever they could find a space. Some hung from the shrouds; some had climbed onto the stored boats. When Will felt that everybody was in place, he read himself in. His commissioning letter was standard to all captains taking over a ship. He stressed the final part; Charging and Commanding all Officers and Men subordinate to him to support him according to the said Regulations, Instructions or Orders; to behave themselves with all due Respect and Obedience to him, their Superior Officer.

When he had finished, he took out the Articles of War. All the sailors aboard should have heard these very often, but it was mandatory for a new captain to read them out aloud. There are 36 of them and it takes a considerable time to read them all through. He started in a monotone until he got to article No. 2.

Here he stopped and surveyed the crew. Standing in front of the line was a short man with a pear shaped bald head; that seemed to be placed on a corpulent body without the intervention of a neck. His face was suffused red, and his piggy little eyes seemed to be constantly blinking. He was swaying gently on his short legs, which Will thought looked suspiciously like he was drunk. Held between his hands in front of him was a starter. Will was pretty clear in his mind that this must be the Boatswain. Either side, but slightly set back stood two big bruisers, with rather vacant faces. He fixed his gaze on the short man, so there could be no mistake to as whom he was speaking.

"All flag officers, and all persons in or belonging to His Majesty's ships or vessels of war, being guilty of profane oaths, cursings, execrations, drunkenness....

(Will paused and repeated)

drunkenness, uncleanness, or other scandalous actions, in derogation of God's honour, and corruption of good manners, shall incur such punishment as a court martial shall think fit to impose, and as the nature and degree of their offence shall deserve.

Will paused again and looked up at the crew. A few were sniggering at the back. The short man turned and scowled at them. The sniggering stopped immediately.

Will continued to read the Articles in his monotone until he came to Article. 19. Here he stopped, cleared his throat and again made a point of looking straight at the short man. Then he took another sweeping look across the assembled crew.

"Article 19.

If any person in or belonging to the fleet shall make or endeavour to make any mutinous assembly upon any pretence whatsoever, every person offending herein, and being convicted thereof by the sentence of the court martial, shall suffer death: (he paused for effect), and if any person in or belonging to the fleet shall utter any words of sedition or mutiny, he shall suffer death, or · such other punishment as a court martial shall deem him to deserve."

Will looked up from the sheet held in his hand that he was reading from and looked straight at the short man again.

" And if any officer, mariner, or soldier on or belonging to the fleet, shall behave himself with contempt to his superior officer, being in the execution of his office, he shall be punished according to the nature of his offence by the judgement of a court martial. "

He stopped to let the words sink in. Then he continued reading. The next article, Article 20. After this he stopped again. From the Port Admirals report he had gleaned that Captain Ballantyne had refused the crew fresh food, even in port. This next Article was going to be of extreme interest to the crew.

"Article 21,

If any person in the fleet shall find cause of complaint of the unwholesomeness of the victual, or upon other just ground, he shall quietly make the same known to his superior, or captain, or commander in chief, as the occasion may deserve, that such present remedy may be had as the matter may require; and the said superior, captain, or commander in chief, shall, as far as he is able, cause the same to be presently remedied; and no person in the fleet, upon any such or other pretence, shall attempt to stir up any disturbance, upon pain of such punishment, as a court martial shall think fit to inflict, according to the degree of the offence."

There was a murmur that ran round the assembled crew. The short man turned again in a threatening manner towards the crew. Silence descended once again. Will continued to read in the monotone he had started with, until he got to Article 29.

"Article 29.

If any person in the fleet shall commit the unnatural and detestable sin of buggery and sodomy with man or beast, he shall be punished with death by the sentence of a court martial."

He again stared at the short man, who shifted uncomfortably. Then he continued down to Article 34.

"Every person being in actual service and full pay, and part of the crew in or belonging to any of His Majesty's ships or vessels of war, who shall be guilty of mutiny, desertion, or disobedience to any lawful command, in any part of His Majesty's dominions on shore, when in actual service relative to the fleet, shall be liable to be tried by a court martial, and suffer the like punishment for every such offence, as if the same had been committed at sea on board any of His Majesty's ships or vessels of war."

Finally he got to the last catch all Article number 36. He stopped and allowed himself a smile.

"Article 36

All other crimes not capital committed by any person or persons in the fleet, which are not mentioned in this act, or for which no punishment is hereby directed to be inflicted, shall be punished by the laws and customs in such cases used at sea. "

He folded the papers and handed them to a Midshipman standing close by.

"So you see I am the third nearest to God in your

lives after, His Majesty, and the First Lord of the Admiralty. So remark it well!

However, you will find that there will be considerable changes aboard this ship. For a start the Purser will be commanded to make sure that at all times ..all times that it is possible, you will have fresh meat and vegetables to eat. It is imperative, even at peace, that you are physically fit and ready to defend our nation. God save His Majesty!"

A cheer started from the back and spread forward so that even the short man could do nothing about it.

"Number One, prepare for sea immediately! Then join me aft."

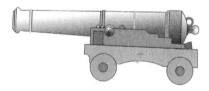

Will walked slowly to the stern of the quarterdeck. He watched as the crew went to their stations. The short man strolled forward shouting something, which Will could not hear and then disappeared down the forward ladderway. Where had he gone? His station should have been on deck. The captains of the tops were leading their men up the ratlines to their yards. The quartermasters were standing at the wheel. A middle aged figure appeared dressed in a plain dress coat and approached Derwent. Derwent took a quick look towards Will and then turned back to the man. There was a short conversation and then the fellow came hurrying aft to Will.

"Baldwin, Ship's Master, Sir. Captain Ballantyne wouldn't let me use the sails to assist breaking out the anchor. He liked to see the men sweat at the capstan - he said. Do I have your permission to use the sails?"

Will replied immediately, "Of course, how else is one supposed to carry out such a manoeuvre?

"Thank you, Sir!" Said the Master with an apologetic smile, then he turned and nodded to Derwent, who raised his voice trumpet and ordered the sheets to hauled in on the Inner and Outer Jibs. He then pointed the trumpet upwards and commanded that the Fore-topsail, the Main-topsail, and Mizzen topsails be unfurled. Then the Braces to the Yards be hauled in, then the sheets taken up.

Gradually *Optimist* began to make headway, from forward could be heard the sound of the seaman on the capstan chanting in time to a fiddler.

Right up in the bows a seaman raised his arm to signal that the Anchor was 'up and down' meaning that it was strait below the bows. *Optimist* seemed to hover for a moment and then break free from the mud at the bottom of the harbour. Will could not hear the shouts up from the bows, but it was obvious that the anchor was hauled up ready for catting.

Derwent raised a questioning eyebrow to his new captain, who nodded his assent, and Derwent ordered the wheel to be put up.

At long last the short man re-appeared on deck still shouting and using his starter on anybody who was un-wise enough to come into his orbit.

Optimist came round, yards were hauled round using the tacks and braces and the sails sheeted in. Now she was moving towards the narrow entrance to Portsmouth Harbour. Will watched every detail of how the ship was handled without saying a word. Once they were out into the Solent, Will strolled forward and told the Master to take her East out of the estuary. Now things had quietened down, Will asked Derwent to join him at the stern of the quarterdeck.

"Well Number One, the crew seem to know what is required of them, without the help of that short man with the bald head!

"The Boatswain!" Derwent said pithily.

"Ah yes, the Boatswain! I think I shall have a word with that gentleman. Have him brought aft."

Instead of staying where he was, Will strolled forward so he was standing to one side of the wheel, well within the hearing of the Quartermasters and all the officers. The short man, now indentified as the Boatswain, came swaggering aft as if he commanded the ship.

"You wanted a word Captain?" He said, but his

words were slightly slurred. Will leant forward sniffed and stood up straight. "You have been drinking! Nobody serves on any ship of mine when they are partaken of drink. I understand you were the Boatswain. It would normally be up to you to set an example."

"I am the Boatswain!" He man said truculently.

"Not any more, you're not! Lieutenant Cranfield, kindly go below and search this man's cabin and remove any liquor."

"You can't do that, I'm a Standing Officer."

"What's your name?"

"Carrick."

"Sir!"

"Carrick Sir."

"Well Carrick, if you hadn't been so drunk, you would have noticed that when I read myself in, I particularly stressed the part that I was directly responsible to the Board of Admiralty and that means I don't answer to any Commodores, Admirals, or anybody else, but directly to the First Lord, Earl St. Vincent himself."

Carrick blinked hard as if trying to understand what Will was saying. He also swayed from side to side and had to move his feet to stop himself from falling over.

"Stand still when I am addressing you!" Ordered Will.

Carrick made as if to use his starter on Will, but two Marines stepped forward and restrained his arms. Derwent had obviously used his initiative.

"I'll bloody kill you!" Carrick whispered.

"You heard the man, Number One? And you Lieutenant?" Will was questioning the third officer Formby.

"Aye Sir!" Said both in unison.

"Take this man down to his cabin and place a guard of Marines outside until further notice. He is to have no intoxicating liquor, and his not to communicate with anybody aboard without my express permission."

Carrick was in a paroxysm of rage. He shouted drunken threats at all around him, regardless of rank or otherwise.

"Have his two Acolytes assigned to different watches and parts of the ship, Number One. Which is the senior of the two Boatswain's Mates?"

"Jones, Sir."

"Have him brought here, if you please."

A tall broad shouldered man of indeterminate age came smartly forward.

He knuckled his brow. "Jones, Captain."

"Very good, Jones. Do you think you could act as Boatswain temporarily until we are sent a new one?"

"Yus, Sir"

"Good, carry on! But see if you can get along without you or your mate using your starters, unless absolutely necessary. Use your voice, and your wit. It works better I assure you."

The man gave the broadest grin, one could imagine, knuckled his brow, and trotted away at the double to consult with his opposite number.

Will turned to his officers. "Now we shall put

this little lady to the test. Mister Baldwin. Let us try every point of sailing, and every variation of sail, including all the fore and aft sails."

For the next four hours *Optimist* weaved her way further out to sea, constantly changing direction and her sail plan. All the time the log was streamed and their speed through the water recorded on the traverse board.

Now well out in the Channel and no other vessels in sight, Will asked for the Gunner.

He checked Derwent for the man's name so when he arrived Will was able to say.

"Mr. Noble, we will now exercise the guns, but not in the normal way. I want two Midshipmen with two chronometers to note the time each individual gun takes from firing the first shot to being ready loaded and in a position to fire the second. When the gun is ready for the second firing, the gun captain is to raise his arm and shout 'ready'. The time taken from the first firing to the 'ready' will be noted by the Midshipmen independently. Each gun will be fired separately, starting with the starboard upper-deck working aft. No gun is to be touched before the first firing. I want to see which Gun Captains have maintained their weapons. Once we have completed on the upper-deck, we shall repeat the performance up on the foredeck. You may inform the men that the fastest gun crew will be rewarded with an extra tot."

The Gunner's mouth had dropped open in amazement. "Begging your pardon Sir, but the Gun's haven't been fired or exercised since the day peace was declared. Captain Ballantyne didn't like the noise, Sir."

Derwent standing to one side said. "I am afraid Guns is right. We were treated virtually as the Captain's personal yacht. The only time we put to sea was when Captain Ballantyne wanted to replenish his wine and spirit store."

Will had read the fact in the Port Admiral's report, so was not surprised.

"Well we shall be exercising the guns everyday from now on. She's all yours Number One."

Derwent nodded his acknowledgement, with the first smile Will had seen from the man. The atmosphere aboard was already subtly changing. Seamen were going about their duties, but with a smile and a joke between them.

It was getting dark by the time they had finished, the gunnery practice. Three guns on the upper deck and two on the forecastle failed to fire. When the Midshipmen reported the timings, there was a wide variation. Obviously a lot of practice was going to be needed.

Leaving instructions for the Master to prepare a plot for the return to Portsmouth, Will descended the stern ladderway, and by the light of the lantern was able to make his way to the entrance to his quarters. He nodded to the Marine on guard and opened the door to the dining area. To his right, beside the cannon, there was a table laden with ledgers held in place by the fiddles. He assumed that these have been laid out in case a new captain should arrive, and that he would've wanted to have studied them before anything else. The door to the sleeping area was open, and he could see a large cot with ornate trimmings hanging from its guys. The very sight of the cot sickened him. He shut the door and opened the one to the main cabin. Lanterns from the deck head showed him that the cabin was lavishly furnished. Across the centre was a fine table with eight chairs set around it. Between the table, and the stern windows were too comfortable chairs with side tables. As he crossed the cabin to sit on the window seat, he heard somebody enter behind him. Swivelling around he found an ancient servant, who bowed low. The man said. "Evening Cap'an, can I get you anything?"

"And you are?"

"Millward, Cap'an."

"And how long have you been the Captain's servant Millward?"

Millward looked rather confused and Will noticed the man's hands were shaking. "Nigh on two weeks, Cap'an."

"So how long have you been aboard?" Asked Will in surprise.

"Two years, and some."

"So how come you have just been made the Captain's servant?"

"Well you sees Sir, it's like this. Captain Ballantyne liked to have the young men around him. Only he ran through all of them, and I think that someone must've heard that I'd been a footman, cause I was taken from the wardroom and made to serve up here. Didn't want to, you understand,."

"Oh, right! A good Claret, Millward, would not go amiss, and if you could find an inkstand, pen and paper. I should be very grateful."

Millward looked very surprised and a smile crept across his face, and Will noticed that he's hands had stop shaking.

A few minutes later, the steward returned with a tray containing a decanter, a glass, writing utensils and paper. These he placed on the table, made a small bow with a smile and retired. Will stood up and moved across to a chair by the table, he poured himself a glass of wine and then sat down to draw the stern quarter of a frigate. Will had been drawing all of his life, his journal was full of sketches. The first sketch did not show any ornamental gold work. He then took another piece of paper and laid it over the first, then by flicking the paper up and down, he was able to copy exactly the previous drawing. He took up the third piece of paper and repeated the copying. On this last drawing, he added a gallery to the Stern of the ship and added in ornamental work. He then put this piece of paper aside and drew in different ornamental work on the page below. To this drawing, he added a ship's boat hanging from davits over the Stern.

Will sat back and took another sip of the wine, then sat for some time thinking, pondering. He then pulled out another piece of paper and started writing. He continued in this manner for the most part of the night.

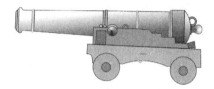

As the first signs of a new day showed through the stern windows of his cabin, Will put down his pen, stood up and stretched, then walked through to go up on deck. On his way he noticed again the door to the sleeping cabin open. There hung the gross cot. It was much wider than normal, and was covered with lavish, rich fabric. He shut the door and continued his way out, and on to the quarterdeck. Formby the third Lieutenant had the watch. Will nodded to him, sniffed the air and looked all around. There were a few white caps to the waves, and there was a good breeze. Vaguely on the horizon he could make out the darker smug of land. He told Formby to summon the young gentlemen to his cabin at the next change of the watch. Then, his hands behind his back, he crossed and re-crossed the quarterdeck, all the time, checking the sails, the wake, and everything that was going on around.

When the watches changed from the Morning Watch to the Forenoon Watch, Will waited for a few minutes and then went down to his cabin. Here the young men who hoped one day, to be midshipman, were assembled. They were a ragged lot ranging in age from perhaps as young as 10 years or so, to their late teens. He asked each one their name and their age. He then set them the task of taking down the cot in the next cabin and taking it out on deck to be placed on one of the carronades. He waited for some time, and then went back on deck. This time it was Cranfield, who had the watch. Will ordered that all the crew be summoned for a burial service.

"Has somebody died Sir?" Asked Cranfield; a puzzled expression on his face.

"No! But I want to bury something!" Laughed Will.

Puzzlement still showing on his face Cranfield ordered the crew on deck to witness a burial at sea. The boatswains' whistles sounded and the crew came piling up from below to gather on the foredeck. Will ordered the gunner to bring up an 18 pound ball in a shot bag. Once the ball in its bag had been brought up on deck, Will ordered that the bag be secured to the cot.

Will stepped forward. "This offensive object does not deserve any religious offering! We'll just commit it to the deep and hope that it will rot in hell for the rest of eternity!" He nodded to the young men gathered around the cot, and they upended it to drop with a satisfying splash into the murky sea. A cheer went up from the crew, and Will turned to see a mass of smiling faces.

Certainly there was a complete difference in the behaviour of the crew from when they had first left their anchorage in Portsmouth Harbour. Then everybody seemed to move about in a morose trance-like state, now they were laughing and making jokes about each other. The Boatswain's Mate, now acting Boatswain was grinning from ear to ear, and cracking jokes at various slothful seamen's expense.

As Will re-entered his private domain, he noticed the ledgers once more. He idly opened the Punishment Book, and wished he hadn't. There didn't seem to have been a day without a flogging. Noticing the Muster Book, it reminded him to call for the Purser.

He opened the door to the Upper Deck and spoke to the Marine on sentry duty.

"Pass the word for the Purser."

The Marine came smartly to attention and repeated what Will had said. The words were echoed from various parts of the ship. Will shut the door and went through to the main cabin, and to his seat of ease on the Port quarter.

When he came out, buttoning up his flies, Purser was announced by the sentry. The Purser flounced in, it appeared to Will that he was on tiptoe.

"Mr. Bennett, the Purser, at your service Sir!" He chirped in a high effeminate voice.

"Oh God, not another!" Thought Will, but he said instead. "I understand that the late Captain wouldn't allow fresh food for the crew. Is that right?"

"Absolutely! He was a very, very mean man. He had all the best for himself, but cared not a jot for anybody else. I was positively forbidden to bring anything fresh aboard, except of course his things!"

"Well that changes the moment we get into harbour. Fresh food for everybody aboard. The officers will be allowed to opt out if they so desire. Fresh beer and rum to be brought aboard.

Then we come to the matter of clothing. You are to provide every seaman aboard with a new blue short jacket, a blue waistcoat of similar cloth, a white jerkin with thin horizontal stripes, a red one with black stripes for the Landmen. Wide white trousers for all. Whilst you are about it, lay in a supply of those black hats, the sailors like so much – various sizes of course. Don't worry I shall see that you don't go short. Oh and do the crew have oilskin coats?

"I have no idea. I never venture abroad when it is wet up-top." The man was all fluttering hands and fingers.

"Well make sure that all those who work on deck or in the rigging are well provided for. That is all for the present. A cutter will take you ashore as soon as the anchor hits the bottom."

After the Purser had gone, Will realised that there was nothing he could do about the ledgers, or logs. He couldn't sign them off; he would have to get Number One to ask the Port Captain what was to be done. Making his way up to the quarter-deck he found the First Lieutenant already up and about.

"Good Morning, Sir" Said Derwent; doffing his hat.

"Morning Number One."

"Looks as if the weather is going to hold."

Will looked about him. "Looks like it." He looked up at the sails, and then aft at their wake. Then he turned to Derwent. "A word with you Number One."

Derwent's face clouded.

They made their way to the stern.

"The Purser will need one of the cutters to go ashore as soon as we are secure. He is to make sure we have fresh food for all aboard whilst we are in harbour. I should be grateful if you could get one of the Midshipmen to take my gig to 'Spice Island' and go to the Star & Garter. He should seek out a Midshipman Tucker, who will be lodging there. I need to see Tucker before I leave for London. I need him to bring a riding horse to the steps. Yes, I have to go to London almost immediately. The gig is to return for me, they can bring back both Midshipmen when I have left. Also I should like you to do a few things for me whilst I'm away. I want the guns exercised twice a day. If any gun can beat the existing rate, then they get an extra tot for the crew."

Derwent's face had changed, he obviously realised he wasn't in for criticism. Will scratched his neck, as he always did when going through a list of things to do.

"Do you know if the late Captain had any family?"

"No, Sir. He never mentioned any."

"Then when you have time, get yourself taken over to the Port Admiral and see if he knows. I shall make enquires in London, if I have time. In the meantime, have all his furniture bundled up ready for putting ashore."

"Excuse me Sir, what about his wines and spirits?" Asked Derwent.

"I am sure he would have wanted to donate them to the Wardroom. In any case, I think they might get broken, if they were taken ashore!"

Derwent broke into a smile. He could see that Will was making a mockery of the former Captain.

"Oh, and any nautical instruments, books or the like, have them parcelled up separately. If no one claims them, then they should go to the Gunroom...if we had one!"

This time Derwent laughed at Will's quizzical expression. The nearby Midshipmen turned to witness a sight they had never experienced on *Optimist,* the Captain and First Lieutenant laughing together.

"What about Carrick, Sir?" Asked Derwent, more sure of his Captain now.

"Oh I shouldn't think he has dried out sufficiently to understand any charges if they were put to him. No, he shall have to wait for my return. However, if by chance you do have to go over to the Port Admiral, you might warn him that we shall be sending the rogue over for Court Martial anytime soon." And Will grinned at Derwent.

The First Lieutenant appreciated the handling of the situation, and was moved to laughter again, mostly from relief.

"Whilst I am away, you can take some time ashore for yourself. Make sure that there are two

Lieutenants onboard at any time. That way each of you should be able to buy yourselves a few essentials. The same goes for the Warrant Officers and Midshipmen. Just make sure they avoid the dives and the prostitutes. I don't want incapable officers on this ship."

"Thank you very much Sir!" Derwent was truly surprised. What a change.

"Permission to speak Sir?"

"I thought you had been... of course, you don't need to ask, fire away."

"I would just like to say that I couldn't have believed that the whole atmosphere of the ship could change in such a short time. I even heard the crew remarking upon it. They would never have dared before. Incredible, truly incredible!"

"Thank you Number One, I hope you are right! But... I don't want anybody to think that I am a soft touch. I expect everybody to do their best, to their ability. I have found that encouragement and rewards work better than punishment. I punish where necessary, but I prefer to know the circumstances of any failure, before making a judgement. Of course you are to continue to listen out for any indication as how the late Captain disappeared. We don't want to have a murderer in our midst." So saying Will walked forward to the wheel.

The coast of Southern England and the Isle of Wight could be clearly seen. They would be turning shortly to make their way up the Solent towards the narrow entrance to Portsmouth Harbour. There was time however to investigate his command. He called on Derwent to accompany him and strolled forward.

"Won't you need a couple of marines?" Asked Derwent; falling in alongside him.

"Why should I?" Will asked.

"Captain Ballantyne insisted on it, Sir!"

"I'm not Captain Ballantyne. I doubt very much if anybody will want to attack me."

As he came to the first members of the crew on the foredeck he asked their names, which ships they had served on and to everybody's surprised asked if they had any questions or complaints.

Most of the men were tongue tied. They had never experienced a captain chatting to them and seeming interested in them as a person. The pair continued the progress forward and then down through the forward ladderway to the decks below. By the time they had reached to bilges, Will had spoken to each and every seaman aboard.

Back in his quarters Will asked Derwent to give his thoughts on the ship and the crew.

Derwent found this difficult because the very recent 'rounds' had been a revelation to him.

Some members of the crew had expressed their hatred for the late captain and his methods. Will had assured them that things were going to be very different under his command.

Will found Derwent's description of life aboard, under Captain Ballantyne, to be almost unbelievable.

When Derwent had finished, Will thanked him for being so frank. Then he had each of the officers in for a chat separately. He even had the non-commissioned officers in, one at a time, for a frank exchange of views.

The news soon spread throughout the ship.

Having finished his meetings Will went back up onto the quarterdeck.

"Mister Baldwin, she looks well set-up!" Said Will to the Master.

"Thank you Sir! I reckon we shall hit the tide just right for entering, and the wind is being kind for a change."

"Good Omen, Master!"

"Hope so Sir!" Grinned the Master.

Will decided to leave them to it, but a further thought crossed his mind.

"We shall be having a new Boatswain shortly Number One. Fellow by the name of Tarrant; one of the best, in my opinion, in His Majesty's Navy."

"And Tucker is to join us?" Asked Derwent.

"Yes, quite so. Very fine young man. Been with me on my last two ships." He purposefully avoided saying 'commands', because he was very conscious that he had only held one command previously.

Just as he was about to go below, Lieutenant Cranfield came panting up. He glanced at Will, but addressed Derwent.

"Been a bit of fracas below. The Boatswain's two 'guardians' have been set about. The Master-at-Arms broke it up, but I thought you should know."

Will decided to leave it to Derwent. He needed all the support he could get if their future mission was to succeed. He went down to his cabin, although he had nothing to do. To occupy himself, he made a list of the furniture he would need, if he was getting rid of the late Captain's.

He waited until the shore lines of both the Isle of Wight and Southsea could clearly be seen, before going back up to the quarter-deck. He nodded to Cranfield who had the watch. The Master came over to speak to Will.

"Tides just right Sir. Not too strong, but will carry us through nicely."

"Very good, Master."

"I'll be taking in the Courses, the Inner jib and the Fore topmast staysail when we've turned."

Will nodded and gave the man an encouraging smile. Obviously the poor man was still used to the ways of the previous Captain. One always took in those sails when manoeuvring in harbour so you could see what you were doing, and to reduce the speed.

The Master glanced at Will, who gave no reaction, and then gave the order for the turn. Immediately afterwards the orders were passed for the courses to be hauled up to their yards. The two fore sails' halliards were released and the sails dropped to be taken in. *Optimist* headed for the entrance.

Will noticed that a gun crew were being sent forward to one of the carronades on the larboard side. They would be firing a salute for the Admiral, but whether it was for the Port Admiral or the Fleet Admiral, Will didn't know. He sauntered over to Derwent who had reappeared on deck.

"I take it we shall be firing only one salute, and leave it to their Lordships to decide to whom we are giving that mark of respect?"

Derwent blinked quickly, but regained his composure and chuckled to himself. The question needed no reply.

Formby had his eye to a glass and spun round. "Signal from Flag, Sir. Captain to report."

"Does the signal give a pennant number?"

"No Sir!"

"Well, how are we to know if he is referring to us or not? If they remember to give a number; Number One, send over Formby with a message that the Captain regrets that he has been called to the Board of Admiralty, which of course takes precedence."

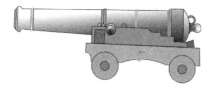

Once they were back at anchor, the cutters and the gig were swung out and placed in the water. The Purser climbed warily down into one of the cutters and left for the shore to see about fresh food. With him he carried an extra purse provided by Will himself from his own funds to make sure there was plenty of the best possible provender.

A Midshipman dropped rather more nimbly into

the Gig and it was off down the harbour towards the entrance where the Star and Garter Hostelry was situated.

Will standing by the wheel was gratified to see seaman grinning at him as they went about their business. Derwent joined him.

"I have put five seamen on report Sir, for fighting. What do you want to do about them?"

"I don't want to do anything about them; Number One. Such a small incident is up to you to deal with. However, might I suggest that you investigate why the fighting occurred. I have a suspicion that it was retribution for past ills. You can't let it go without some form of punishment, but I have always found that a number of times up the ratlines and down, of each mast in turn, concentrates the mind wonderfully. The men are fit for duty within a very short time. Besides we have no Surgeon aboard at present, so we can hardly flog anybody even if we wanted to do so."

"Never stopped Ballantyne!" Remarked Derwent.

"Well she is all yours again Number One, look after her kindly. I have a distinct feeling that this peace is not going to last. The Corsican is now firmly in power, and he is ambitious! Very dangerous in a ruler!"

Derwent nodded and smiled his agreement.

Will passed the word for Millward and when he appeared ordered him to bring up his bag and his cloak. Then he paced the quarter-deck to await the return of the Gig. Millward appeared with the old leather bag, containing the pistols and the cloak.

"Going to be ashore long then Sir?" An emboldened Millward asked.

"Yes Millward a few days. I have to go back to London. The First Lieutenant will be arranging for the late Captain's furniture to be taken ashore. Make sure you pack his instruments carefully and keep them aboard. Oh that reminds me, I have forgotten to speak to the carpenter about a new cot."

"Would you like me to speak to him Sir. We's are mates, so to speak. Both come from the same town, see."

"Very good. I just want an ordinary cot, nothing gross like the late Captain's."

"Quite so, Sir. It shall be done."

Formby came up and stood hovering.

"Yes Lieutenant?"

"Pardon me Sir, but the frigate down there is repeating the signal about the Captain to repair aboard the Flagship. Still no number!" And he grinned.

"Well they will realise soon enough, so you will have the pleasure of making a visit to Flag. Won't you?"

"Aye Sir."

"Captain's Gig returning!" Came a cry from the bow look-out.

Derwent came hurrying up to accompany Will to the exit port.

"I have asked Millward to have a word with the Carpenter about a cot for myself. Just thought you'd better know!"

"Thank you Sir. Have a good journey!"

Will dropped effortlessly into the Gig; the Midshipman taking the leather bag from his hand.

"Midshipman Tucker will be waiting for you at the South Jetty steps, Sir."

"And you are?"

"Midshipman Crawley, Sir."

"Well Mr. Crawley, your little crew made very good time. I hope you haven't exhausted them?"

The stroke oarsman smothered a chuckle. Crawley looked embarrassed, until he realised that the new Captain was smiling at him.

"I hope not Sir."

As the Gig pushed off from *Optimist's* side the crew gave a cheer. Will looked up to see rows of smiling men crowded everywhere along the ship's side and in the rigging. It brought a lump to his throat.

Tucker was waiting for them at the Dockyard's South Jetty steps. He was holding the bridle of a well formed mount. Will climbed the steps and greeted him warmly.

"So how goes it Thomas?"

"I have been advised that you should not take a house in town. It is very noisy and smelly...besides I don't think Mrs Calvert would appreciate 'prossies' walking past her door day and night. So.... I hope I have done the right thing, but a Naval Captain had a new house built just outside Portsmouth itself, in the village of Southsea. It has a very fine view of the Solent. He is hoping to rent it, as he is on half-pay. Well I imagine that is the reason. I took a look late last night, and it seemed just the thing."

"Well, you do surprise me, I had thought that you would be still looking. I trust your judgement. You know both of us well enough by now. If I had known you would have been free, I would have got you to come with me to London, for the sake of company. As it is I must be on my way. Lieutenant Derwent is the First Lieutenant. He is expecting you. Go to Midshipman Crawley in the Gig. Arrange for him to make sure you are picked up when you have arranged the house. My orders. See you when I get back. Oh! I shall come back to this jetty when I return. Be a good test for the lookouts to see if they spot me."

Will swung himself up onto the horse and relieved Tucker of his bag, which he placed on the saddle in front of him to take out the two pistols and put them in the holsters that Tucker had remembered to bring. He dropped the bag to Tucker, retained his cloak, which he rolled up and placed between the straps on the back of the saddle. He gave a wave to the Gig crew, then turned and set off for London.

The rain held off until he was just past Cobham. He therefore arrived at Kenton House dripping wet. That didn't stop Isabella showing her pleasure at his return by giving him a hug. Laughing together they went up to their room, where Will undressed and changed into civilian clothes. Merrick, who doubled as footman and valet, took away the uniform to dry it and press it ready for the morrow.

Will had to wait for two and a half hours the next morning, in the crowded waiting room, with less fortunate Captains, Commanders and Lieutenants, who all sought an audience to plead their case for a ship.

Finally he was called, and shown along the usual corridor to Lord St. Vincent's office. He was announced and found that Sir Nepean was seated with his Lordship.

"Ah Calvert, didn't expect you back so soon. Trouble?"

"Good Morning My Lord, Sir Nepean; trouble? No not that I know of! Are we at war already?"

There was a glint of amusement behind his Lordship's eyes. "So, what brings you back so soon?"

"To discuss details; and to show you some of my ideas."

"What about *Optimist*?" Asked Nepean.

"Oh fine Sir. The crew are happy to be about to get fresh food for the first time for months. The Boatswain is under guard in his cabin awaiting my return. He was rolling drunk when I went aboard and threatened to kill me when I ordered him to his cabin. So I had all alcohol removed. I thought that was good enough to have him court-martialled, without having to put the young men through the painful procedure of giving evidence if he was accused of sodomy. We put to sea to test out the crew. The guns hadn't even been exercised since peace was declared, so we now have a competition to see which crew can achieve the best time. The crews' sail handling was remarkably good. We tried every point of sailing, and we varied the rig. The Master knows what he is about, and I think that Lieutenant Derwent is beginning to recover. We did have a little ceremony, I am afraid to report...probably rather naughty of me, but ... well we had a burial at sea of the late Captain's cot. It went down very well with the crew, especially the young men."

Earl St. Vincent raised an eyebrow to Sir Nepean. "Well let's get down to your plans."

Will outlined his ideas, before Sir Nepean excused himself, and left Will alone with his Lordship. Lunch was brought in by servants, so the two could continue. Will produced his drawings which drew many comments.

"The long barrelled bow-chasers; you're planning to use the same tactics as you used on *Snipe*?" Queried His Lordship.

"Aye Sir. I intend to try and hit them where it hurts!"

Late in the evening the First Lord called it a day.

"I shall put this to the Board tomorrow. You get back here in the afternoon."

Isabella and Will spent a pleasant morning walking in town, and had lunch in a well known hotel. Then Will put Isabella into a chair, and walked back to the Admiralty. This time there was no waiting, he was shown straight up to the First

Lord's Office. Here he discovered a few other members of the Board. They quizzed him about certain features of the secret undertaking, but seemed on the whole satisfied with his answers. Some of his ingenious ideas, caused few shaken heads, but Jervis, the First Lord, assured them they were practical. Will realised that these gentlemen were not sailors. They were probably members of the House of Commons or of the Lords.

When the other members of the Board had departed, Sir Nepean reappeared.

"I have had permission from the Prime Minister to order from the Ordinance Board the special long barrelled 18 pounders, Captain Calvert asked for. He was very intrigued. I have made ready the instructions for the Master Shipwright at Portsmouth, as well as for the sail-makers. If the board agree, perhaps you could sign them, My Lord, and they can then be sent out."

"My we are keen Nepean!" Laughed His Lordship, and Sir Evan Nepean smiled at Will.

"What about the extra crew at Gibraltar?" Asked Lord Jervis.

Nepean shrugged. "So long as we are not at war again, I see no problem. We have surplus of Lieutenants. However, if war is declared, every Admiral within range will want to snaffle them."

"I know!" His Lordship got up and began to pace the floor. "Send them to Malta. Nelson is in charge out there. He will see the reason. And what is more he will make sure it happens. Can't trust others nearer home, what?"

"Agreed! We send them by transport to Malta, to await *Optimist*."

"Will they be privy to what we are up to?" Asked Will.

"No! Fewer who know the better. Been hard enough bloody work, getting the Board to swear to their secrecy: same with the Dockyards. We won't tell them why we are doing things, if asked we say we are experimenting. That should shut them up!"

It was extraordinary how fast the Admiralty could move, now that Lord St. Vincent was in charge; thought Will. He was required to return to the Admiralty the next day in case there were any problems that needed to be resolved. These turned out to be few and minor. So when he left the Admiralty it was to return to Portsmouth, and days of dockyard work. He had managed to look in on the clerk who dealt with Commissioned Officers, and discovered Captain Ballantyne didn't seem to have had any known immediate relations.

The next day the Calvert convoy started out again, this time for Portsmouth. Messages had gone out, with Admiralty blessing, ordering Tarrant and Dr Henri de Cornes, to repair aboard the frigate *Optimist* currently at anchor in Portsmouth harbour. Allwood had been put on the half-past seven mail coach from the Sussex Tavern, Fleet Street, to warn Tucker that they were coming, so that they could go straight to the new rented house.

They were grateful to find Tucker waiting for them at the last mail stop, before Portsmouth, Cosham. It was late afternoon, and Tucker led them directly to Southsea and the house. The place was smaller than they were used to, but it had a first floor sitting room with a fine view out over the Solent. Tucker had arranged with the housekeeper that she employ a local cook, so a meal was soon on the go, after their arrival. There were not enough rooms for all the staff, or for the horses and carriages. The housekeeper had arranged with a local hostelry so that the second coach, the van and their horses could be stabled there, with accommodation for those who were not immediately necessary in the house.

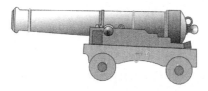

Next day, the lookout on *Optimist* must have been on the ball, because almost as soon as the Calvert light coach arrived in the Dockyard, the captain's gig could be seen leaving the ship.

Allwood was at the helm, and he gave his cock eyed grin, when he had successfully brought the boat alongside the steps. The boats crew looked much smarter than before, wearing their new sweaters and sporting black hats with dark blue ribbons. Will and Tucker got in, and were rowed out to *Optimist* anchored in the Harbour.

Will received a proper Captain's reception as he climbed through the entry port, to be greeted by a smiling Derwent. Walking together towards Will's cabin, Will asked the Lieutenant if he had had time to go ashore.

"Yes thank you Sir, and so did the others. Made a great change for all of us, I must admit."

The Marine sentry came to the present as they went through into the deserted cabins. Without furniture they looked very bare. Millward popped out to see if anything was required and coffee was ordered. They had to sit on the bare wood of the window seat, as the cushions had gone the way of all the furniture.

"My wife has undertaken the job of finding furnishings. I have described what I need, so she will be on the trail very soon."

"You are married Sir?" Derwent seemed surprised.

"Yes Jasper, I am married and my wife is here in a little village called Southsea, next to Portsmouth." It was the first time Will had used the First Lieutenant's forename.

"So tell me how are things aboard here?" He continued.

"Well, Sir. We have exercised the guns twice a day, and the Master-at-Arms has started sword drill again. I visited the Port Admiral...well actually I spoke to the Captain, but they are prepared to receive Carrick as soon as we wish. The Flagship finally got their act together after you had left and Formby went over to appraise them of the situation. He suggested to me that he thought it might clear the air if you could possibly pay a courtesy visit. I understand the old man was not very happy! I did as you suggested and the men who took part in the fracas, were very surprised at the punishment. There was quite a lot of banter about it. It is an experience I don't think the participants want to repeat very soon. Oh and you have a cot...it is about the only thing you do have, but it is up and ready. No trimmings or sheets etc."

"Well I doubt that I shall be sleeping aboard for the next few weeks. We are to go into dry dock very shortly. One of the frigates in Ordinary, will be brought down stream, and our crew will transfer to her whilst the work is being carried out. Cranfield and Formby will be with them, You stay aboard here.......Thank you Millward!"

The Captain's servant placed a tray with two cups of coffee on the seat between the two officers.

"Millward, tell the cook that I shan't be eating aboard today, will you?"

Millward shuffled out.

"Now Number One, I have to ask you to give your solemn promise on oath that you will not reveal to anyone what I am about to tell you?"

"Of course Sir!"

"Good. Well this ship has been chosen for a very secret mission. I can't tell you exactly what until we are at sea. However, when we go into dock, we shall have our paintwork changed to 'Nelson' yellow. We shall also be measured for 'gauntlets'... I can't think of a better word at the moment... canvas covers for our bow rails and fancy work and for the sides. Our ornate scroll work at the stern will be removed, re-gilded and replaced, but with a different method of fitting. Our name plate will have the same treatment. A gallery will be made to fit the stern, but this is removable too. We shall be taking delivery of two new long barrelled 18 pounders, but they will be mounted on special skids, very like those of the carronades. This will mean that there will be new gun-ports right up forward, with extra decking. There will be special rails for the new cannons to slide on, as they won't have the normal wheels. They will be sliding on their axles. We did this on a ship I commanded and it was very successful. These are to be installed at the bow. We shall also be taking onboard extra canvas, in different colours, as well as yards.

You are to make sure that the Carpenter has extra timber to erect the framework for extra officers' cabins. Extra canvas will be supplied. We won't construct those until shortly before needed.

We shall need extra barrels for water, for a long voyage."

Will lowered his voice. "I need your help in another matter. You are to go ashore, taking civilian clothes... if you haven't got any, let me know... then you are to purchase from where ever you can find them, foreign officers' uniforms to fit our own officers. Don't worry about swords. Oh, and the Master-at-Arms, will be supplied with extra powder, and pistols. He is to train every member of the crew in firing them accurately."

Derwent stared at Will for a moment and then a smile spread across his face. "Sounds interesting, Sir."

Later Will had himself rowed over to the Flagship, where he had a short interview with the Fleet Admiral. It was short because Will apologised for not attending sooner, then handed the Admiral a sealed letter from the First Lord of the Admiralty. This short missive informed any senior officer not to interfere in any way with anything that *Optimist* or her captain did, as they were under direct command of the Admiralty, to carry out experimental work..

Thomas Tucker settled into the Gunroom (frigates didn't have wardrooms), but said very little about himself or his Captain. He had decided to let Captain Calvert's highly regarded record to slowly become known to his messmates, which would take seconds to spread over the entire ship. His Captain had expressly forbidden him to see to the sea-chests. These were brought over in the cutters when the van arrived at the quay. At least Will had something extra to sit on, although not that comfortable.

The next day, the ship was all agog, when the Captain returned, bringing his wife with him.

Everybody aboard pushed their way to an advantage point to see the lovely lady hoisted aboard by boatswain's chair. Once aboard she turned and smiled at everybody and gave them a wave, before being shown down to the Captain's suite. Here she was introduced to the Officers. They asked if they might 'dine' her and her husband, which was graciously accepted.

When the officers had left she turned to Will and whispered. "It's a lot bigger than *Snipe*. Lots of light. Now tell me what you require."

So Will showed her the new bare cot hanging from the deck head.

"You don't sleep in that do you?" She asked; staring at the object hanging in front of her.

"Of course. The seamen have hammocks, which in my opinion are a lot more sensible. It wouldn't seem right for a Captain to be seen sleeping in one unfortunately."

"However do you get into the thing?"

Will demonstrated the first part, but since he was fully dressed and the cot had no mattress or bed-clothes he didn't get into it.

Isabella was laughing as Millward entered carrying a tray.

"This is my servant Millward. Millward my wife."

Millward looked startled at having been introduced to the fine lady. He bowed low over his tray and mumbled something.

Isabella sipped her wine, presented by Millward, and then got down to business with her measuring tape. She was going to make all the cushions and cot covers herself for her husband.

They discussed furniture, and she measured the size of the cabin spaces. At the sound of six bells (3pm), the First Lieutenant came to invite Will and Isabella to join the officers in the Gunroom, for dinner.[2] This meant that there were fourteen to sit down at an extended table.

As was his right Number One sat at the head of the table with Isabella at his right hand side. Will sat at the other end of the table with the Midshipmen. The cook had really tried hard, and the food was edible, though Isabella left most of hers. She said she didn't eat much. Will knew that she loved her food! The Officers were dazzled by her vivacious demeanour. She knew exactly how to put men at ease, without being flirtatious. If the officers weren't in awe of their Captain, they certainly were after the dinner. Anybody who could catch such a wife must be pretty special.

The next day, *Optimist* retrieved her anchor and sailed the short distance to the Pitch House Jetty. Here she was warped into the lock and through the basin to the starboard dock. Once firmly in place, the crew carried their possessions and hammocks back to the jetty and were taken out by a series of wherries to the frigate in 'ordinary'.

The dockyard workers immediately set about propping the ship, and then as the water was pumped out of the dock, scaffolding was erected all round. Then canvas screens were fixed to the outside of the structure, so nobody could see what

---

[2] This was the normal time for the officers to dine.

was going on behind. The only persons still aboard were the warrant officers that always stayed with their ship, except of course for the Boatswain, who had appeared before Will to be sent for Court-martial.

Will spent part of each day checking on progress, but otherwise left the ship to Derwent. The rest of the time he spent with Isabella, much of it on expeditions to seek out furniture for his cabins. In the evenings Isabella sewed the fabric she had chosen for the cushions and cot. Will was relieved that she had chosen very masculine designs.

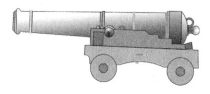

Three days after *Optimist* had gone into dry-dock Boatswain Tarrant and Surgeon Henri de Cornes, both late of Will's last command, the schooner *Snipe* appeared. Tarrant immediately set to work to find out who were the 'Topmen' of the ship. These were the younger men who served on the top most yards. These he then took to *Optimist* in the dock and proceeded to lead them to the very top of every mast to check methodically every stay, and all the cordage. The fact that such a large man could still climb and work high up the masts, whilst joking and making the others laugh, soon got back to the rest of the ship's crew. This was a totally different type of Boatswain. Carrick had never ever been seen anywhere higher than the top deck. Tarrant also employed members of the crew to lower all the yards, sand them, and then give them multiple coats of varnish.

Will knew that his men had their needs. He had authorised the sending of letters to wives and sweethearts inviting them aboard the frigate in ordinary to satisfy these needs. He had deliberately done this by invitation, because otherwise the ship would have been over-run by prostitutes. One thing Will did not want on this expedition was seaman too ill to do their duty. It was for this reason that he had the Surgeon check the health of every member of the crew below Warrant Officer. De Cornes used the captain's sleeping cabin on the frigate in ordinary as his surgery. The Midshipmen had been ordered to come up with a poster to advertise for fresh crew. Now that it was over a year since peace had been declared it was felt that there might be seamen, who needed to get back to sea for one reason or another. The final poster called for fine seamen to join the 'Merry crew of the frigate *Optimist* under the Captaincy of the young brave and well regarded Captain William Calvert, late of the famous schooner *Snipe,* on a new adventure!' Will was much amused, but it had results. Nine experienced hands were added to the roll-call, after less suitable applicants had been rejected by Derwent.

Derwent had drawn up a list of those members of

the crew he felt were the weakest or who were trouble makers. To this list Will added the purser and one quartermaster. This list was then sent to the Port Admiral, who arranged for transfers.

Aboard the frigate in ordinary there was a lot of discussion below decks as to what all the preparations were for. Those who had been employed painting the entire Gun Deck white, were intrigued by the new slots cut in the deck head at intervals along the side, which were repeated through the upper deck. It was only later that they found out that they were new ducts to provide more air to the mess-deck. This hinted at the tropics.

It was two and a half weeks before the screens and scaffolding came down. *Optimist's* bottom had been scrubbed and the copper plates replaced where necessary. The beak-head, sides and stern quarters shone bright, with the new yellow paint and gilding. The figurehead had been removed, repainted and then re-installed. The dock was flooded and the ship was warped out into the great basin. Once out through the lock gates, the crew strained at the oars of the cutters to tow her out to a vacated buoy. The crew had returned to their ship, expecting to set sail. Instead the masting hulk was manoeuvred alongside, and four long barrelled 18 pounder guns and their newly designed carriages were swung aboard. Next it was the turn of the ordinance hoys to bring out the fresh gunpowder. The gunner was surprised to find that most of the powder was already in the canvas charges. There were also a number of extra long charges that had the cannon ball sewn into them. Will explained that this was an experiment to see if it shortened the reloading time, as only one charge had to be rammed home, instead of a charge, then a wad, then a ball, then another wad.

Finally the victualling hoys came alongside and the ship was provisioned ready for sea and the new water barrels hoisted aboard.

Will said a fond goodbye to Isabella. She would wait and watch her love as *Optimist* sailed down the Solent and then return to Devon. She was determined not to cry, but all her will-power was not enough to stop her eyes filling with tears as she said farewell to her husband. Will was in an equally bad state, but hoped that he could dry his eyes by the time he had to leave for his coach.

When Will at last climbed aboard for the start of the new venture, *Optimist* was looking in a very fine state. At last his cabins were furnished and habitable. The Master came to report on the most suitable time to leave harbour, and Derwent followed to tell him that all was ready for sea. At long last at seven bells of the forenoon watch (1130am) the mooring to the buoy was cast off, the sails' sheets hauled in, and *Optimist* turned to face the mouth of Portsmouth Harbour and the sea beyond. As they passed Southsea, Will heaved himself into the mizzen mast shrouds and waved towards the shore. He would not have been able to see Isabella, but he wanted her to know that he was not too busy to wave goodbye.

Optimist cruised down the Channel towards the Western Approaches, making long tacks as the wind was from the West. The crew were happy; they had a new cook, who seemed to make the food taste that much better. Lashed amidships, under canvas sheets were two new cutters and two new jolly boats. The cutters were fitted for swivel guns, and the jolly boats were painted in different colours. Each jolly boat had its own fitted cover so nobody could see the colour of its paintwork. As they sailed down the channel they tested for the first time the new long barrelled 18 pounders. At first they loaded them the traditional way, and then they timed the difference it made if they used the new all-in-one charges. It was found that it shaved a half minute off the already impressive time the gun crew had achieved. The days of competition in exercising the guns had worked marvels. Their times were down to two minutes.

Their track took them through the passage between the island of Ushant and the French mainland down the Chenal du Four. As they sailed

South in the early evening, they could all see the mouth of the Raz de Brest. Thomas quietly recounted to his fellow Midshipmen the extraordinary story of the way their Captain had sunk two French frigates within minutes as he was left in charge of the quarter-deck during the last hostilities. Within minutes everybody aboard had heard the story, and its heroism was growing as it was retold.

They were not lucky as they progressed south. The Bay of Biscay decided that it didn't like the weather being too good for them, so built up a storm to test their metal. It now became apparent to the crew who had to work the forecastle, waist and quarterdeck, that the new southwesters and oilskins were a blessing. Will was determined to make good progress. He had been secretly warned by the Admiralty that it was very likely that Britain would declare war on France at any moment. He didn't want to waste time fighting the French. He had more important matters to perform. Driving the frigate meant that the waves were constantly bursting over the bows, sending walls of water rushing head long astern along the decks. The helmsmen were eternally grateful to their captain for having a 'V' shaped bulwark erected in front of the binnacle, which deflected much of the stinging salt spray that would otherwise have soaked them. It wasn't 'macho' but all those going aloft in the storm were ordered to attach themselves to lines led to the various positions on the masts, so that if anybody fell, they were caught before they hit the deck and then could be gently lowered. Will didn't want to lose experienced members of his crew for no good reason. As they raced past Cape Finisterre, the wind eased and the sun came out. During the trip to Gibraltar, Will was able to assess his officers and many of his crew. Derwent, the First Lieutenant had gradually come out of his shell. The brown rings around his sunken eyes had all but disappeared. He was smiling a lot, and Will had witnessed him having a joke with some of the hands. He had proved be a very efficient Number One, and obviously was an experienced, though Will suspected, overlooked seaman officer. Will had invited each of the officers to dine with him, so he could get to know them better. After the first round he had included Derwent at each of them, as he found it easier. Number One was also battle hardened. He had seen action in a frigate at Copenhagen, under Nelson's command, not Admiral Parkers. His ship had been badly damaged.

Cranfield, the second officer was a short stocky Welshman, with a bustling air. He was a very serious character, who did not seem to be able to relax. It was as if there was a demon on his shoulder driving him along. Will suspected that he lacked connections, which was a great disadvantage in the Navy, unless you were lucky enough to gain recognition by merit or in action. Both of which had propelled Will up the ladder. He was very self contained, never raising his voice unless necessary. He was a fine navigator, and seaman. It was noticeable that the crew seemed to respect him, even if he was a bit sour faced. He had been on a frigate at the Battle of the Nile, but his ship had not actually taken any part in the action.

Formby, the third, was the complete opposite. He was outgoing, cracking jokes where appropriate and seemed to have a permanent contented outlook on the world. He was also well respected by the crew. Seamen soon sussed out if an officer knew his business. Formby was always the same, even in a minor crisis. He would often lighten the mood with an apt remark. Formby was also battle hardened, having served on a two deck fourth rate at the Battle of Camperdown.

Baldwin the Master had been a Merchant Navy Captain, and had extensive experience of sailing both sides of the Atlantic and beyond. He had no battle experience, but he was very wise to the ways of the sea and seamen. When he walked the deck he could have been taken for a jockey, his legs were so bandy. He had an equitable nature, and was well respected by all.

The Midshipmen ranged from the most senior, an elderly 24 year old Grantly Harris, a tall skinny individual with a permanent stoop. He was fast losing his hair and looked even older than he really was. He had seen action at both Camperdown and the Nile, being aboard 74s both times. He was rather a depressed character. Will observing him, soon realised that he knew his business, he was very good at taking sights and plotting them. When challenged he revealed that he fell to pieces at interviews. He had never had a captain prepared to push him, or to recommend him.

Hinton, the next Midshipman in line, was a young 18 year old who was full of his own importance. He strutted the decks on beefy calves, his barrel chest puffed out. He was unreliable, as he considered he knew it all.

Thomas Tucker, Will knew all about. He might not have been in the rank very long, but he knew his navigation better than any of the others, thanks to Will's tutelage, and was right up there with his seamanship skills. He never needed to be told anything more than once. He was utterly reliable.

Midshipman Crawley was younger looking than his 16 years. He had a round cheery face under an unruly mop of blonde hair. He was a very pleasant sole, but a slow learner. It was obvious that he had connections, not that he bandied these about, to his credit. He needed to be watched carefully.

Midshipmen Trimble and Weeks were 13 and 12 respectively. They were still boys and it showed. Eager to please, but lacking in knowledge and maturity; both were extremely nervous, and Will suspected that they might well have been abused by the former captain and his side-kick boatswain.

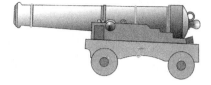

Then it was down past Portugal, through the area of the Battle of Cape St. Vincent, where Will had served on HMS *Victory*, and round to drop anchor off Gibraltar Rock. Here Will had to be rowed ashore to pay his compliments to the Commissioner, but really all that *Optimist* required was to top up her water barrels. Here he discovered that Britain was at war with France. Spain had not yet joined them. Having shown herself to any agents on the Spanish coast overlooking the Rock, *Optimist* upped her anchor and sailed on round the south coast of Spain, keeping in sight of land.

It was part of Will's plan, but it surprised the Spanish when *Optimist* entered Cartagena Harbour, the home port of the Spanish Mediterranean fleet. Henri de Cornes spoke passable Spanish. His father had been a diplomat under the ancient regime, and Henri had spent a number of years in the country as a boy. When challenged, Henri shouted back that they wanted to purchase Oranges and Lemons. This caused a considerable amount of confusion. *Optimist* was forced to drop her anchor, whilst the officials sorted themselves out. All aboard *Optimist* could see the Spanish Pinazas, a large rowing boat, scuttling around the harbour. Eventually a rather better rowing skiff arrived alongside and a Spanish officer was welcomed aboard. He would have been hard pressed to detail any weaponry, because all the guns were covered in canvas, specially made for the job. After some discussion with Henri and laughter the officer left. An hour later an invitation arrived from the Admiral aboard the *Santisima Trinidad,* the Spanish flagship. This huge ship, reputed to be the largest in the world had been at the battle of Cape St. Vincent, only to escape capture by the skin of its teeth.

It was not Villeneuve who greeted Will and Henri, acting as interpreter, but an Admiral with an unpronounceable name. They were entertained with fine wine and little trays of delicacies called 'Tapas'. Will caused some amusement by expressing the hope that this time the Spanish would not support the little Corsican who had seized power in France. He said that he could not understand how the Spanish could support a Republican State. There was a lot of shrugging of shoulders and smiles, together with plentiful toasts. Will was grateful to get back to his command in one piece and sober enough to climb up the side of his ship.

The next morning a flat bottomed craft came alongside and they were able to hoist baskets of oranges and lemons aboard. When Will ordered the Purser to pay, the Spanish flatly refused payment.

Once the new cargo was safely aboard, *Optimist* upped anchor and sailed majestically out into the Mediterranean, to turn and head North within sight of the land. Once it was really dark, the helm was put up and she turned out to sea, to then sail back out of sight in a southerly direction. By first light she had changed course again and was heading north, just in sight of land, enough for anybody ashore to identify a British frigate heading north. The alteration made during the night was the erection of the two davits at the stern and the working round of a jolly boat to hang from them. Not only did this obscure the name of the ship, but to a casual observer she looked an entirely different frigate.

After passing Capo de Palos, they headed north east towards the island of Formentera. As darkness descended they reduced sail considerably. Will wanted to arrive off the south eastern tip of the island at first light. Having identified their position, when they were first able to see land they headed for the Cala Codolas on the south eastern corner of the island. The long barrelled 18 pounders in the bows were put on stand-by and they sailed away from the cove, then turned and slowly made their track straight towards the centre of the deserted bay. By constantly triangulating their position, at 3,000 yards with an approximately 7° angle they fired the first shot. It fell into the water. At 2,750 yards they fired the next. It still dropped in the water, but at the water's edge. The first gun, reloaded fired at approximately 2,500 yards. This time it hit the rocky foreshore. Satisfied they now knew the extreme range of their new guns, when fired from their ship, they prepared to sail away. First though the jolly boat was lowered and brought forward to be hoisted aboard and the davits removed. *Optimist* was back in action.

Will sent for the carpenter and had him make up two quadrants which were then set so that they were marked for different types of ship's mast heights. The angle being set from a sextant. These would mean that the gun captains could set the quadrant up for, say a frigate, the usual height of their masts being about 220 feet, and by holding it in front of them had a pretty fair idea of when they were in range.

Each day the frigate exercised her guns, with the same competition to see which gun crew was fastest that day. They didn't actually fire the guns every day; they had a team who hauled the gun back as if it had been fired. *Optimist* carried a larger crew than normal because she mounted extra guns, and the upper deck guns were 18 pounders rather than the usual 12 pounders. The heavier guns took more men to handle them. To give the crew more space, the off watch members of the crew were allowed to hang their hammocks on the upper deck as well as on the gundeck/messdeck.

Now that Britain was at war with France, it was pretty certain that the fleet would be blockading Toulon again. Two days later the fleet was sighted to the west of Toulon. *Optimist* set course to intercept them, but had to amend her course as the fleet turned to patrol back along their original course. The signal was hoisted to tell everybody who had a telescope to their eye that *Optimist* carried dispatches. As they approached the flagship the hoist was made 'Captain to prepare aboard', this time with their pennant number. *Victory* obligingly backed her sails, so that *Optimist* could lay a few yards off and the jolly boat was lowered to take Will across the tossing sea. It was quite a struggle to keep up with the progress of the flagship let alone successfully come alongside. Allwood urged his crew on with encouragement rather than abuse, and finally a rope was thrown to them that the bow man could catch hold of and they 'planned' up to the side of the great ship. Will managed to grab the handhold lines either side of the steps up the side to the entry port and scrambled aboard to be met with considerable interest as well as the usual ceremony required for a captain visiting a ship. Will was met by Lord Nelson's flag lieutenant and shown straight to the admiral's cabin.

"You come not before time Sir! I need more frigates, I really do!" Said Nelson greeting Will as the later walked across the great cabin towards the hero of the Nile.

"I know you, don't I?" Queried His Lordship.

"I doubt if you remember me, My Lord, I was

but a humble Lieutenant when I saw you over the side of this same ship."

"Young....Calvert, am I right?"

"My Lord I am very flattered that you should remember my name!"

"Not at all. Lord Jervis pointed you out to me. 'That young man is going to go far.' Was what he said. I won't flatter you any more as to the reasons he gave! Anyway you are very welcome."

"I am afraid, My Lord, that I only bring you dispatches from the First Lord himself. He wanted you to know exactly what was planned."

"Planned? You intrigue me. Take a seat to recover from your alarming crossing. Don't worry about the cushions, they'll dry!"

Will handed over the canvas covered package. Nelson sat down on the window seat and using a thin bladed knife slit open the package. He took the letter out, flicked the seal apart and started to read. He stopped once to regard Will and then went back to reading. He must have read it all twice, Will reckoned.

"Oh Dear! I had hoped you were one of the long awaited extra frigates I have been calling for, but it appears that I am wrong. I can see the point of the operation. I should like to hear more of how you propose to carry it out." Nelson rang a small bell and a servant appeared.

"Some refreshment for our guest." He ordered; then he looked out of the stern windows.

"I see that this is for my eyes only! Pity, I should have liked to discuss this with you over dinner, but I

128

have some of the other captains joining me. So when we have the wine, let us get down to the detail."

The wine appeared, and Will outlined his plans. Nelson listened intently, never interrupting. When Will had finished, Nelson asked about detailed points. He had some ideas of his own, of which Will took note.

They were interrupted by the arrival of the first of the visiting captains, so Will said his goodbyes.

"I understand exactly why Jervis picked you out. I wish you the best of luck. If I was younger, I should like to be serving with you! God bless you and your crew."

After having had to wait for another captain to come aboard, Will was seen over the side for another hair-raising trip back to *Optimist*. Dipping her ensign in salute, *Optimist* made a smart increase of sail and speed to turn out of line and to head south.

It took over a week of fluky winds and then sudden storm force winds to reach Malta. The Island was well out of her direct route, but it was here that they were scheduled to pick up their extra crew, provisions and water. Once anchored in Grand Harbour, Lieutenant Cranfield was sent ashore to locate the extra crew members. A couple of hours later the new additions filed aboard. The new crew were signed in, the Lieutenant shown to his new, temporarily erected cabin, and the loading commenced. Nobody else went ashore, except Will to show his respects. In charge of the extra crew was a stocky Lieutenant, who went by the name of Stuart Ross. Obviously he came from the border country. He had a reddish tinge to his hair and his face showed that his skin was not suitable for being in the sun for any length of time. He had a square shaped head, with a thin mouth and startlingly green eyes. He was of a serious countenance. Will was not quite sure where he rated in the Navy list. He was determined that his First Lieutenant would take command of any captured vessel. The question was where this newcomer rated? Was it above the second, Lieutenant Cranfield or even the third Lieutenant - Formby. In Malta there was no such thing as a Navy List. Will would have to interview the new Lieutenant to find where he was supposed to rate in the command structure. There were 30 extra members of the crew counting the Lieutenant. There were two Boatswain's mates, 10 topmen, a carpenter's mate, a sailmaker's mate, a cook, and 14 rated able seamen. It was up to Will to decide which would serve on a prize, if they were lucky enough to take such a thing.

Two days later, at first light, *Optimist* was towed out of Grand Harbour, the cutters recovered and she turned her bow towards the west.

Once well out of sight of any other ships, the first of the planned transformations took place. Just under topsails alone, the crew hoisted up from the hold, the huge sacks that contained some of the canvas that had been made in Portsmouth. A net was slung under the bowsprit, lines passed above it and hauled tight to support the figurehead. The Carpenter then went to work to undo the bolts holding the figurehead in place. It was then carefully lowered slightly, and men on life lines, clabbered down to secure other ties round the carving, for it to be gently hauled up and over the bows to be stowed below. Then the second stage began. Tarrant explained carefully exactly what each member of the crew involved had to do. He went over it twice, making sure each man completely understood his roll. Only then was the bow end of the long roll of canvas unrolled and worked inside the foremast shrouds against the side to be attached to the beak. Once this had been achieved the aft end of the canvas was worked aft round the inside of the main mast shrouds and then the mizzen shrouds. Then the stern crew, again on life lines, climbed over the stern quarter and passed the cords that had to be threaded through the new holes below the windows to the stern. These were tied to the eyes and then the crew inside hauled them tight, stretching the canvas taut as possible so it covered the whole side of the ship's yellow side and gun ports. Other men then threaded lines through the holes drilled all along the side on the upper deck at deck-level and deck-head level. These were then secured. The whole operation was then repeated on the Starboard side.

When completed *Optimist* looked like a merchant ship, with guns visible only on the forecastle and quarterdeck. Now the ship made her way to towards the Straits of Gibraltar, with the aim to pass through at twilight, on the fast flowing tide. It was hoped that any ship they passed or anybody on the Spanish shore would assume she was merely a merchant ship going about her trade. The officers were ordered not to wear uniforms, as a ship passing within telescope range would be able to make out that they were naval officers. When they became becalmed a hundred miles before the Straits, a cutter was lowered and rowed out to see at what distance it was possible to realise that the new sides were canvas covers. At two cables it was impossible to tell the difference. They now knew to keep at least that distance away from any other ship.

Because of the calm weather, estimates of when to pass through the Straits had to be altered, as it was imperative that they went though in the late evening and on the tide to aid their speed through. It lost them three days in the end, and the tide was not as strong as they would have liked, but luckily there was a slight fog, caused by the different temperatures between the Atlantic and the Mediterranean seas.

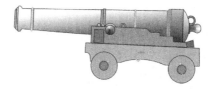

At last out in the Atlantic *Optimist* turned south to catch the trades. The crew began to appreciate the thought that had gone into providing the extra air ducts to the gundeck. The canvas covers were removed from the top of each duct, and small wind socks mounted to force the air below. Once they were well clear of land, the canvas side pieces were carefully retrieved and stored in their bags. Now a different group of bags were hauled up onto the foredeck and quarterdeck. These had hazel twigs sewn into the sides to hold them open, once the neck of the bag had been undone. These bags contained special lightweight staysails.[3] Instead of being attached to the stays as in normal practice, these sails had their own extra stays which could be hauled up through blocks from the deck, to ride just below the existing stays. This meant that they could be set far quicker than normal.

Two nights after leaving the Straits, Will was woken by a sudden loud crack. He slid out of his cot, crammed on his sailor's white trousers and a shirt and raced up to the quarterdeck. The wind had been building since midday, and it was now just

---

[3] Staysails are fore and aft sails, which allow a ship to sail much closer to the wind.

after first light. Will could just make out Lieutenant Ross standing by the binnacle holding a voice trumpet. Forward he could just make out the burly shape of the boatswain. Ross was screaming at the top of his voice, but it was difficult to understand what he was trying to achieve. Tarrant was calmly organizing things.

"Lieutenant Ross, you are relieved. Go below!"

Ross turned, and for a moment Will thought the man was going to hit him.

"But Sir!"

"I said, go below!"

Ross made his way forward and down the ladderway. Will could see quite clearly that Tarrant had everything under control. A yard on the foremast was being lowered. Will was not sure of the reason but he ordered the sheets of all sails to be eased. Making his way forward, holding onto a lifeline, he joined Tarrant.

The boatswain turned to find who was there and knuckled his brow.

"Seam gone on foretopsail. Think it must've been one of the originals. We'll have another up in a jiffy" He shouted above the wind.

"What happened?" Asked Will.

"I hear it go, so raced up here. The Lieutenant didn't seem to understand the problem, Sir, if I may be so bold. I am afraid I had to ignore him, because if they had done what I think he wanted them to do, it would have made matters worse."

"Yes, I gathered that. When you've finished here, you get your head down....and thank you

Sydney." It was not often that he used Tarrant's christen name, and only when they were alone. He knew the Boatswain liked to keep the name to himself.

Will returned to the wheel. "I have the watch." He said to the quartermaster.

The new sail was secured to the yard, and the yard re-hoisted. Only then did Will have the sheets trimmed. He noticed that the Quartermaster and the seaman at the wheel were grinning, their faces revealed by the light of the binnacle.

It was a very surprised Formby who came on deck to take over the watch. He frowned, swept the deck with his eyes and turned to look questioning at Will.

"I thought I was relieving Ross, Sir."

"You were, but I sent him below. Carry on, on this course. You have the watch."

"I have the watch, Sir." Replied Formby.

Will made his way back to his cot. He would have to have a word with Ross in the morning.

As four bells of the forenoon watch sounded, Will sent for Lieutenant Ross. The man came in looking exceedingly nervous.

"Lieutenant Ross, this morning you made yourself an object of contempt amongst the crew, something that will be very difficult to correct. You lost your nerve, in a very mundane situation. What are you like under fire, I ask myself. What have you got to say for yourself?"

"I couldn't see what had happened. It was all

confusion. I did my best to sort it out, but the Boatswain came up and usurped my authority, Sir."

"You had the watch, it was your responsibility. Never ever pass the blame. Boatswain Tarrant, is one of the best in His Majesty's Navy. He knew instantly what had happened and dealt with it before further damage could be done. You on the other hand just shouted at everybody, confusing them. You never went forward to see for yourself what was the problem. Had you moved your arse, you would have been able to do something about it. I don't know your date of rank, but I can assure you that if I had the mind to do so, I might very easily drop you back to Midshipman, because frankly many of them would have handled things better. You came from a 2nd rate, didn't you?"

"Yes Sir."

"And you never actually kept a watch on your own, is that right?"

"Yes Sir."

"I thought so, it shows. In future, as you are extra to compliment, you will stand watch with Lieutenant Formby, and try to learn from him. We are all put in a position where we are not sure what to do. Shouting, never achieves anything. Stop! Think, then act. Have you ever seen action?"

"No Sir."

"Well you might very well do so this voyage. I shall be watching you like a hawk from now on. I hope that your nerve will hold under enemy fire, when all around you is chaos. I suggest you go and put your apologises to Mr. Tarrant. You need him on your side...Oh and lest you think that it is beneath you to apologise, let me tell you that I offered to put Mr. Tarrant up for a Commission, he turned me down asking to stay as my Boatswain. I suggest you make a point of quietly asking his advice. He knows more about handling a sailing ship than anybody else I know. And don't be shy in asking the advice of your fellow wardroom members. Nobody will think the less of you. You may go now."

Ross thanked his Captain and left.

A day later they made land fall, and confirmed that it was Selvagem, the largest island in a group between Madeira and the Canaries. The Master was extremely surprised when Will brought up his old journal, from when he had sailed with his father, and compared the sketch he had made with the outline of the island. If he had needed further confirmation, he could have also consulted his father's journals, because Tarrant had brought them together with all the charts, when he came aboard.

From the island, it being spring time, they were able to turn west to pick up the westerly trade wind. This was a fairly constant wind and they were able to average a good 7 to 8 knots. It helps to have a clean bottom. It was a pleasure to run before the wind with the stud-sails[4] set.

Each day the watches practised their gunnery.

---

[4] Square sails set on extra yards set out from the usual ones. Used in fine weather to run before the wind.

The starboard watch one day, the larboard the next during the forenoon watch. The Master-at-Arms made sure every member of the crew knew how to handle a cutlass. The Gunner taught everyone how to load and fire pistols and their new Baker Rifles. The Americans had used this type of rifle during their war against the British. They were far more accurate than muskets. The Marines used the slops as target practice from the stern of the ship. During their leisure periods, the crew were encouraged to have tag races between groups up and down the deck.

Swivel guns, normally for use on cutters were mounted at intervals around the deck. Their barrels protruded between the hammocks lining the sides. These fired grape shot, and had been added to clear the musketeers that the Spanish tended to use from their cross-trees to shoot down at the deck of an enemy. It was for the same reason that the 'V' shaped breakwater in front of the binnacle, at action stations had more hammocks stacked against it, to protect the quartermasters at the wheel. The swivels were the responsibility of the Marines.

Just over two weeks after leaving the smaller of the Canary Islands, *Optimist* was able to drop her anchor in Tyrrel Bay in the small West Indies Island of Carriacou.

It had not all been plain sailing on the journey, however. There had been very little need for punishment during their trip to the Med and during their time in the area. There had been the usual petty problems, which had been dealt with by the

First Lieutenant. Now for the first time there was a dramatic fight on the upper deck. The exact cause of the fight was obscure, but one seaman stabbed another in the abdomen. It was lucky for the stabbed man that Boatswain Tarrant had heard the start of the argument and was near-by when it took place. He wadded in fist flying and laid the knifeman to the ground, then chopped hard on his arm holding the knife. The next moment the man had his arm painfully twisted up his back and was on his knees sobbing with pain. The injured man was quickly taken below and the Surgeon called. The Master-at-Arms had been called, but he stood by as Tarrant hauled the knife wielder up to a standing position and marched the man below. The Master-at-Arms followed and the man was shackled to the deck on the Orlop deck close by the Marines' store. Tarrant sniffed the man's breath and pronounced him 'taken of drink'. It was a flogging offence, and Will had no compunction in ordering 12 lashes. It was the first time anybody had been bound to the grating to receive the 'cat', since Will had taken command. It had one benefit though, it showed the crew that their captain was quite capable of punishing anybody who offended. The man was also denied his tot for a month, which was considered by some to be a greater punishment than the cat. The effect was that the Master-at-Arms was ordered to carry out random searches of the crews' effects to see if anybody was hording their rum, or had hidden away extra tots given for services rendered.

Tyrrel Bay was an eye opener for those who had never served in the West Indies. Will had chosen Carriacou, because it was supposed to be free of the dreaded Yellow Fever, which decimated crews throughout the area. The clear blue watered bay was on the west side of the island, so did not suffer from the Atlantic swell. There was also water to be had on the island. It helped that the few residents were British, or their slaves. The bay was about half a mile wide with small cliffs on either side. The sandy beach led up to higher ground. The bright blue of the sea reflected off the few white painted craft that lay anchored close to the shore, making their hulls look pale blue.

The cutters were lowered over the side and the water barrels hoisted up and then down to the cutters, which then ran a ferry service ashore. Marines were posted at intervals to make sure nobody tried to abscond. Two local land owners came to see what was going on, and then offered their slaves to help roll the empty barrels up to be filled and then to roll the full ones down to the beach. Awnings were stretched across the forecastle and the quarterdeck, so that the land owners could be invited for drinks aboard. They were fed deliberately false information as to the frigate's next port of call. Other than water, the island had little that was needed aboard. They were able to purchase a few pigs to refill the sty in the bows, and some laying chickens and feed to provide at least a few eggs. What delighted the officers most was that for some reason the locals had a trade going with the

Spanish colony of Venezuela in coffee beans.

It was Henri de Cornes idea, that the seaman should be allowed ashore in small groups to wash their clothes in fresh water. De Cornes was a physician as well as a Surgeon. He would normally have been placed aboard a ship of the line, but because he was French, he was overlooked. The fact that he had volunteered for the British Navy when he had escaped France, being an Aristocrat, had made no difference in Whitehall.

As always Marines were posted to make sure that the sailors didn't go native, but also to make sure that no slaves swam out to the ship to become freemen. It had been a condition made by the landowners for any help or supplies. Any sailors who could swim were allowed to frolic in the waters beside the ship; scaling nets allowing them easy access to regain the deck. Most sailors could not swim, but those that could, encouraged others to join them. At least one barrel of fresh water was set up on the foredeck so that the swimmers could wash off salt water when they returned aboard. It was the last barrel to be refilled.

It was impossible to stop clothing becoming impregnated with salt when one had been at sea for any length of time. The salt could cause sores. As a result for the five days that *Optimist* lay at anchor in the bay, she looked more like a floating clothes horse than a ship.

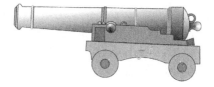

Refreshed, replenished, the virtual holiday was over. *Optimist* hauled up her anchor and trimmed her sails to sail due west. A day and a half later they sighted the small island of Blanquilla. Two days more and the island of Bonaire was confirmed. In another day they were off Aruba. Their next reference point was Cap Gallinas, and from here they moved further out to sea but still headed west. The area that Will wanted to patrol was about 100 miles north-west of the port of Santa Marta, for this was the area through which the Spanish ships could be expected to pass after they had left Cartagena on the Gulf Coast of South America. Where the intelligence came that this was the main port of export, Will had no idea, but it was all he had to go on. The prevailing wind was from the north of east, so any ship leaving Cartagena would have to sail on a course NNE. Will felt that it was highly unlikely that any Spanish ship would use the passage to the south of Cuba for the Atlantic. That would take them too near to the British Island of Jamaica. And being this far from Europe there was no knowing whether Spain would be at war once more with

Britain. The original route of the Spanish treasure fleets had been up round the northern tip of Cuba to rendezvous with others at Havana, before rounding the tip of Florida and then riding the Gulf Stream up the coast of America and across the Atlantic. Another route might be that they would tack all the way to the southern tip of Haiti, as this was now independent, and there was little likelihood of Spanish ships being attacked.

All the way from Carriacou, they had been converting their ship. Again a net had been spread below the bowsprit and a new figurehead brought up and manoeuvred into place. 'Gauntlets or spats' as some called them were brought up and laid out. Then each was carefully fitted to the bow rails. They were painted white and hid the original yellow. Then new canvas, also painted white was laid over the sides and fitted between the gun-ports and behind the shrouds. The davits were re-erected at the stern and used to hoist the dummy 'gallery' into position. Then they were moved to the starboard side to support the white painted jolly boat. Each gun-port lid was carefully hoisted aboard and turned upside down to be re-fitted the other way up. Horizontal pintles had been fitted below each port for this very reason. Now the gun-ports could be dropped at an instant. The British ensign and the commissioning pennant were taken down and replaced by the current American flag, a blue flag with a ring of stars. The next pieces to be changed were the ornamental gilded carvings on the quarters, which were replaced with different work painted white. Then finally the name plate was taken inboard and a new plate fixed which carried the name in white paint *Dependent*.

Now the ship looked to all intense and purposes an American frigate, and America was not at war with Spain. The previous Sunday, after 'Church' which consisted of a few prayers, the crew were all summoned on deck before lunch. Will, using a speaking trumpet, explained exactly the plan of action. The Youngmen, having the best eyes, were to be strapped to the fore-topmast with a telescope securely attached to the mast. They would be changed every half hour every hour of daylight. They would report immediately the first sighting of any masts on the horizon. The crew would then go to Action Stations. The gun-ports would remain shut. Nobody, but nobody was to show their heads above the hammocks that lined the sides. The topmen would be brought down as would the Youngman. Some of the sails were to be let loose, to look as if they were not being tended. The Jolly boat was to be suspended off one fall from the davit on the starboard side. One of the cutters, already prepared was to be lowered on the larboard side and turned bottom up, but still attached by its painter. Small barrels had already been lashed to the thwarts. *Optimist* had to look as if she was no longer under command. She would still move forward due to the sails that were still sheeted home. Steering would be maintained by using block and tackle attached to the tiller arm below decks. The whole concept was to make the captain of a

Spanish ship think that the American frigate was in trouble, and come to investigate. It was doubtful that the Spaniard would come too close, in case of fever, but they would have to come within range, if they were to be able to ascertain what was going on. Once the Spanish ship was within range, the carronades would fire grape shot at their rigging and at the top deck. If any of the Spanish ship's gun-ports opened, then one of *Optimist's* gun-ports would be dropped and the gun fired immediately at the offending void. They didn't want to sink the ship, they wanted to disable her enough to capture her and her cargo.

Will carefully instructed the Youngmen as to what they were looking for, which were ships or frigates that were low in the water. It was known that the Spanish were using frigates, rather than merchantmen. They were to report any sighting, and then keep reporting everything about the ship or ships as they approached. Directly the ship was hull up, a Midshipman would take over at the tops.

Optimist was prepared to sail at any point of the wind possible. To aid sailing as close to the wind as possible the staysails were ready in their sacks, to be hoisted at a moment's notice. It was extremely unlikely that the Spanish ships would have been careened recently, so *Optimist* should have the speed advantage. It was surprise which was the ultimate weapon.

The Marines were not wearing their red coats. It was a great relief to them, because it was really too hot for the thick cloth. The officers didn't wear coats, because they would be recognised as British.

Optimist patrolled up and down across the chosen area for a week, and nothing appeared on the horizon. Tempers were getting a bit frayed, as the boredom factor clicked in. Will encouraged singing in the 2nd dog watch,. Formby had an unexpected talent. He played the squeeze box, so it helped with the enjoyment. As yet the fresh food collected from Carriacou had not run out, so the crew were still eating well. It would not last many more days, but it helped.

Another week of nothing followed, then yet another week. Will ordered that water was to be rationed, and the cook ordered to cut the rations. The heat and inactivity was having its effect upon the crew. Petty squabbles broke out. For Will the worry was whether he was patrolling the right area. Time and again he went back to the charts and studied them, trying to put himself in the position of a Spanish Captain leaving the port. Each time he came to the same conclusion. He got Baldwin to do the same thing and he showed Will his track on a chart and it virtually matched Will's.

One month and two days after they had first reached their patrol area, a lookout reported sails on the horizon. The only thing was they were sailing in completely the wrong direction. They were sailing towards the port. Will ordered *Optimist* to close the ships until it could be ascertained exactly what type of ships they were. Tucker was sent aloft with the most powerful scope aboard. After three hours, he came swiftly down to the deck and reported that they were two Spanish frigates. *Optimist* turned away to sail back the way they had come.

"Just one thing, Sir." Reported Tucker.

"What's that?"

"One of the frigates seemed to be unusually high in the water."

"Interesting! Thank you Thomas!" Said Will. Perhaps these two frigates were coming to pick up a cargo of bullion. The question was ... how long before they set sail again, and would *Optimist's* victuals last out?

Another week and the lookout at the top mast reported first one mast then two masts appearing over the horizon. They were heading north the boy thought. Midshipman Harris surprised Will by asking to relieve the boy. An hour later he reported that there were two frigates, with about two or three miles separating them. An hour later he reported that their hulls appeared to be low in the water.

Will had not passed on the intelligence, that the frigates were thought to have removed their guns from the upper deck, because of the weight of the bullion. It did no good to get too confident. However two frigates together were not what the intelligence had expected. They had stated that the Spaniards were using a single frigate at a time to try and avoid suspicion. Now Will was faced with engaging two virtually at the same time. He had to in some way separate the two. Would the tactics he had used on the schooner *Snipe* work with a frigate?

He sat thinking through each move. He realised that it was before a battle that he found most frightening. He had to be decisive! He must not show any doubt, otherwise it would communicate to the crew and unsettle them. He pondered the problem through once again and decided on his tactics.

Will called his officers to his cabin.

"We have two Spanish frigates, and they are a mile apart. It is hoped that the leading frigate will change course to investigate. If she does, then we shall allow her to get within carronade range as previously explained to the crew. I want her to be forced to surrender if possible, or at the very least her rigging so damaged that she can't get away. I intend to leave her once that has been achieved and use the new long barrelled 18 pounders to show the second frigate that we can strike with impunity. It will all depend on how the first frigate behaves. If the first frigate sails past, and ignores our supposed difficulties, then we attack the second. It will take time for the first to come to the other's aid. In that time we must inflict a decisive victory over the second ship. If we fail, then we fall back onto our third option. We out-gun either frigate. We have a longer range than either, so we dodge about, making it difficult for either to hit us, whilst we keep hitting them hard. Remember though that, if possible we are to take possession of their cargo, if we can't do that then we sink them. Either way the French are not going to get the bullion they so desire. If and I say if, advisedly, we are fortunate to capture one, we shall be very rich men indeed. Thank you gentlemen." The officers raised their glasses. "To a great victory!" Lieutenant Jackson the Marine Lieutenant said. "Here, here!" Came the response.

It was an agonising wait to see what the first of the frigates would do. It would be unfortunate if she backed her sails, shortening the space between the two Spanish ships. All they could do was to wait and watch. It would take another hour before the first frigate was within telescope distance to be able to make out if there was any life on *Optimist*. It would be another hour before she was within range. *Optimist* had the weather gauge, she was 'six points large' therefore she had the wind on her quarter. The Spaniard was close hauled. What would he do if the two frigates closed and they tried to engage *Optimist* from either side. He had to keep them at arms distance, or rather at long barrelled 18 pounder distance. Because the use of the bow chasers as a main weapon was not something that frigate crews were used to, he had exercised the crew in the attention to speed in manoeuvring the ship. Practise had improved their performance markedly. The crew knew exactly what was expected of them, and because they did it every day, it was virtually second nature.

Will had the sheets eased slightly, he wanted the leading Spaniard to pass on the windward side, because there was no way the Spaniard would turn into the wind so close to a strange ship. Directly it was clear that *Optimist* would cross the Spaniard's track, Will ordered a very slight change of course. By putting the helm to larboard a couple of points,

Optimist would very gradually come round to sail three points large or one point abaft the beam, so travelling on a parallel course to the Spaniard, but in the opposite direction; north-north-west to their south-south-east.

There were no nets rigged over *Optimist's* decks which would normally be in place to protect her crew from falling yards and masts in an action. Nets would have given the game away. The remaining cutter and gig were tightly covered by tarpaulins. This would stop some of the splinters if they were struck by cannon balls. Will was up on the forecastle, telescope to his eye watching the leading frigate. He was hidden by the hammocks, but square funnels made of wood had been placed between some to give observation points. These were placed all along the side in between the hammocks to give the marines a clear view, yet a protected firing point for their rifles.

So that they had some control over the ship, only the Fore Topsail, Fore Topgallant, Main Topgallant, Main course and Mizzen topsail were sheeted. The rest of the sails, other than royals which were not set, were flapping wildly. The Mizzensail's gaff was right out to port, with the sheets trailing in the water. The gun crews waited on the upper deck, crouching ready by their respective guns. Lying flat out, face down, close to the foreward ladderway, Tucker repeated everything Will said for the benefit of those below. Aft, lying propped up against the bulwarks, Marine Lieutenant Jackson was in a death pose. When the ship rolled slightly he could see the sails of the lead frigate. Tarrant was on his back by the main mast pin rails. Scattered about the deck, crew men lay in death like poses. You could almost physically feel the tension!

Derwent was crouched beside Will, listening to his captain's running commentary. Below Cranfield, Formby and Ross stood at their gun stations, making sure everybody was quiet. Above each gun port a hole had been drilled through the side so that the gun captains could squint at their target before the ports were dropped. The aft hatch cover had been removed, and a space made. Here Midshipman Hinton could pass down any orders to the steering crew based in the gunroom. Sailors had taken up position between the carronades, some lying over them, to give the impression that they were dead.

It was part of Will's tactics to make the Spanish fear the Fever, so that they could use *Optimist's* long range guns. He didn't want the Spaniard to lay alongside. The North East Trade wind was a steady moderate to fresh breeze from North East by East, with the sea having long breaks between gentle curling white wave caps. It was ideal weather for fighting.

Another half hour and the leading Spaniard took the bait, she was seen to alter course slightly to close *Optimist.* Derwent slivered to the foreward ladderway and slid past Tucker to run aft along the upperdeck out of sight. Slowly, very, very slowly the Spanish frigate came round to make a course that would allow her to pass a cable's length away from *Optimist.* Will crawled aft, flat on his face as close to the starboard side as possible, which was the side the Spaniard would pass on. If anybody saw him, he made it look as if it was a great effort; stopping frequently to rest.

Directly the leading Spaniard's bow was level with *Optimist's* foremast, a whistle indicated to Will that the Carronades could do their job. He gave the hand signal, and the three forecastle carronades fired grape at the deck of the Spaniard. As soon as the Spaniard was within range the aft carronades poured bar and canister shot into the rigging. Within seconds, the Spaniard's sails were shot to pieces, Yards came crashing down, men could be seen hurrying to get to the Spaniard's guns on the forecastle and quarterdeck. Derwent nodded as Will brought his arm down. Positioned with just his head above deck level the First Lieutenant was able to immediately transmit to the Officers on the upper deck to fire when necessary. As the crew of one Spanish gun went to their weapon forward, an *Optimist* gun-port crashed open and an 18 pounder's canister shot scattered them or left them dead and wounded. Only a cable length away, they could hear the screams of the wounded and dying. It was in less than two minutes that *Optimist's* carronades again sent grape shot across the Spaniard's deck. The smoke was quickly whipped away by the wind. Marines, protected by the hammocks, picked off any remaining musketeers in the Spaniard's rigging using swivel guns and their new Baker Rifles. These were far more accurate than muskets, had a far greater range and had been specially asked for by Will.

The Spaniard had been caught completely unawares and hadn't managed to fire one shot, other than a few muskets from her crosstrees. It was obvious that intelligence had been correct. The Spanish frigate appeared not to have any guns on its upper deck, as there had been no attempt to open any of the gun ports. The Spaniard's sails were in ribbons; there was no tell-tale ripple at the bows, which showed that she was dead in the water.

Will shouted the order. Sheets were hauled in, *Optimist* began to gather speed and leave the stricken Spaniard. The up-ended cutter was cut loose. *Optimist* had the advantage of the wind. She was still sailing with the wind one point abaft the beam. Another order and the studdingsails'[5] yards were hauled out and the sails set. Sheeted in, she now was going at a spanking rate, fast closing the distance between herself and the second Spaniard.

The first Spaniard had been caught unawares. The second had plenty of time to prepare. The Spaniard turned so as to present a broadside to the oncoming frigate. This meant that the long barrelled 18 pounders had to be swung round to give a wider arc, as their first shoots were supposed to straddle the ship. Will didn't want to hit the ship, if possible,

---

[5] Yards extending from the usual yards on which extra sails could be set for running before the wind.

just intimidate her so she would haul down her ensign and surrender. The two gun captains were ready with their quadrants. It was up to them when they fired. It was clear to see that the Spaniard had hoisted his gun-ports. Will suddenly had to change his previous instruction; he had thought that the second frigate might be under gunned like the first. He sent Midshipman Weeks rushing forward to give his command to the gun captains. The two guns were hauled round so they now aimed straight at the side of the Spaniard. At the same time the order was given to bring in the studdingsails. They didn't want to over-run the Spaniard. Sheets were eased and *Optimist's* head-long rush slowed. Allwood, well, used to this type of fighting from his days as quartermaster on *Snipe* was at the wheel, there was no pretence any longer.

The use of the quadrants worked, the two long barrelled 18 pounders fired almost simultaneously. Both shots were observed to hit the Spaniard at the level of the gundeck, which like a British frigate meant the deck where the men eat and slept. There were no guns on this deck. The Spaniard fired a broadside, but all her shot fell well short of *Optimist*. In less than two minutes, another two shots from Optimist's long barrelled 18 pounders hit the Spaniard, this time piercing the larboard upper deck, where its guns were ranged. The 'cartridges' of powder and shot combined had brought the reloading time down even further than normal. It must have been terrifying to the opposition to realise just how fast their enemy could fire her guns. The smoke from the two bow chasers rolled away partly obscuring the target.

Will immediately ordered all sheets to be let go. He wasn't going to allow this Spanish frigate get within range. Intelligence had only been partially right. This frigate still mounted guns on the upper deck.

The Spaniard responded by coming back onto her original course. She was obviously intending to fight it out, broadside to broadside. It must have surprised the Spanish Captain, when *Optimist* turned so her bows remained facing the Spaniard. Again and again the long barrelled guns wrought havoc to the Spaniard. Her foretopmast must have been hit, because it swayed and then came crashing down, taking its topgallant mast[6] with it, to hang over the starboard side of the ship. Every time the Spaniard fired a broadside the smoke smothered her. Still all their shots fell short, splashing into the sea a hundred yards away from *Optimist's* sides.

Will wondered what size cannon the opposition mounted, whether they were 18 or 12 pounders. Everybody on the forecastle could see that the Spaniard was putting people in the rigging. *Optimist's* Courses[7] were taken up. This was normal when in action. It gave the quarter-deck a clear view of what was happening. Still heading towards the

---

[6] The masts of square rigged frigates were made up of three lengths, mounted one above the other. In this case Foremast with topmast then topgallant.

[7] The lowest and biggest square sails to Foremast and Main mast.

Spaniard, another two rounds from the long 18 pounders again struck. The larboard gun ports were dropped, and the ordinary upper deck 18 pounders run out. It would be a menacing sight, and Will hoped that the Spanish Captain would think that these guns had the same range as those in the bows.

It was to be assumed that the Spaniards would be busy chopping away the rigging holding the foretopmast to the ship. If they were successful, what would the Spanish Captain try to do then? His opponent held the weather gauge, and had not suffered any damage. It would be futile to try and run for it. The enemy held all the cards. Would his fellow frigate be able to come to his aid?

Optimist now had a choice, did she continue to snipe away at the Spaniard, or did she close for the kill. If she chose the first option, there was always a danger that the first Spanish frigate would be able to replace her sails and join in the fight. There was time for one more blast from the long range guns before Optimist would have to turn and use her upperdeck 18pounders. There would be a short interlude until the distance was shortened to make that possible. The gun captains up in the bow had knocked out the wedges, and the long barrelled guns now were aimed at the upper deck of the Spaniard. They hit their targets which were near the bows and amidships, but it still left probably about ten guns that might be able to fire. It was a risk that Will had to take.

Lord Jervis' orders came back to Will.

It is imperative that the bullion does not get to

France. However many ships there are in any convoy you encounter, you must sink as many as possible, even to the extent of sacrificing your own ship in the process. That gold is keeping the French Army and their Navy in business.

This he had not passed on!

Optimist turned smartly to starboard. As the range shortened Will only altered course a point. If he came round any further he would be sailing closer to the wind, and *Optimist* would begin to heel, so preventing the larboard guns being able to bear on their target. Tarrant was well aware of this problem and Will could see him anxiously checking the sails against the angle of the hull.

It was the Spaniard who fired first. It was more likely to be an over eager crew than a command from the quarterdeck. The Spaniard's larboard side guns nearest the bow were clearly out of action. It was two guns four or five gun ports aft, but they just did not have the angle and the shot fell into the sea short of *Optimist's* bow. Cranfield had held his nerve. Minutes passed and still *Optimist* did not fire Then, in an orderly manner, one at a time, *Optimist's* upperdeck guns began to fire. Some of the shots went high, but most slammed into the side of the Spaniard. However as *Optimist* got nearer, the Spaniard was able to return the fire. *Optimist* was struck first on the larboard side upperdeck, taking out one of the guns, then further aft at gundeck level, then just forward of the quarterdeck

157

at that level, taking out two of the carronades and the pintail rail, killing and injuring members of the crew. Yards and sails came crashing down. Everybody standing near the wheel involuntarily ducked. The yards and sails crashed down just ahead of them. *Optimist's* upperdeck guns were still keeping up a withering fire, together with the quarterdeck carronades firing grape, and the forecastle carronades firing bar shot at the rigging. From under a pile of canvas Will was relieved to see Tarrant appear, already ordering the afterguard to clear away the mess and re hoist the yards which carried sails.

As each of *Optimist's* upperdeck 18 pounders had a target they had fired. The quarterdeck rail of the Spanish ship disintegrated. One shot must have struck her mizzen mast, because it began to rock. Another shot was seen to hit the ship's boats stacked over the well. Disciplined firing, and lots of practice, meant that at least one shot out of two found their intended target. *Optimist's* guns were firing three times to every Spanish shot. Now *Optimist's* 18 pounders were concentrating on the Spaniard's upper deck gun-ports. Because of the smoke from the Spaniard being blown back across her decks, it was obviously blinding the Spanish gunners. *Optimist's* gun crews had been taught to gauge their target by the position of the enemy masts, so were less affected by the smoke. Some of *Optimist's* shots smashed into the heavy planking, others sailed through the open ports. The carronades, loaded with half the weight of grape

158

shot, but with a full charge were now clearing the quarterdeck and rigging of marksmen. *Optimist* was not immune; her larboard side was receiving a battering, but for some reason most shots seemed to be aimed high and passed between the masts. It might have been a ball or bar shot, but whichever it was the Spaniard's mizzen mast took the brunt of it and finally gave up the uneven struggle and toppled over the ship's side to act as a sea anchor slowing her down to a stop.

Now *Optimist* could circle the Spaniard at will, whilst keeping a weather eye out to watch what the other Spaniard was doing. It was obvious that the latter was having difficulty replacing her sails. Will suspected that they might be short on crew now. The Spaniard which they had just subjugated sat mournfully stopped as *Optimist* sailed round her. Her name on the stern read '*La Bruja del Mar*' which de Cornes informed Will meant the 'Sea Witch'.

The problem for *Optimist* was that with the mizzen mast gone from the Spaniard, there was no way of knowing whether she was prepared to strike. No alternative ensign had been hoisted, but the Spaniards could play dirty as well.

Derwent was standing beside Will, smiling broadly. He had been quick to anticipate Will's orders. It had contributed greatly to their action so far. They must not make a mess of things now. As *Optimist* turned with the wind behind her to pass close astern of the Spanish frigate, a couple of figures were seen to run to the stern and hang out a white sheet over the ship's name.

The order was passed not to fire unless fired upon, or if a gun was seen being rolled out prior to firing.

Optimist circled round the Spaniard. They were well within range of the Spaniard, but they had stopped firing. However all the Spaniard's starboard guns appeared be serviceable. Would she fire, even if a couple of the crew had decided to surrender? It was a nail bighting wait as *Optimist* sailed majestically down the length of the ship. Were they going to suddenly spring a surprise and fire an apology for a broadside? To make sure they didn't catch onto such an idea, Will had the 18 pounders seek out open gun-ports and aim to send their ball straight through. Nothing happened!

Harris suddenly shouted. "The other frigates getting under way!"

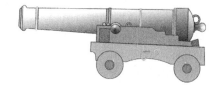

Will brought a scope to his eye. The first Spaniard was beginning to show a wake. By now *Optimist's* fallen yards were back up and the sails sheeted in to be secured to anything available. "Main Courses and Staysails, Mr. Tarrant." Shouted Will. Tarrant turned, grinned, nodded and the men were up the ratlines before the call had been made.

Soon the Forecourse and Maincourse were up and being bowlined[8] in to allow *Optimist* to sail as close to the wind as possible. Then from their sacks the staysails rose to their stays and were hauled out. *Optimist* gathered speed to sail as close to the wind towards the first Spaniard as possible.

After a bit it was clear that *Optimist* was easily overhauling the leading Spaniard. As they came within range, the Spaniard hauled down his colours. Grappling hooks were brought up together with pistols, cutlasses and boarding axes. Mr. Tarrant went round deciding which of the men should be in the first party to board. Will turned to Derwent. "It's your honour Number One, she will be your command."

Derwent stared at Will for a moment and then a smile spread across his face. "Thank you, Sir!"

As they came up to the Spaniard it was possible to read the name of the ship for the first time; it was *Don Alvaro de Bazan.* De Cornes had no idea who he had been.

Optimist came to lie alongside the Spaniard's weather side. Whooping and shouting the boarders swung across using whatever was to hand to gain the Spanish frigate's deck. Jackson the Marine Lieutenant was at Derwent's side when he crossed, along with a party of marines. These swiftly took up firing positions covering the deck, whilst those

---

[8] Lines attached to the lower part of the outside of a square sail allowing it to be brought closer to the wind.

aboard *Optimist* pointed the 'popguns' as the marines called them, the small swivel-guns normally used on the cutters. The prisoners who were still able to walk were herded to the stern of the Spanish quarterdeck. Then the decks below were swiftly searched, and more men came up. Derwent sent Harris to inform Will of the situation below. The grape shot had wounded over half of the crew including her Captain and First Lieutenant. The Spanish surgeon was trying his best to save men down in the Orlop. Will asked de Cornes to see if he could assist. All along the forecastle, galleries, and quarterdeck of the Spaniard, bodies lay where they had fallen. The deck was slippery from blood and guts.

Harris came up on deck again and clambered back aboard *Optimist*, it was obvious he could hardly contain himself.

"Captain, Sir. The bilges are full of gold as are the cable tiers and sail locker. There are no guns on the upper deck, that's where they have stored their sails and cables. There are also metal bound chests, but we haven't broken them open. Lieutenant Derwent wants to know what he should do with them?"

"I suggest he leaves them. You Harris are now the Number two to Lieutenant Formby who will be Captain Derwent's Number One. Yes you are an acting Lieutenant. Congratulations!"

Harris shook his head as if he could not believe it.

"Thank you Sir, Thank you very much. I shall

not let you down."

"It is Captain Derwent, you must not let down!"

"Oh! Quite so Sir!" Harris replied with a chuckle, before crossing back to his new ship.

When Derwent finally reappeared on the Spanish deck, he came across to speak with Will.

"Very little structural damage. If you could pass across any spare sails, that would be appreciated. What do you want me to do with the prisoners?"

"Hold them where they are whilst you sort out your new crew. Then once you can get underway, come and find us, we shall be taking over the other frigate. We can't unfortunately crew three ships, so I intend to check if the other ship is carrying bullion. If she is I mean to transfer it to *Optimist* and then put all the prisoners on the other ship, and leave them to get themselves back to port. We will work out exactly how we divide the crews when we have dealt with the other ship."

Once he was sure that the Spaniard was secure, Will ordered de Cornes back aboard *Optimist*. He might be needed on the other ship.

Optimist let go of the grapples, backed her sails and let the wind push her bow round, before cruising back to the second frigate. Will had ordered that only the topsails, Jib, foremast staysail and Mizzen be set. He didn't want his gun crews diminished in case the second frigate had decided to oppose them. With all the port gun-ports hanging down and the guns protruding through them, he hoped that *Optimist* would look sufficiently warlike to intimidate any idea of fighting again. The upended gun below had been righted and now joined the others in a show of force. Two men had been killed and ten injured. The injured had all been treated by the Surgeon de Cornes, before he had checked on the first of the enemy injured. Now he stood beside Will watching their approach to the Spaniard. He would be needed for any interpreting that was needed. The frigate was a sorry sight. The foremast had now been cut free, but the mizzen still lay across the stern of the quarterdeck, and there seemed no move to cut that free.

The coir fenders were out on the larboard side, and the grappling hooks ready, as *Optimist* ghosted in alongside the frigate. Blood curling yells signalled the assault by *Optimist's* crew as they charged up the ladderways, pistols in belts, cutlasses in hand, to swarm over the Spaniard. Will for the first time in his life led the boarding party with Tarrant to one side and Allwood watching his back.

There was no resistance, and it was obvious why. Sitting in a chair near the remains of what had been the ship's wheel sat an elegantly dressed man with both of his legs bound up with bandages, the blood oozing through. He held out his sword to Will, who took it and then handed it back. The Spanish Captain looked very surprised. De Cornes stepped up and in Spanish said.

"The Captain respects your gallant defence."

The Spanish Captain tried to smile, but the pain

was obviously too great.

"Why do you attack? You are American?" The Spanish Captain managed to get out between clenched teeth, for Henri to interpret.

"Nothing is that clear cut! We are after your gold!" Stated Will.

The Spanish Captain nodded his head sadly at Henri's words. "Greed!" He managed to spit out.

"Have this man taken down to his cabin." Ordered Will.

It was a repeat of the other Spanish ship. The dead lay heaped against bulwarks waiting to be buried, whilst the few who had not suffered some form of injury helped those that had. Below, the Upper deck was in chaos. Guns were lying on their sides, blood was everywhere. The badly injured were laid out on the deck in groups being tended where possible. On the gundeck, hammocks had been hung to take some of the most badly injured. Down in the Orlop, the Spanish surgeon was frantically chopping off limps, whilst his assistants moved the injured up the queue. Others were bandaging wounds. Will as he wandered through the ship, couldn't but be impressed on the one hand by the way members of his crew were assisting the wounded, whilst on the other hand he was sickened by the whole sordid scene. Was it really necessary to fight wars? Was all this wanton destruction just down to a few egos?

Taking a lantern he followed Midshipman Hinton to the bilges. There instead of normal ballast there lay bars of gold and silver. Will stood transfixed.

"Right Mr. Hinton, what would you do with this lot?" He asked.

The over-awed Midshipman spluttered a bit and then replied. "Take it aboard *Optimist*?"

"Well, yes, that, but what have we also got to do?"

"Open the hatches, Sir!"

"That too, but there is a very important thing we have to do first."

The Midshipman stood pondering the problem, whilst searching this way and that.

"We have to exchange what is in our bilges for what is this bilge, otherwise we would be top heavy, and this ship would probably turn turtle." Will answered for him.

"Oh! Yes I see Sir."

"Now ask Mr. Tarrant to come down here, and quietly Mr. Hinton."

"Aye Sir!" Hinton rushed up the ladderway.

There was no way that Will could estimate the number of bars, or their worth. Tarrant arrived promptly. He gave a sharp intake of breathe when he realised what he was looking at.

"I want this transferred to *Optimist*; to replace our ballast." Said Will.

"Very good Sir. Need net slings, but they would have to be strong. I wonder if this ship has any? If not it will take a bit of time making them up. Very heavy I would think this lot!"

"Very!" Replied Will and they grinned at each other, both realising that they were going to be very rich indeed if only they could get this lot back to Britain.

Tarrant managed to locate the net slings that had obviously been used for loading the ballast originally. The hatch covers were removed and blocks attached to the yardarm[9] of *Optimist's* main yard and that of the Spaniard.

Lines were run through blocks to the capstan, to make lifting easier. Members of the Spanish crew were detailed off by Tarrant for certain duties, each under the watchful eye of a boatswain's mate or Midshipman. Canvas buckets appeared from the boatswain's store together with a couple of shovels. For each bar of gold or silver, there had to be at least a full bucket of gravel lifted out of *Optimist's* bilges. There were metal bars as well, but these had to be checked to make sure there were no English marks on them, before they were removed. Gravel and metal was then lowered down to the Spaniard's bilge, replacing the bullion, which was transferred to *Optimist's* bilges.

The work went on all night by lantern light, with frequent changes made to the crews' positions during each watch. An extra tot of rum was doled out at the end of the watch as an incentive, although the very fact that it was gold, was really enough, because every man aboard was full of the fact that their Prize Money was going to be very great indeed. The Spanish prisoners were extremely

---

[9] Yardarm: the metal end cap to the yard, with eye for attaching ropes.

surprised when their cook was made to provide them with a meal, and they too tasted for the first time, British Navy rum.

By the end of the morning watch, the last of the bullion had been transferred. The heavy trunks, full, it was discovered, of rare stones, had been lifted over and stored in Will's cabin aft.

Up on deck the *Don Alvaro* could be seen lying a few cables off.

Signals were hoisted to tell the *Don Alvaro* to lay alongside the *La Bruja*. Half an hour later, all three ships lay rafted up. Will then called Derwent over, together with Boatswain Tarrant and the Master. Mr. Baldwin. Over a glass of celebratory wine, they discussed the division of the crew. Since the *Don Alvaro* had no guns on the upper deck, there was no need for a large gun crew, whereas *Optimist,* acting as guard, would need as many as possible. The extra crew really had not been enough to completely crew a prize, but they helped a lot.

Once this had been agreed, Will had the magazine of the *La Bruja* emptied and added mostly to *Optimist's* depleted magazine and the remainder to *Don Alvaro*. Water barrels from *La Bruja* were transferred to *Optimist*, along with some of the provisions, still leaving enough for the Spaniards for a week or so. All the prisoners, including the injured were moved across from *Don Alvaro* to *La Bruja.* A priest who had been found hiding aboard *La Bruja*, was taken over to *Don Alvaro* and made to take a funeral service for the dead of the *Don Alvaro*. He was then forced to repeat the whole service again aboard *La Bruja*. Once that had been completed, Will took Henri de Cornes over to the Captain's cabin of the *La Bruja*, where there were now two Spanish Captain's each nursing their wounds. De Cornes interpreted as Will addressed the Captains.

"Gentlemen, we have made sure that there is enough cordage to stay your remaining mast. You have sufficient yards still intact and sails to be able to make it back to Cartagena. We have left you enough water and fodder; none of our crew have purloined any personal belongs of any of your crew. All we have taken is the gold, silver and gems, which would have been passed on by your government to the French to pay their Army! We feel that we have every right to purloin your gold, why we might even assist our cousins, although we might not always see eye to eye with them. The wind is fair for Cartagena, you should be able to make it in a week or so. "

Will waited until de Cornes had finished the translation, then he bowed to the two seated Captains and he withdrew with de Cornes close behind him.

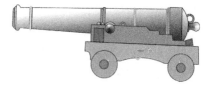

Once the British crews were all back on their respective ships, the grapples were cast off, and they set off heading North-north-east. *Optimist* led the way. They sailed close hauled for two days and nights, during which time their dead comrades were assigned with the usual respect to the deep. Well away from the area of the battle, they slowed to make alterations. The 'gauntlets' were stripped off *Optimist,* the figurehead replaced by the original and the ornamental work put back, together with her name plate. Aboard the *Don Alvaro* there was less that could be done. Will had the carpenter prepare a board, and an ex-signwriter was ordered to gild the word 'DERWENT' on the board. This was then rowed across between the two ships, much to the amusement of both crews. It was obvious the Admiralty would not see the joke, so another board had been prepared with the name *Leucothea* proudly spelled out on it. *Leucothea* was a Greek sea nymph, so would be more acceptable it was thought, to their Lordships. *Optimist's* gauntlets were rowed across and placed around the captured vessel. Then the crew started to paint the canvas yellow to match *Optimist's* sides. Union flags were hoisted at the mizzen gaffs' ends. *Optimist's* commissioning pennant was hoisted to her masthead once more. The *Don Alvaro* seeing this

170

soon had a mock up made to fly from theirs. So that no British ships or their Captains would interfere with their progress, *Optimist* hoisted a broad red pennant to show that she was under direct orders of the Admiralty. Just in case Will had a Commodores uniform packed in his trunk, although he had no right to wear it. It had been Lord St. Vincent's idea.

The sheets were hauled in and they continued to make a fair progress to the north-north-east with the aim to start to tack about a hundred miles south of Kingston, Jamaica. They would then have to work their way between Jamaica and Haiti and then through the passage between Cuba and Haiti.

Three days later just north of Navassa Island they came across a British brig which altered course to intercept them. It would have looked very strange if *Optimist* had tried to avoid the Brig, so very quickly the name plate was exchanged for one saying *Alba.*

The brig came round and sailed alongside *Optimist* close enough to exchange information through the speaking trumpets.

"Did you know we are at war with France?" The shouted question came.

"Really!" Was the response.

"Where are you headed?" Was the next question.

"Where are you out of?" Was the reply, as it was up to the senior officer to do the questioning, not a Lieutenant.

"Kingston."

""We are on diplomatic duty, As far as you are concerned, we never existed! Is that clear?"

171

"Not really!"

"Well If I hear any prattle that you have seen either of our two ships, your time in the Royal Navy will be over! Do I make myself clear!" Shouted Will; through the speaking trumpet.

"Very! Have a good trip!" The Brig turned away and headed back on her course.

Will laughed to himself, when he thought of the Lieutenant looking up *Alba* in the navy list and finding no mention of her. What would he think?

The pair of frigates rounded the southern tip of Cuba and turned to head North between Cuba and the Turks and Caicos Islands, before cutting out below the Bahamas into the Atlantic. Here they hoped to pick up the Gulf Stream.

They were lucky with the weather; late June and early July meant that they just missed the start of the stormy hurricane season. One month less a day after leaving the Bahamas Ridge, they sighted Lands End. Derwent had handled the *Leucothea* very well. She had kept in sight of *Optimist* nearly the whole time. There had been a couple of occasions when early in the morning there was no other sail in sight, but by prudently slowing down slightly, soon the mast, then the sails of *Leucothea* had appeared out of the haze and she had caught up with them. She was not as fast a sailer as *Optimist,* lacking a copper bottom, so allowances had to be made.

Cheers greeted the sighting of the British mainland, but the winds were not kind in the South-western approaches. An area of high pressure over England meant that the winds came from the East. Both ships had to make short tacks to advance up the Channel. Will did not want to risk the French side with their cargo. So it was galling to keep seeing recognisable land marks as they tacked their way up Channel. They could have put in at Falmouth or Plymouth, but Will was determined to end the voyage at Portsmouth. Start Point was a major landfall, before they altered course away again. They could have sailed past Torbay, but Will was determined not to get into a signals war with the Channel Fleet Commander. They tacked just within sight of Portland Bill then back towards land and St Albans Head. Then sailing with staysails and foresails only, they passed St Catherine's Point, before being able to begin to turn for the Solent. They lay all night off Bembridge before picking up the tide in the morning and sailing up the Solent to turn and head between the two forts that marked the entrance to Portsmouth Harbour. *Optimist* saluted the Port Admiral and waited for the Guard Boat to come to first *Optimist* and then *Leucothea* to find out where they should anchor or whether they should come to a buoy. In the event they were told to anchor further up the harbour.

Optimist was securely anchored, the sails had been taken up to their yards, the gaskets tightly drawn -Will was particularly anxious that they should be perfect this time. Tarrant made sure there were no bulges to be seen. The Jolly boat was lowered. Will then reminded the crew of the secrecy of their recent voyage, and that anybody known to have let drop even a hint of what they had done, would lose their share of any Prize Money. He told Cranfield, as acting First Lieutenant that nobody, not even an Admiral was allowed aboard whilst he was away.

"If anybody tries to insist, tell them that the ship has a fever, and it is very catching and can be fatal. That should suffice!" Cranfield was much amused at the idea of being able to turn nosey senior officers away. Will was then rowed to *Leucothea*, where he was welcomed aboard with the normal pipes. Derwent seemed to have blossomed during the trip. He looked much more confident, and greeted Will with the warmest of smiles. Will repeated his injunction against visitors, asked if there was any post and then was rowed over to the Port Admiral. Here he had a short interview, where he asked that the telegraph to London should pass a signal.

Optimist plus one returned.

The Port Admiral was eager for any news, he had been able to see that both frigates had been in action. Will bluffed his way through the interview suggesting that it had been an encounter with the French. Where, he did not explain. He reminded the Admiral that his ship was on secret duties, reporting direct to the Board of Admiralty.

Back aboard Optimist Will sent Allwood to invite Derwent over for Dinner. The mail, including a number of letters to Isabella, had been left with

174

the Flag Lieutenant for onward transmission. It was a convivial meal, with Cranfield, Formby and de Cornes joining them. Much of the discussion was about how to unload the treasure, without it becoming common knowledge.

"I am expecting a signal at any moment." Stated Will. He was not wrong; the Flag Lieutenant was shortly announced. He came with a short signal from Admiralty.

Captain Calvert to London - immediate.

Will hired a riding horse for the journey, but had to travel sedately as he was no longer used to the saddle. He changed horses, and left the last at the Kenton stables at the back of the London Kenton House. He decided it was too late to go to the Admiralty, so took advantage of the offer of a bath and spent the night in a comfortable bed. He did not sleep too well, as he missed the swaying motion of his cot. The next morning he was an early arrival at the Admiralty, so expected to have to wait. He was amazed to be taken straight up to the First Lord's apartment over the premises. He found his Lordship having breakfast and was invited to join him.

"So; Optimist plus one. Sounds intriguing!" His Lordship said; when the servants had left the room.

Will decided to make the most of the moment. He sipped his coffee and smiled over the lip at the Admiral. "Yes, we managed to bring back a frigate, which might help the war effort."

"Good, but I have the feeling you are playing with me, Captain."

"Well My Lord, I have to admit to a certain amount of satisfaction, yes. We captured a Spanish Frigate, whose bilges were filled with bullion... and a couple of trunks of gems." He let the announcement hang in the air.

His Lordship slapped the table. "By Jove, that's absolutely brilliant young man! I knew we had chosen wisely."

"We also captured another frigate with even more bullion and gems. Unfortunately we didn't have enough crew to bring both back."

His Lordship's mouth was open in surprise.

Will continued, "So we transhipped the bullion and gems to Optimist. We then left all the Spanish crew on the second ship. It had lost two masts in the altercation, and was somewhat damaged. I was wondering how we were going to unload all this gold and silver without it becoming public knowledge."

Earl St. Vincent sat staring at Will. Then he slapped a thigh and throwing his napkin on the table stood up. "Follow me!" He barked.

They descended to the office floor, but instead of entering his Lordship's office, they continued on to Sir Evan Nepean's. Without knocking, the Earl opened the door and marched in. Secretary Nepean looked up considerably startled. Earl St. Vincent stood to one side and with a sweep of his arm made Will enter.

"Captain Calvert! What might I ask is going on?"

"Ha!" Exclaimed the Earl; marching up to

Nepean's desk. "You tell him, Calvert."

"We arrived back to Portsmouth but the day before yesterday, Sir. We brought back with us a captured Spanish frigate." He paused.

"So?" An unimpressed Nepean said.

"Ha! The fellow loves to tease... go on Calvert."

"I have to inform you Sir; that we also brought back the cargo of two frigates, which consisted of much bullion and a large quantity of gems."

Nepean's expression was a wonder to behold. He held his mouth with his hand, then leapt up and came round the desk to shake Will's hand. "I can hardly believe it. Napoleon will be furious. How much do you estimate it to be worth?"

"I have no idea Sir."

"Got to come up with a way of unloading without anybody knowing." Added Jervis.

Nepean scratched his head.

"Any ideas, Calvert?" Barked the Admiral.

"I did think that if we were to lie alongside the timber wharf of Portsmouth Dockyard, then we might unload straight onto wagons. We shall have to cover the nets each time, but I have never observed much activity at that end of the dockyard."

"Capital!" Cried his Lordship; rubbing his hands together. "We shall need an escort for the wagons to London. Can you see to that Nepean?"

"I should imagine so, My Lord. Though it will take a little time to arrange."

"I am afraid you will need to strengthen the bottoms of the wagons. The bullion weighs rather a lot." Commented Will. Nepean nodded his head smiling.

"Now Calvert, you come with me. I am off to the palace to report to his Majesty." Lord Jervis added for Nepean's benefit.

It was a very strange journey for Will. His Lordship wanted to know every detail of the engagement. He asked particularly about the long barrelled 18 pounders, which Will had to report were very useful during the battle, but his Gunner had reported that they had not stood up to the pressure well, and were now dangerous. His Lordship made him repeat the sequence of the battle again, this time dwelling on the wind gauge, the sea state and the discipline of the crew. He was amazed to discover that a crew, who had been on the verge of Mutiny, a few months later, had quitted themselves with valour.

Will had not realised that they would have to travel so far, but King George was as usual at Kew Palace, for the summer. As a result, Will was closeted in the coach in the heat of the summer with the First Lord of the Admiralty.

On arrival at Kew Palace, they were greeted by a Major-Domo who led them up through the steps and through the front entrance to face a long passage. His Lordship was shown through the first door on the left, whilst Will was led down the passage to wait in an anti-room. Will waited for some time; during which he was surprised by an attractive young lady bursting in, giggling, to stop with great surprise writ large on her expressive face. Two

178

older young ladies came in a few seconds later as if looking for her. They recovered their dignity, and the first held out her hand as if Will was to kiss it. Confused, he came to attention, which made the three laugh.

"I am Princess Amelia. These are my sisters, Princess Mary and Princess Sophia. Pray why are you hiding here?" The first arrival announced.

"Your Highness, I am not hiding. I am waiting upon Earl St. Vincent."

"Very well, carry on!" She said with a coquettish laugh and they all left through the door they come in by, laughing.

A few minutes later a footman arrived. "Captain Calvert? This way please."

Will was led back down the passage to the door His Lordship had been shown through. The room was lined in linen panelling, which looked as if it was of some age. Here Will was asked to wait. Then the doors at the other end of the room were opened and he was announced. This room was also panelled, but was obviously a library. It was no bigger than his own in Calvert House, which surprised him. The King was sitting in a chair to the left, whilst Earl St. Vincent and another man stood facing him to the right.

"Your Majesty, may I present Captain Calvert of your Majesty's frigate Optimist." Said the Earl. Will advanced; wondering if that was the correct thing to do.

"Captain Calvert! I am delighted to meet you. We have been hearing great things about you, eh?"

179

Will just smiled and nodded.

"Of course you probably know Henry Addington, here, my Prime Minister."

Will gave a little bow of the head towards that gentleman. "I have not had that honour, your Majesty."

"Well you have now, what?" And the King laughed at his own joke. "Made us much richer I hear. Can always do with that, what? Addington, here hasn't come up with quite such a beauteous idea, what? So tell us how you managed this feat."

Will then gave a potted version of what had happened.

"Come, come, Calvert, I feel you are making it all sound too easy. Tell you what; I like the bit about making it look as if you were American... pesky critters. That'll sock it to them!"

For the first time the Prime Minister spoke. "His Majesty would like to reward you. He suggested a Baronetcy. Earl St. Vincent has pointed out that we must keep this a secret. So I have thought of a way through this dilemma. I suggest that His Majesty has graciously agreed to your request to the hereditary title of a former Calvert. Was there such a fellow?"

"Indeed your Honour, I think it was my Great, Great Grandfather who was Sir William Calvert."

"There you go then, Sir William Calvert, Baronet. Not got any cousins in the way, have you?" Queried His Majesty.

"Not that I know of, Majesty."

"Addington, get the Royal College of Arms to

see that it is done." Commanded His Majesty.

The Prime Minister inclined his head, which Will took as being a sign of assent.

The meeting was obviously over, because both Addington and Lord Jervis bowed to the King and started to move backwards out of the room. Will was unfortunately in the way, so had to quickly turn, bow and shuffle backwards himself. Miraculously the doors opened behind them before they backed into them.

"See you outside Calvert." Said Lord Jervis.

Will took the hint and left the outer room to find his way out to the front steps. As he waited for the First Lord, a coach was brought up to the steps. After a few minutes Addington emerged, smiled at Will and said. "Good day to you Sir William" and climbed into his coach which immediately departed. Lord Jervis' coach now drew up, and as it did, so did his Lordship, grinning hugely. "Well that cheered the old boy up!" He said as he climbed into the coach. Will followed him and settled himself as the coach started to move.

"He was having a good day, today. Poor fellow, not been at all well, as you have probably heard. Been better of late though. When he is feeling himself, he is great company. Knows a lot about agriculture, you know. Breeds those sheep you see there."

A King breeding sheep seemed rather bizarre to Will.

"So you will be going back to your ship, will you?" Asked His Lordship.

"I had thought to do just that. I shall have to arrange for the repairs to be carried out to both ships. Which reminds me, My Lord; how are we going to explain the arrival of a newly captured Spanish frigate?"

"Confusion, my dear Calvert, confusion. We announce that we have taken out of reserve a previously captured Spanish frigate and renamed her in honour of our northern brethren the good ship Leucothea. I doubt if anybody will ask any difficult questions. We just omit to say what she was called when we captured her."

Will was not totally convinced, but refrained from saying anything. The rest of the journey was taken up with discussing lines of battle, types of ship and their build, as well as the training and discipline of seamen.

When Will was finally dropped off outside the arches to the Admiralty, he quickly managed to find a chair and was taken to Kenton House. Here he sat down and wrote a letter telling Isabella that he had just met the King. The next day it was back in the saddle and the ride to Portsmouth, marred by it pouring with rain as he left Petersfield. Late in the evening he finally made Portsmouth. There little chance of attracting Optimist's attention, but he chanced the steps in the hope that somebody might be returning late to their ship.

He had to wait for an hour and was about to give up and find a hostelry, when a Captain's gig arrived at the steps. On enquiry, it turned out that a Captain off a Fourth rate was expected. After another long wait the gentleman arrived, slightly worse for wear. When Will asked to be given a lift to his ship, the man barked "What ship might that be, pray?"

After being told the name, the man said. "Can't recall that ship, what is she, and who are you?"

"I am Sir, Sir William Calvert, I am the Captain of the frigate Optimist recently returned."

The other Captain, a more senior captain as he wore two epaulettes, grunted, but his manner changed. "Sir William, I see no reason why not, but pray why is your boat not waiting for you?"

"I am just from the First Lord: been riding back. My ship had no knowledge of my likely return."

The senior captain lurched into his gig, helped by his coxswain. Will nipped down after him. The Captain did not say a word on the journey over to his ship, just a "Good night to you Sir." As he climbed up the boarding steps of his ship.

"Optimist is up channel, isn't she Sir?" Asked the coxswain. Will agreed and was swiftly returned to his ship.

It was a very surprised sentry who was answered by the call "Optimist", but the side was manned for his arrival, and Formby was there to greet him.

The next day, Will was rowed ashore to visit the Master Shipwright of the Naval Dockyard. This gentleman was slightly surprised by Will's request for unloading facilities at the Timber wharf, and asked why a frigate was carrying timber. Will told him that it was a secret cargo, for the Admiralty in London. Will also explained that it might be some days before the wagons arrived, but when they did, first *Leucothea* and then *Optimist* would need to unload. The Master Shipwright asked why both couldn't lie alongside at the same time. Will agreed that this was a good idea, and might save time. Will then ventured to ask about repairs to both ships.

"I sees you've been in a bit of a pickle. I wondered when you were going to get round to asking for dockyard assistance. I better take a closer look. Got your boat here?"

So *Optimist's* gig took Will and the Shipwright round both ships. "Which comes first, the unloading or the repairs?" The fellow asked after close inspection. "Unloading" Replied Will.

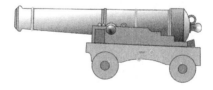

The harbour routine seemed very mundane to the crew after their endeavours. Formby in his capacity as acting First Lieutenant did not allow them to idle about. What repairs could be done inside the ship were undertaken. The sails were taken down one at a time and their seams checked. The Quarterdeck, galleries and forecastle were holystoned until they were shining white. Tarrant had all the standing and running rigging checked and replaced where necessary. The most badly wounded who had not recovered from their injuries were taken across to Haslar to the Naval Hospital. Re-watering and re-victualling was undertaken. The seamen on the top decks were required to wear their smartest gear, as were a side party that was ever ready for any visitors.

Two days later, the Master Shipwright was rowed out to *Optimist*. He was welcomed aboard by Midshipman Tucker who was acting Officer of the Day. Thomas took the Shipwright straight to see Will. A surprised Will, invited him into his day cabin and offered refreshment, which was gladly accepted.

"I expect you are wondering why I am back so soon, aren't you? Well I had a missive from the Admiralty. It appears that I am allowed into the secret. That being the case, as I understand it, your ballast is.... well shall we say, slightly unusual! That being the case, and the necessity for repairs, I have moved you up my list of priorities. Next dock off the Great Basin that comes free will be prepared for you. As it so happens, that will be, opportunely, the northern one."

Will thanked the man, who having sipped his Claret, continued.

"You will need replacement ballast, so I shall arrange that. However, I think it a good idea to check the timbers whilst we can. So, this is what I suggest. We bring in new ballast and leave it on the quay. Anybody being nosey will think, 'Ah, their changing their ballast.' Off course the old ballast is pretty noxious, so it needs to be carted away, doesn't it? Well, there are quarries on Portsdown Hill which would be a quite normal place to dump old ballast, wouldn't it? One or two are quite near the London Road. What I suggests is that the wagons with the 'ballast' are driven up to there. They can be easily guarded there, though what to do about their journey out of Portsmouth I leave to you. Then what's more natural than a convoy of troops and their wagons going to London. How many people are going to notice the difference?"

"I like your idea. I suggest that we put marines in every fourth or fifth wagon under canvas, so as not to draw attention to the convoy. I can supply the marines, after all they already know all about the bullion, they have been guarding it for long enough. Any news on the wagons, bye the bye?"

"No, the Admiralty said in their missive that they were having extra strong flooring put in the wagons. I should hope so! Don't want all the gold dropping out on its travels, do we?"

Five days after he had arrived back aboard from his trip to London, news came that they would be going into the dockyard the next day. Later that same day, a letter was delivered to *Optimist* by a waterman. The Midshipman on duty was young Porteus Trimble. He read the assignee and a puzzled frown crossed his face. The letter was addressed to Sir William Calvert. Bt. Not wanting to make a fool of himself, he took the letter to Lieutenant Ross who was the Officer of the day. Ross was equally puzzled, but told Trimble to take it to the Captain. On entering the Captain's day cabin, young Trimble waited for the Captain to notice his presence. Will finished his writing, sanded it and turned to Trimble.

"Yes Mr. Trimble, what can we do for you?"

"Well Sir, I have a letter just been brought out, but it is addressed to Sir William Calvert Bart. I wondered if it was for you or if there had been some mistake.

"No Mr. Trimble, no mistake. That is my correct title."

The Midshipman stepped forward and handed the letter to his Captain. Then he fled. He had NEWS for the gunroom! An hour later, when his deck duties were over he burst into the wardroom/gunroom and blurted out the information. Surgeon de Cornes, who was reading at the table, looked up and quite calmly said. "Yes he inherited the title whilst we were abroad." Will had told him a couple of nights before, but being Henri de Cornes, he had kept the information to himself. It only took minutes for the information to spread right round the ship.

The letter, as Will turned it over in his hands was written in Isabella's unmistakable hand. He held the letter to his nose and sniffed, hoping that perhaps her scent had lingered on the paper. Finally he tore it open.

My Darling,

I have been waiting so long for news of you.
It was such a great relief to hear that you
are safe and well! I hope you will forgive me,
but knowing the Navy demands so much
of your time. I have taken matters into
my own hands. I have travelled to Portsmouth
to see you. I was very fortunate to rent the
 Captain's house once more.
I pray that you will be able to find time
to visit your loving wife.

Everything at the Estate is fine.

All my love.

Isabella

Will found his eyes fill with tears. He had so wanted to see her again and she was here close by.

He had written to Isabella telling her about meeting the King and his being made a Baronet, though he did put in the letter that the title had been passed down, just in case anybody read the letter. He would tell her the whole truth when he saw her next. He had congratulated her on now being a Lady.

Will grabbed his sword and called for Millward.

"I shall be going ashore very soon. Call for Midshipman Tucker and Allwood."

Millward rushed off to get the marine sentry to pass the word. Very shortly Thomas appeared.

"Thomas, you know the place where you hired the horses before? Well get me one and bring it to the steps as soon as possible. Isabella is here in Portsmouth...er Southsea."

Thomas grinned hugely and rushed off. He knew the Captain would need his gig, so he called for the Jolly boat to be brought alongside. Then he sought out Formby to inform him as to the reason he had to leave the ship. Will, in the meantime had sent a message by Millward to inform de Cornes what he was about to do. Then he called for Formby and told him that he had the ship whilst he was away. He would be back next morning in time to organise the transit to the dockyard. A look of relief was very evident when he received the last piece of information. It was one thing to look after a ship at anchor, quite another to take the responsibility of moving a ship into a dock in front of all the other ships.

Will was in such a hurry to get to see his wife that for once he was on edge, willing Thomas to hurry up. Finally Thomas arrived riding a horse; then slipped from the saddle and held it for Will.

"I shall be back tomorrow!" He called as he rode off.

On arriving at the house that had such a fine view of the Solent, Will threw his reins to a groom and ran round the side of the house and in through the Kitchen entrance, as it was nearer. He hurtled down the corridor and out through the servants door to nearly flatten his mother-in law who was crossing the Hall.

"What the.... Why Will, it is you! Isabella is in the sitting room."

Will gave his mother-in-law a peck on the cheek and rushed to the Sitting Room door and burst in. There sat Isabella in a chair by the fireplace, which was not lit, it being Summer. Opposite her, although Will hardly took the fact in was her father.

"Will!" Isabella shrieked as she rose to greet him. He just enveloped her in his arms and kissed her neck.

There was something different about Isabella, Will realised as he let he go. She had a small protuberance at her stomach. Isabella laughed delightedly.

"So you did notice! Yes I am with child! And before you ask, yes we are both doing very well thank you!"

Will took her in his arms again, and then noticed for the first time his father-in-law sitting smiling at him.

"Hello Will." Grinned Banker Kenton.

"I apologise Sir. I am afraid I did not notice you when I came in."

"If you had I should have been disappointed in you, Sir William."

Will laughed. "I hope you are treating my wife with the due respect she is entitled to!" Said Will with a laugh of pure delight. He was still holding his wife's hand.

Kenton got up, put his newspaper to one side. "I shall leave you two, to it." He commented as he left the room quietly shutting the door behind him.

What Will found most awkward was explaining to Isabella how he had been made a Baronet. He explained it away by saying that he had carried out some very secret diplomacy on behalf of the King, so had been rewarded.

Will was as good as his promise and was back aboard well in time to organise the shifting of position. When the tide was about to become slack, the capstan was manned, the nippers were ready, the cutters crewed ready with tow lines attached. The order was given and the men started to push on their bars, both on the quarterdeck and the upperdeck. The topsails helped to take the pressure off the anchor cable and it was brought up, hosed as it came with the fire-pumps. Once it was up and down, the Cutters were given the order to start rowing. The tow ropes came up out of the water and strained to pull the bow round. Slowly as if reluctant to leave her place *Optimist* began to obey her small consorts, and turned. The anchor rose from the water, and the hoses were turned on that.

Sheets tightened, helm over and *Optimist* followed her tugs towards the quay. As she neared the opening to the Great Basin, which had its gate open ready to receive her, lines already secured and coiled in the gig and jolly boat respectively, were taken across to the quay. These were then used to haul heavier cable across, to be passed through large blocks on the quay and then to the giant carthorse teams that took the strain. The cutters swung to each side, and *Optimist* glided gently between the sides of the lock. Warps were passed aft to act as brakes and she slowly came to a halt with her bowsprit thrusting out over the lock gate. They rested there until the tide turned and the water level came up to match the level inside the Great Basin. Only then were the gates opened and *Optimist* was dragged into the Basin and then to larboard and levelled up to slide into the dry dock on the north side of the basin.

Behind them, on the same tide *Leucothea* was brought through to the Basin, but the entry was not as smooth as that of *Optimist*. Well, it was the first time that Derwent had ever tried such a manoeuvre, and by now the tide was trying to play with its toys. *Leucothea* was tied up immediately aft of *Optimist* but in the Great Basin itself.

Normally once a ship was in the dock, the workers would have been crowded round it. This time only the Master Shipwright and his side-kick appeared once everything was secured. They walked round the three sides of the ship on the hard, pointing and making notes. Finally the Master

Shipwright came up the newly erected gang-plank to be greeted by Will.

"We shall start pumping out in a bit; then the prop-boys will be here to do their business. We won't start any work on the ship, until the ballast has been taken out. I am told that the wagons should be here in about five days. I shall come back tomorrow and we can both have a look at the old girl's bottom." He must have noticed Will's look, because he added. "No need for you to take a look really, Sir William. Better to check it when all the work is finished before we flood the dock. I expect you want to get off to see your folks."

"Well, that is a very kind thought. Actually, my wife has arrived and is staying in Southsea. Means I get the best of both worlds!"

The Master Shipwright slapped him on the back with a friend gesture, then apologised for touching a Baronet. Will just laughed at the absurdity of it all. "I am still the same fellow you know. No need to change your tune, my friend!"

Will stayed to see the draining of the dock and the insertion of the many props as the water went down. Late in the evening satisfied that all was well with his ship. He called for his horse and returned to his wife.

Each day he returned to his ship to check all was well and to attend to any defaulters. The second time he came by carriage, bringing his wife, followed by his in-laws. He invited Derwent, Cranfield, Formby (as acting First Lieutenant), and de Cornes to dine with them. Although Will had told Millward to expect his guests the day before, he had deliberately avoided telling Formby, as he wanted to see whether he would have the crew up to the mark, whatever was happening. He was more than pleasantly surprised to find that every member of the crew within sight of the gangway and upper deck was wearing the smart uniforms that Will had purchased before they left Portsmouth. The men showed a pride in their ship. They had a secret; their ship was one of the two most valuable ships in the Navy at that moment. They all knew they were going to be relatively wealthy men, and they were not going to put a foot wrong that might jeopardise that.

When Formby saw the coaches turning to come to a halt under the bowsprit, he had called Tarrant. Mr. Tarrant had seen to it that every man knew what to do. As a result, the marines were ready at the entry port, all red coats, white breeches, white gaiters, pipe clayed cross belts and their black hats. Behind them the Petty Officers were ranged in their best dress, then the other ranks in their best dress. As Will led the way through the entry port, the pipes shrilled their salute, the marines came to a smart port. Then there was a shout of "Three Cheers for the Captain!" and the whole ship reverberated to the three shouts at the top of everybody's voice.

Isabella was over come and started to cry from happiness. Banker Kenton and his wife looked rather overwhelmed. Formby as acting First Lieutenant, formerly welcomed the guests aboard and then led them aft to Will's quarters. As the guests made their way aft, they couldn't but notice the damage that had been done to the ship, although it had been tidied up as much as possible.

That night Isabella took him to task, asking about the damage to the ship. He told her that they had been in a slight altercation with a French frigate, but she should have seen the Frenchman.

Isabella was as usual upset that her husband had risked his life. She wanted him to leave the Navy. They had enough money and he would be safe. He told her that neither of them would be able to hold up their heads if he did that, when others were risking their lives to keep the country free. She understood his feelings, but still resented the fact that he faced such dangers.

The benefits of being in dry dock were not lost on Will. He was able to spend time with his wife. He tended to visit the ship in the morning and then leave before dinner, which was at about 3pm. On the fifth day of *Optimist* being in the dock, a very breathless Thomas Tucker arrived at the Calvert's rented house. He came rushing in asking for the Captain. Isabella heard the commotion and came out to see what was wrong. Thomas blurted out that he had seen Lord St. Vincent coming out of the Star & Garter. He had taken a horse from the nearest stables to get there to warn his Captain, in case the First Lord visited *Optimist*. Isabella calmed Thomas down and told him William was already on his way to the ship and was probably there already, but that she much appreciated Thomas' efforts in trying to protect his Captain. An embarrassed but grateful

Thomas took the horse back to the stables and ran all the way to the Dockyard. He was very out of breath when he entered the ship through the entry port. Lieutenant Ross, who happened to be on the upper deck checked him and asked what all the rush was about. Directly he heard the news he told Thomas to tell the Captain whilst he told the men around him to get into their best gear, and to pass the word. As a result Will tarried longer than usual and had his dinner aboard. Just as eight bells sounded at the end of the afternoon watch, Young Weeks spied a party of gentlemen approaching the ship on the hard. He notified Lieutenant Formby, who was on tender-hooks for such an eventuality. The side party was ready when the First Lord mounted the gangway. The Marines presented arms, and the pipes sang. So as to make it look as if they were not expecting the visit, Formby met the Earl and sent Weeks scuttling off to fetch their Captain. When Will came across the upper deck to meet the visitors, he was surprised to find that Sir Evan Nepean had accompanied the Noble Lord.

"Hope we are not too late to take a gander at your Ballast Sir William." Said the First Lord; with a broad grin and a chuckle.

"Still holding onto it for dear life!" Commented Will as he shook hands with first his Lordship and then Sir Evan Nepean. "Let me show you, but first may I introduce my acting Number One, Lieutenant Formby,"

Formby knuckled his brow, but the look of surprise and then pleasure was a picture to behold.

"This is Lieutenant Ross, who joined us as extra for our trip. The Master Mr. Baldwin, Midshipmen Hinton, Tucker, Trimble and Weeks." The Noble Lord smiled graciously at them nodding his head .

"And this Sir, is a gentleman I am sure you remember. Mr. Tarrant, our Boatswain."

"Good to see you again Tarrant. Still keeping your Captain up to the mark I see. A very fair turnout." His Lordship said after a swift glance at the seaman standing behind in their best rig.

Will led the group of gentleman that included the Master Shipwright, down the main hatchway to the gundeck and then round to the aft ladderway and down to the Orlop. He took a lantern from a boatswain's mate strategically positioned for that purpose, and called Henri de Cornes from his medicine chest to be introduced. Then it was necessary to call for hands to remove the hatch cover to the bilges. Here there was a wait and Sir Evan Nepean commented on the neatness of the cables and the stowage of the sails.

"Never doubted it would be so!" Commented the First Lord. Once the hatch covers had been withdrawn they were all able to see the gold bars that now acted as ballast.

"By God, I never thought to see such a sight!" Said Lord St. Vincent.

"I assure you that *Leucothea* is an even more impressive sight." Said Will, and then regretted it as he feared that Derwent might not have got news of the visit and his ship might not be in such a fine state for an inspection.

They all wanted to see for themselves after that, so Will led the way, as technically he was still the Senior officer of *Leucothea*.

As they made their way down the gangway and walked towards *Leucothea*, Sir Evan Nepean was kind enough to introduce the other three gentlemen as members of the Board.

Will should not have been quite so worried; the crew were not smartly dressed, and the upperdeck was littered with the sailor's personal belongings. Derwent met them at the entry port, so he must have been warned in some way. The group were more than slightly surprised to find the gundeck being used to store the cables and sails, but when it was explained that the Orlop was being used for 'cargo' it was partly explained. This time when the group stood at the bottom of the ladderway and surveyed the Orlop, they were very quiet. Instead of ropes and canvas, there laid out on deck under nets were bars of gold and silver stretching out of sight into the darkness.

"And the bilges are the same as on *Optimist*?" Queried His Lordship.

"Aye Sir!" Replied Will and Derwent together. "Would you like to take a look?"

"No, no, I believe you. So how much is gold and how much silver?"

Will stepped in. "About three quarters is in gold; that includes gold coins, and the rest is in silver. However that does not include the gems."

"Gems?" His Lordship was seen to turn smartly round to look at Will in the half-light thrown by the lanterns.

"Aye Sir, There are two trunks of gems in Lieutenant Derwent' s quarters, and two, plus another containing coinage in mine."

They started to climb back up to the upperdeck of *Leucothea*, but on the way Will invited the members of the Board to drinks in his cabin aboard *Optimist* at the same time as viewing the contents of the trunks.

The whole party, including Derwent, then made their way back to *Optimist* and down to Will's cabin. There a smartly dressed Millward had laid out glasses and decanters for the visitors. He withdrew at a sign from Will, and then the assembly gathered around the first trunk. This was a heavy wooden affair with metal strapping. The three locks' clasps were tightly shut. Will produced the keys which he had taken off the unfortunate Spanish Captains and began to undo the locks, one at a time. There was a group gasp as the lid was raised. There, lying mixed together were various precious stones, and gold ornaments. The sunlight coming through the stern windows, sparkled back throwing multicoloured reflections on the deck head. There was a long silence, before anybody spoke.

"When do you expect the wagons?" Asked His Lordship.

"I am having extra oak bottoms fitted to ten, My Lord." Said Nepean.

"Will that be enough to transport the lot?" Asked one of the members of the Board.

"I calculate that each wagon can carry about 75

bars of gold each. Rather more of the silver bars." The Master Shipwright had done his sums.

"But that won't be enough to shift the lot, will it?" Reposted His Lordship.

"No My Lord, there will have to be a number of convoys."

"Can't we get more wagons?"

"Not from our naval sources, My Lord."

"So how many convoys will it take?"

"Three, My Lord."

"Three! And how many days will it take?"

"It depends where we intend to store it."

"I suppose it better be the Tower of London, don't you?"

"Yes!"

"So how long will it take?"

"About five days, My Lord."

"Five days?"

"Per convoy. That is from loading to the completion of unloading."

"Five days! We have got to do something! Sir Evan, what do you suggest?"

"My Lord, the problem is the weight capacity of normal carts. I suggest that we could not rely on hiring in farm carts. We could not guarantee their load carrying capacity. Might I suggest that the Army be called in?"

His Lordship pondered the idea. "Pity we didn't get Calvert to take the ships round to London."

"Ah, but My Lord, there would be no way we could unload in that city secretly, none at all." Commented Sir Evan Nepean; glancing at Will.

Then the Master Shipwright spoke up. "Pardon me, My Lord, but I should point out that each ship will have to be unloaded separately, so if we could take the Trunks by some other type of cart, it would only mean two trips."

"And are we still hiding marines in covered carts to guard the convoy?"

"I have arranged My Lord, for the Army to take over guarding the convoy from the quarry. We have arranged for a large quantity of hay to be sent there, so that once the wagons are in the quarry out of sight, the hay can be piled on top. It would then be feasible for a small number of mounted troops to be seen on the move together with fodder for their animals." Sir Evan Nepean looked rather pleased with himself, as His Lordship regarded him with mild surprise.

"So what about the trunks?" His Lordship queried.

"Not unusual for a senior officer to travel with a few trunks and some furniture1" Added Nepean.

"You're enjoying this aren't you?" Said the Earl, but there was a smile playing around the corner of his lips.

That night it was an exhausted Will that arrived back to join Isabella for supper. He was surprised to find that she knew the First Lord had been in town. When she explained that Thomas had come to warn him, he said that he must thank Thomas the more. He knew he had brought the intelligence, but had not been told that Thomas had gone to the house first.

"I shall have to thank him again, tomorrow. Typical of the young man to think of alerting me; wherever I might be."

Three days later the convoy of wagons came into view to draw up in line on the dockside. Mr. Tarrant went into action. First he had tarpaulins laid across the bottom of each wagon, with the ends hanging over the sides and both ends. Then the *Optimist's* hatches were opened, the main yard, which had been ready for days, set in motion. Each load of gold came up wrapped in canvas inside the net. It was swung out over the wagon and gently lowered into it. Seamen from both *Optimist* and *Leucothea* stood ready to receive the gold in the wagon. Each bar was carefully taken out of the net and canvas and stowed in a balanced fashion on the new oak floor of the wagon. Dockyard workers were allowed to stroll past, but none even bothered to take a second look. As far as they were concerned it was just cargo, there was no way they could ever have seen a hint of the gold.

When seventy-five bars had been placed, the four sides of the tarpaulin were hauled over and secured. Then the next wagon would be pulled up to replace the one before, the four massive shire horses then patiently waited for their wagon to be loaded.

It was early evening when the convoy at last set out. Beside each driver sat a marine in plain clothes, but with a brace of pistols hidden behind his seat. Taking up the rear was a covered wagon, with marines in full dress, hidden by the canvas cover and the front and stern flaps. A little later a heavy van rolled up. It was of the type used by prosperous families to transport their luggage. One of the trunks was gently lowered, and manoeuvred into the interior. Nobody was quite sure of the weight, and they had to test to see if the springs and axle would take the weight. Any heavier, and it would have pushed the springs to their limit, but it was felt that there was enough play for the springs to survive a trip to London, so long as it was driven slowly and carefully.

Lieutenant Jackson of the Marines, in civilian dress was joined by one of his men; dressed as a gentleman. The fire power they carried, could have wiped out half of all the highwaymen in the country. They would drive straight to London.

The next day single axle carts arrived with the shingle and metal bar ballast to replace the bullion ballast. The Master was very busy making sure it was properly stowed, so that the trim would be right.

It was another five days before the Master Shipwright passed the repairs that had been made to *Optimist*. The water was allowed back into the dock and the supporting props removed. The gates were opened ready for *Optimist* to be warped out. Whilst the water had been flowing back into the dock, *Leucothea* had been moved to the other side of the Great Basin using heavy horses to pull the warps. Now lines were thrown from the stern of *Optimist* attached to heavier warps. These were then hauled out by the berthing crew and attached to the heavy horses. Other warps were taken round land based capstans. Slowly *Optimist* was pulled out stern first from the dock, until she was where *Leucothea* had rested for the last couple of weeks. More lines were taken to the south side of the Basin and she was hauled round to lie sideways on to the entry gate. Now a small rowing boat was employed to take a line across the basin to the East side, so that another warp could be pulled across. Then *Leucothea* was warped past to have her stern worked across *Optimist's* bows so she was ready to be put into the dry-dock, *Optimist* had just left. Once *Leucothea* was safely inside the dock, the warping of *Optimist* began again. The last warp that had been laid, was now used to pull the stern right round so that she pointed towards the harbour. There she waited until the tide was at the right height and then the gates were opened and she was hauled through, to be taken over by her cutters pulling her the last bit. Once clear of the entrance, sails could be unfurled and she turned north to drop anchor very near where she had first been when she arrived back from the West Indies. She no longer sported her extra long barrelled 18 pounders. These had been taken off earlier, as they were deemed to be unsafe. They had only been fired about 15 times in all.

It was a strange feeling just lying at anchor at harbour when Britain was at war with France. Will was surprised that no orders had come to join the Channel fleet or the Mediterranean Fleet. He took advantage whilst he could. Derwent had been given leave of a week, so Will made it his business to visit both ships during the day. At the end of the second week the wagons returned to the dock. This time a proportion of the cargo was made up of silver. There were still the original ten wagons, but these accommodated the cargo easily. A second heavy van joined the first for the transfer of the final trunks to London. This time Midshipmen Harris and Hinton were allowed to travel with the vans, so they could have a couple of days leave in London. The Warrant officers of both ships had been allowed into Portsmouth during the time the two ships had been in dock. Cranfield and Formby as acting First Lieutenants had missed out. Will now let them have leave of a few days to visit their parents. *Optimist* still had to be re-victualled and resupplied with ball and powder. The September days were relatively balmy, yet no orders arrived. The crew were back to exercising the guns twice a day. Boredom could very soon start to afflict the crew. All the Officers arrived back from leave. *Leucothea* remained in dock, her repairs not yet finished.

Then at last a signal arrived, but it was not for Will it was for Derwent. He was commissioned as a

Commander, to take command of a fine Brig Sloop. She was at Plymouth, so he would have to travel by land to that city to take her over. Lieutenant Ross then was ordered to join a frigate, fitting out at Chatham. Cranfield returned to *Optimist* as First Lieutenant. Will was still spending as much time as he could with Isabella acutely conscious that the happy times could not last. He heard rumours of an impending change of Government, and wondered what effect that might on his own future. He was very well aware that he was Lord St. Vincent's man, and that the gallant Earl was not popular in some quarters for his efforts in trying to stem the endemic corruption within the Dockyards and supply chain. If William Pitt was to become Prime Minister it was almost certain that Lord Jervis would have to resign. So who would take over?

On the 2nd of October a signal arrived summoning him once again to London. Now certain that he was to be called back into the fray, he suggested that Isabella should accompany him to the Capital, and then go back to Devon for the birth of their child. So the Calvert convoy, as Will termed it, set off the next day for London. Once he had made sure that Isabella was safely settled in Kenton House, he hurried round to the Admiralty the next day.

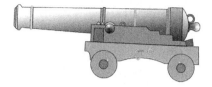

There was no long wait; he was taken straight up to the Admiralty Boardroom, where he found Lord St. Vincent seated at the table. "Ah Calvert! You made good speed as usual. Follow me."

His Lordship picked up a cloak hanging over the back of a chair and led the way out through the door where normally the clerks entered. They went a short way down a corridor and then down two flights of stairs to emerge at the back of the building where a hackney carriage stood waiting. His Lordship climbed up and Will followed him. Immediately they were safely aboard the driver clicked his tongue and they moved off.

"Sorry to kidnap you in this fashion, Calvert, but we have to: this trip must remain a secret, and off course you have never met the gentlemen you are about to meet. Get my drift?"

"Aye, My Lord."

"Good man."

They didn't speak another word. Will, not knowing London well, had no idea where they were being taken, though at the end he was sure they had gone round in a circle. The carriage slowed, and then turned through a narrow arched entrance to a mews. Coaches and curricles were parked on either side, with horses being groomed and a farrier shoeing a horse, before they turned sharply to the right and stopped. Earl St. Vincent did not wait for the carriage door to be opened, he did so himself and climbed down heading straight for an open door beside a coach house. Will followed him. They moved down a passage; then along a roofed arcade, with an open side to a garden, which looked distinctly wintery. Then it was through another door, past a dusty window that revealed a kitchen in full swing, up some steps and into a hallway. Here a Butler, nodded his greeting and led them up a sweeping staircase and knocked on a door on the landing, opened it and stood to one side. The Earl led the way. Sitting in a group either side of a fireplace with its welcoming blaze was a group of well dressed gentlemen. Will thought he recognised the Prime Minister, only to realise immediately that he had made a mistake.

"Ah, Jervis! Good timing, we have only just arrived ourselves. I take it this is Captain Calvert?"

"Yes your Royal Highness, this is Sir William Calvert."

"Heard a lot about you from my father, the King. Take a pew Calvert and you Jervis."

Lord Jervis and Will sat on the two vacant chairs that faced the fire at the end of the low table that divided two couches on which sat the rest of the gentlemen.

"Don't know if you have met these gentlemen, so I shall introduce you. Mr. Pitt. Mr. Hiley Addington, the present Prime Minister's brother, Mr. Wickham, Viscount Castlereagh, Colonel

Smith, and General Smith. I take you know who I am, but just in case, I am the Duke of York." He smiled at Will encouragingly.

Will nodded at each as they were introduced.

"Over to you Jervis." The Duke settled himself back on the couch.

"Thank you your Highness. As all of you know Captain Calvert probably knows the North French Coast, better than most. He undertook a lot of work for you during the last fracas. This time, we shall listen to him and not push him or his ship to the limit!"

There were nods of understanding all-round.

"We have been having long and frank discussions about the invasion threat. Lord Keith's North Sea Fleet is responsible for making sure that the invasion cannot happen. And of course the French cannot invade without a fleet to protect them, which is why the Channel Fleet is still blockading Brest. However the best laid plans can go wrong. I suggested to these gentlemen that you might have some original ideas on how to deal with the threat. I know I did not warn you, but that is exactly what I wanted. I wanted you to throw out your ideas, without any outside influence. You can say whatever you want. None of these gentlemen here will hold anything you say against you. We all deal with the unseen battles behind the scenes, if you see what I mean. So Sir William, we should like you to think aloud, so to speak."

Will sat in a state of shock. Here were some of the most influential people in the country and they wanted his opinion; it seemed surreal! He looked round nervously. Fighting the French or Spanish was much less terrifying than this.

"I am afraid that I am not really up-to-date on the situation. However I suggest that if the Corsican is in charge, then there has probably been more effort put into the whole operation. If that is the case, what was relatively easy for us, is going to be a whole lot more difficult from now on. I hear he is based on Boulogne. That port is almost impossible to attack without great loss. The entrance is extremely narrow, and the harbour well set back. On either side there are sand banks, so you can only make a full frontal approach. The last I heard was that the French had gunboats moored off the entrance. To get within range of the inner harbour - extreme range, even a frigate would be in danger of running aground. Even a sloop would have problems, and anyway they would be in easy range of any artillery that must be set up near the mouth of the river, and that is if all the defending gunboats had been sunk in one go. And of course the French gunboats outside are probably mounting 24 pounders with a greater range, I suspect, than even our 18 pounders. Further south the River Bresle is the most probable place that they would gather landing craft. That is very narrow and has constantly changing sand banks. The French would, if they have any sense, place their craft near Ètaples, up the river, so anything trying to get within range would be ambushed. Travelling further south, St Valery-sur-Somme, is where they gathered a fleet of landing craft last time. We had *Snipe* at that time and were able to get in; destroy a large number of their landing craft and get out without the French being able to do much about it. Mark you; we had silenced the fort at the mouth first. I should imagine they have now positioned artillery on the other bank and reinforced the fort."

Will paused, they were still attending to his every word, so he paused a moment longer to summon his thoughts and continued.

"I must admit, it is a subject that I have thought a lot about. I am afraid that my ideas would probably be an anathema to the Admiralty."

"I think we can be the judge of that, don't you your Highness?" Said Lord St.Vincent.

"Aye, fire away Captain. We shall think no less of you, even if we don't agree." The Duke of York gave a throaty chuckle.

"Well, Your Royal Highness, My Lords, Gentlemen, If it was up to me I should attempt to try to outflank the French. By that I mean use Frenchmen against Frenchmen. I would train a special squad of French volunteers to attack the harbours from inland at night. At the same time I would position shallow draft ships with as much firepower as possible to attack from the front door, to act as a diversion. The object would be to burn as many of the landing and assault craft as possible. I should use schooners to get in and out as quickly as possible and go back to the middle ages and use canisters of burning oil in the harbours. It is a pity that Mr. Congreve's ideas on rockets are not further advanced. We could do with a weapon that we can fire further than 2,000 yards. I would undertake the raids on both Boulogne and the River Bresle on the same night. We could only achieve a result, if we have surprise on our side. After that I would concentrate on their supply lines. They have to construct enough ships to carry out an invasion. They have only a certain number of timber yards in the north. They will have to use yards further apart to construct the craft and then they have to sail them round. I would augment the Channel Squadron to stop that happening. I would use the French Royalist volunteers to travel inland, to burn their supplies of seasoned timber."

The Duke of York had been listening with his chin on his chest, and he made no movement when Will had finished. Lord St. Vincent was smiling. "Bravo! Calvert. A new approach as usual! What do you think your Highness, Gentlemen?"

"I think that Calvert has raised a lot of interesting ideas." The Duke looked up and looked Will straight in the eye. "How would you land these men?"

"A couple of nights before hand, they would be dropped at known landing places. They would have to be trained to navigate on land by night. During the day they would have to melt into the surroundings. Their landing would be covered by marines landed ahead of them to make sure the surrounding area was secure. That was the way we always covered agents landing. The marines would be used to hold any peasants whilst our Royalists borrowed their wagons for transporting the equipment. They would also cover any withdrawal."

Mr. Pitt nodded. "Where would you get these Frenchmen from?"

"I should imagine that there is a large group of Royalists that are known to the Government, from whom we should be able to pick and train at least twenty to thirty."

"It would be a suicide mission!" Hiley Addington said rather tentatively.

"Not necessarily, Sir. We landed and destroyed over twenty or more craft when we attacked Barfleur. We managed to retreat without losing a man."

"And how, pray did you do that?" Asked the General.

"We caused confusion, total confusion. We used French patois to make some of the soldiers think we were rescuing the craft, whilst setting the fuses."

General Smith glanced at the Duke. He rested one arm on the other and stroked his chin. Then he suddenly sat up straighter, turned to Lord St. Vincent and said. "Right. As we all know here, my cousin Sir Sydney Smith has been sounding off about invading with troops. I know he means well, but it seems to have slipped his mind that there is a whole army waiting over there. He is very impressed by Mr. Francis, sorry Sir William; Mr. Francis is the name we use for Fulton the American inventor. He tried to persuade Napoleon to build a submarine...well he did make a prototype we understand, but it was destroyed. Fulton is now over here....the Corsican wouldn't pay him enough.... advocating something he calls torpedoes. Sir Sydney thinks that he can sink the blockade with them. However, if he succeeded, as Sir William has pointed out, the inner harbour is beyond our range, so the bombarding ships would have to come within range of the entire artillery of Napoleon's Army. No I think Sir William's ideas have merit. What do you think gentlemen?"

"I should like to study the whole project in more detail, but in broad terms I think the idea has merit." Said the Duke.

Mr. Pitt sat thinking. "Well Jervis, you certainly can pick the exceptional spirits. I too would like to see the whole idea expanded into what it would need in resources, costs and an estimation of its feasibility. Charles, you have been very quiet."

Colonel Charles Smith smiled. "I am frankly amazed that a Naval Captain has such a broad picture. I think the whole thing has exceptional merit. Whatever else it does; if it is only partially successful, it will have an effect on the moral of the French troops..... and their so called First Consul!"

"Addington?" The Duke turned to the gentleman on his right.

"What I should like to know is whether Captain Calvert has discussed this with Lord Jervis, or if, as we are led to believe, this is straight off the cuff?"

"I have not discussed this with Captain Calvert. From my past experience of this gentleman, I have come to realise that he thinks out strategy on every front. He does not use conventional methods. That is what sets him apart. His planning for the Caribbean adventure is a case in point."

"Ah yes, the gold! So why was that so very different?" Asked the Duke.

Will looked to Lord Jervis.

"He came up with the idea of being able to change the appearance of his ship; to fool anybody into thinking it was American, so as not to bring the Spanish into conflict with us. He also tried specially made extra long barrelled 18 pounders, mounted in the bows. These were on carronade type carriages. They worked brilliantly, only the forging wasn't too clever and they could not be used again. You see gentlemen it is the attention to detail that sets him apart. Why I remember when we were on *Victory* before the battle of the Cape, he was instructing his gunners to remember the position of the gun ports relative to the positions of the enemy masts, so they could fire through their open ports even if they could not see them."

Will found this talk acutely embarrassing.

"Right, I suggest that we get Calvert to write a detailed report for us, which we will await with interest. Thank you for coming Captain. I hope to see you again in the near future." Said the Duke.

Will realised that he was no longer required. He stood up, bowed to the Duke, nodded to each of the gentlemen and made his way to the door.

"I'll see you back at the Admiralty this afternoon. Take the hackney, and tell it to come back when you are finished." Said Lord Jervis; from his seat.

Back at the Admiralty, Will had to kick his heels. One of the porters took pity on him and fetched him that day's Gazette. It was close to two hours later that he was summoned to the First Lord's Office.

"Come in, Sir William. I thought that went very well. You made a great impression, which will stand you in good stead in the future. I suggest that you go away and think very carefully and write up a report on your ideas. Fill them out."

"Very good, My Lord. I think it might be a good idea if I took *Optimist* on a scouting trip up the coast to get an up-to-date picture of what exactly is happening along that coast. The only problem is that I should be encroaching on Lord Keith's domain!"

"Leave him to me. I am First Lord still you know! Oh by the way I have a note from Castlereagh, he asked me to give it to you."

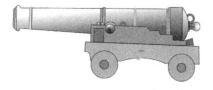

Will remembered to open the note as he was leaving the Admiralty. It invited him to supper with the Viscount. It even added that if Lady Calvert was in town, that would be even better.

Will was very surprised as Castlereagh hadn't

said a word during the whole meeting. Hurrying back to Kenton House, Will explained the extraordinary invitation to Isabella, who was insistent that they replied immediately and that they should accept.

It was a strange supper party as Will and Isabella were the only guests. They were introduced to Amelia Castlereagh who immediately took Isabella off as the men settled for a pre-supper drink.

Castlereagh dismissed the footman and poured Will a glass of claret from a splendid cut-glass decanter and after handing Will the glass poured one for himself before flipping back the tails to his jacket and sitting himself down comfortably. After sipping his wine he said.

"I was fascinated by your ideas. I must say I thought the way you thought on your feet was outstanding. Made some enquires and was allowed into the secret – the big secret, so I thought I should get to know you. Jervis said he thought your wife was in town. I must say you seem to be as lucky a man as I consider myself to be; very beautiful and very charming your wife!"

Will was at a loss for words. He was not used to Society or its ways. Isabella of course knew exactly how to behave, so obviously had carried the day. Castlereagh surprised Will by his knowledge of naval tactics, and became convinced that he must be very highly thought of. Castlereagh also seemed to have a very profound knowledge of Indian affairs, and was interested in Will's descriptions of India, which he had visited with his father as a boy. By the time they joined the ladies for supper, it was obvious that Amelia and Isabella had become friends. Amelia insisted they called her Emily.

That night, Will told Isabella that he would have to take *Optimist* to sea for a short run to keep her crew up to the mark. He did not tell her what had transpired, nor that he was taking the ship into enemy territory. He suggested that she might like to stay in London as he would only be away for a week or so, and had to report back to the Admiralty on his return. This seemed to delight Isabella as Emily Castlereagh had invited her to join her on an outing, and she had thought she would not be able to attend.

Back at Portsmouth, the arrival of the Calvert coach was noted by the watch keepers aboard *Optimist* and the gig set out immediately to fetch him. Once back aboard, he ordered *Optimist* to be victualled for sea, and that she have fresh powder taken aboard. The next day, the hoys lay alongside and there was much bustle on deck. Below in his cabin, Will started work on his report. He had brought his own charts from London, and they lay on the table ready to be scrutinised. There were times where he sat gazing out of the windows in a trance like state, trying to think. Then he would write at length. Millward had been warned not to disturb him, except for meals and refreshment.

They left Portsmouth on the ebb tide as soon as it was light enough to see. They were heading for Ètretat a small village on the French coast about 20 miles NNE of Le Havre. Here there was a hole in the cliff which was a well known landmark. Will was on the quarterdeck as they left Portsmouth, but as soon as they were out in the Solent, he was down in his cabin again. They were not racing, The crew exercised the guns as usual, but this time with charges, so the crew was again familiar with their guns and their recoils. He had left orders that they were to cross to a position within about 50 miles of the French coast and then they were to wait, using tide and wind to hold their position. Directly it was daylight they were to sail to the French coast to begin their 'cruise'. Cranfield as number one was in charge; Will did not want to be disturbed. That night he worked late into the night, until he felt that he was not making progress so took himself to his cot.

The crew had just finished their breakfasts when the first sighting of land was made in the pouring rain. Both Will and the Master had agreed that a depression was on its way, and they were proved right, because the winds had moved round to the West. Now if the tide tables were correct, they would be arriving at their destination at about four and a half hours before high water. This would mean that they would have both wind and tide in their favour for the next five hours, by which time they should be turning north so the tide would stay with them for another hour, before two hours of virtually slack water.

The Midshipmen would be taking it in turns to act as lookouts on the mainmast. Youngmen would be positioned on the other two masts, all with telescopes to search the coast. Positioned in the rigging, members of the crew would relay any information to literate crew members to write the results. Will would correlate their findings later. The sea state was showing a few white horses and was likely to build. At just after nine o'clock in the morning, *Optimist* turned to sail up the coast about a mile and a quarter off, depending on the charted bottom. Leadsmen were positioned on either side calling out the depths the whole time. Up in the bows, sharp eyed boys were suspended on nets to watch for any sign of a change of colour in the sea ahead.

For the first hour there was little to see except cliffs and small coves, then quite suddenly the cliffs dropped to sea level and there was the fishing village of Féchamp, where the reports started to be passed down. A gunboat started out from the little harbour, but *Optimist* was well past by the time they had got their act together. It was back to cliffs, with the occasional small bay with a sandy beach, but other than a few fishing boats drawn up above the tide line, there were no signs of any French naval vessels. They passed small fishing boats off the coast which ignored them. After two more hours and it was another sudden break in the cliffs and the mouth of a very tidal river. This time the reports came down thick and fast. Will standing by the main mast listened with interest. Apparently there were quite a considerable number of flat bottomed boats on either side of the river lying on the mud. On the cliffs either side of St.Valery-en-Caux were signs of gun emplacements. This time there was no reaction from the French and no reports of any craft of any significant size. Another couple of hours of much the same low cliff coast line, with the occasional cove breaking the monotony and there was Dieppe. To the eastern side of the entrance, there was a fort set on top of the cliffs. The lookouts had a field day. Not only were there landing craft, there were bigger wherries or caiques[10], interspersed with three different types of gunboat, a number of peniches[11]; and with their masts standing high above the others, six prames[12] and three chaloupes[13]. One of the chaloupes was seen to try to get underway, but once again *Optimist* was gone before she got her nose out into the sea.

Next it was the small village of Le Tréport, where there were a few 2nd class gunboats, but they did not seem to be manned. Shortly after St Valery-sur-Somme came into view, a place Will knew well having destroyed a large number of landing craft there in the last war with his schooner *Snipe*. Here judging from the masts. there were a number of Peniches, a group of 3rd class gunboats of various classes, as well as a large number of flat bottomed Caiques. They were lying on the mud opposite the

---

[10] Caique: two masted flat bottomed rowing boat with lateen sails, 2 carronades.

[11] Peniche: three masted barge type with main mast much taller than others, 60ft long with 2 howitzers.

[12] Prame: Flat bottomed gun boat, three masts, 10-20 guns.

[13] Chaloupe: Two masted gunboat approx 110 ft long with 12 guns.

village. Tied to the quay were two Prames, but they did not seem to have any crew aboard. Will was rather doubtful of the information as they all were observed at a distance of over five miles. The entrance to St. Valery-sur-Somme, is a mass of moving sand banks. It was four hours after high-water, so they could not get any closer inshore. As it was they only had half a fathom under their keel for quite a period of time. The officers were on edge, but Will knew this coast so well, he knew exactly what he was doing. There was quite a bit of activity around the fortifications on the south bank, but they were too far off, for the French to use their cannon.

The weather was closing in, rain once again coming in a steady down pour. Visibility would soon get worse as the evening drew in. Will ordered *Optimist* to be taken out into the Channel, out of sight of land, to once again lie to wind and tide, keeping her station off the coast. Come the morning they were off the mouth of the River Bresle, another sand bank strewn estuary. Once again it was difficult to get a good picture of things because the rain cane down intermittently. Once again the Caiques, and Peniches, could be seen hauled up on the river bank. The reports from up the masts all agreed that there was only one small 2nd class Gunboat in evidence. What were interesting were the reports that there were a great number of tents on the north bank, with some thatched buildings amongst them. When the rain lifted enough, the lookouts reported horse activity. There also appeared to be embrasures thrown up on either side, with artillery pieces behind them.

Boulogne was a different matter. As they approached they could see that there were three masted, two masted and single masted gun boats at anchor off the port. Added to which there were two prames cruising further out. *Optimist* had been at action stations all the time, but now Will ordered that the 18 pounders were to be loaded with ball and shot alternatively. What was worrying was that some of the gunboats were known to mount new improved 24 pounder guns. Whether they were cannon or carronade, he did not know. Here from only a mile and a half off they were able to see that the harbour was jammed full of all types of vessel. There also seemed to be a lot of construction work going on at the harbour. Luckily the rain held off, though the wind was getting up, which suited Will as it gave him more flexibility and also meant that the flat bottomed gunboats would have great difficulty finding their target. The calls from the crosstrees came down thick and fast. *Optimist* did not change her course she kept straight on, cannons protruding from their open ports. It was a great pity she no longer had her long range 18 pounders in the bows, but the standard ones would have to do. One of the Prames altered course to engage *Optimist* but a gunboat was the first to fire. Immediately the port bow 18 pounder returned the compliment with shot. The gunboats ball passed close by on the larboard side, but *Optimist's* shot was a direct hit and the gunboat slewed away, her sails in tatters. Still the Prame came on. The minutes ticked by as they closed. The larboard chaser 18 pounder was reloaded with ball. Will primed the Master as to what was required and a message was passed to the bow gunners. It was classic *Optimist* engagement tactics. His hand fell, Allwood at the wheel turned to starboard bringing both bow chasers into line with the Prame. Nobody moved, they were transfixed. A gunboat rudely broke the silence by firing at *Optimist*; the ball struck her on the starboard side just below the upper deck, but did little damage. Everybody was conscious of the vibration that told them they had received a hit. A couple of starboard 18 pounders replied and the gunboat disintegrated before their eyes. Then the bow gun captain holding the ranging quadrant gave the order. The lanyards of both guns were pulled and their explosions intermingled as two shots hit the oncoming Prame. The wheel was put back, bringing the whole starboard upperdeck guns into range. At the same time another pair of larboard side guns, picked off another gun boat before she could manoeuvre her gun to line up with the British frigate. The first Prame had been hit but was still capable of returning fire. The larboard side's rolling barrage was met with balls flying all over the place. Two went through the foresails, another hit the larboard cathead which meant that the anchor fell in the water. Tarrant was on to the problem immediately; an axe came down slicing the wreathing anchor warp in two. Another had torn through the top main gallant and a third struck the mizzen gaff, which now hung down with part of the sail, but didn't fall on the deck. The Prame on the other hand was a complete mess. *Optimist's* guns had been aimed at the hull, unlike the French fashion of trying to dismast an enemy. A quick look was enough to establish that she wasn't going to engage again. The other Prame was now coming down on the starboard side bow. Again the bow chasers opened the proceedings with little effect. Still the Frenchman came on. Will did not move. A report from the stern quarter informed him that a corvette was leaving harbour.

He concentrated on the oncoming Prame. Her Captain was a brave man. With so few guns he did not stand a chance against the heavily armed British frigate. He also had the problem that he was sailing against the wind, so would have to tack across the frigate's bow, in doing so the Prame would heel away from *Optimist* showing more of her bottom, and making it almost impossible to fire her guns. All that the Prame Captain could do was to come about and then let his sheets fly, so that the ship did not heel, but then he would lose way and be directly in the path of the frigate. The guns ashore attempted to join in, but soon realised that *Optimist* was just out of range.

The Prame did just what Will had predicted to himself, she came about, but as she did so the bow chasers opened up again, They had been loaded with shot, rather than ball this time, and the confusion aboard the Prame was clear to see. Her crew must have been cruelly cut down.

She lay wallowing in front of the oncoming

British frigate. Will ordered a slight adjustment, and *Optimist* swung away to pass close by the bows of the stricken Prame. From below the upper deck guns picked their target with ruthless efficiency. Then from astern as *Optimist* turned the two stern chasers, placed facing aft through Will's cabin windows, opened up. Will swung round to see the foremast of the corvette sway in an ever enlarging circle to then crash over the side, pulling the Corvette around with it. Two minutes later and the two stern chasers fired again, this time into a tempting target lying broadside on.

Will was very proud of the fact that the lookouts had not stopped what they were supposed to be doing, but had continued to pass down information. There were now twenty gunboats at anchor off the entrance to the port. It now was certain that the harbour of Boulogne was crowded with vessels of all sizes from Corvette down. What was also clear to see was that the harbour was in the process of being enlarged. One strange report was that up on the cliffs overlooking the Port, there was an army camp, but in the midst of it a strange building was being erected. It had rounded ends and a rotunda facing out to sea.

Sailing away from Boulogne, reports came in of some kind of construction going on at Wimereux. It looked through Will's scope as if they were trying to build a harbour there at the mouth of the narrow river. They sailed on with the wind increasing and the sea building with the white caps becoming ever more frequent. As they turned around Cap Gris Nez they became slightly more sheltered from the sea state, but the wind was still strengthening. This was a part of the coast Will knew only too well. They gained more sea room, but this was going to make Calais more difficult to research, given that the rain was back and the shore line kept disappearing. The foreward lookout warned of a number of ships off the Port. He could not make out their size as the rain obscured his view. There was nothing for it, but to give up and go home.

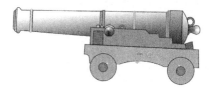

Two days later they were anchored in Portsmouth Harbour. This time they were nearer the dockyard as more ships were at sea. Will had spent the entire time after they left Calais working in his cabin, once it had been re-erected and his furniture brought up. He only appeared on deck as they were entering harbour and stood by to watch as Cranfield and the Master brought the ship to anchor. Once the anchor was pronounced as 'holding', Will went back to his cabin. Except for meals, he worked a four hour shift. He then walked the quarterdeck alone thinking, planning, and taking the air, before descending once again to his desk. He slept for short periods only. He would wake up, dash to the desk and jot down something that had come to him and then go back to bed. Cranfield excelled, getting on with the ship's business, having the damage put right by the carpenter and his team, and the sails patched by the sailmakers. The mizzen gaff was Tarrant's zone of responsibility, and he had that splinted and re-varnished.

Finally Will decided he had done as much as he could, and it was time to present his report. Rather than get his clerk to copy it in fair hand, Will decided to take it to the Admiralty for them to make copies. It was then Lord St. Vincent's responsibility as far as secrecy was concerned. He felt too tired to ride to London, so he ordered a carriage be hired and to be ready to take him to London.

The streets of London were once again a muddy mess. The rain had mingled with the earth and horse droppings to form a sticky glutinous mass, which stuck to any shoes or boots. Isabella was delighted to see Will again, and to show him her bump, which was now quite evident. He could even feel the baby kicking in the womb. With Isabella enfolded in his arms, he slept soundly for the first time in a week. The next morning he had his coach take him to the Admiralty. He had to wait for a few hours, because both Evan Nepean and the First Lord were in conference. He asked to see the First Lord's clerk, who came busily down to greet him and explain once again that the First Lord was in conference. Will waited until the man had finished and then explained about copying his report. The Clerk was extremely apologetic, there were so many who wanted to gain the First Lord's ear. He could certainly get it copied. Will then explained that it was very secret, and therefore perhaps he should consult the First Lord before giving it to anybody to copy, other than himself of course. Will would go home and await His Lordship's summons. The Admiralty porter found him a chair, and suggested that it had not been a good day for the Captain. Will was amused by his concern and cheerfully reported that he was only dropping something off.

The next morning, very early, there was an Admiralty messenger at the front door. Will had warned his coachman the night before to be ready to drive him to the Admiralty from the earliest. The Admiralty messenger was extremely surprised to be offered not only a coffee whilst Will put on his coat and said goodbye to his wife, but to be a passenger back to the Admiralty. Will was shown straight up to the First Lord's private quarters.

"Hello Calvert, read your report. Having it copied at this moment. Got to get a copy round to His Highness as soon as possible: and the others when they are ready. I think everyone is in town. So how was your cruise?"

"Interesting My Lord. I have a report with me. I did not include it with the plan." Will pulled out his closely written report from his pocket and put it on the table in front of his Lordship.

"Good man!" Lord Jervis rang a bell and a servant appeared. "Coffee for Sir William, and some toast, would not go amiss, me thinks. Sit yourself down man, we are just sailors together."

Will pulled out a chair at the table and sat down, whilst his Lordship opened the papers and began to read. The servant brought a tray with toast, a fresh jug of coffee and a cup and saucer. There were grunts and exclamations from behind the papers.

"Wouldn't be a bit surprised if that building above Boulogne wasn't Napoleon's headquarters. Pity it is out of range; it is out of range, isn't it?"

Will drinking coffee nodded.

"Thought so, Pity. So I gather that you estimate that he has about, what seven hundred craft ready?"

"I have estimated the number for Calais, because the weather was too inclement to see. However, I think that would be a roughly correct estimate. I suggest that he has many more being built elsewhere."

"Humph! Very probably right. Now I haven't got your report to hand, it is still being copied, but from what I remember, you say to land the troops; or whatever we are going to call them, to attack Boulogne and Ètaples at coves about five or so miles away. Once ashore they borrow transport. I like your 'borrow', one gets the feeling someone will get them back. Am I right? Thought so! And you think that you can hide these fellows of ours in the midst of the French Army/"

"Where better to hide them?"

His Lordship chuckled. "You never fail to

surprise me Calvert! Where better indeed! Well I suggest you go home and take your wife out shopping or something. Forget about all this. I shall call you when I have the other gentlemen's reaction.

Another very short meeting. Will had no illusions. If the plan was adopted in any way, he would have nothing to do with it. Some General or Admiral would take it aboard as their idea. They might make it work, or they might ruin it. It was out of his hands.

Will was grateful that Isabella had not yet left for Devon, as they were able to walk out together when the weather permitted, and to visit various theatres and other shows with their new found friends, the Castlereaghs. They were introduced to many of the most fashionable people who remained in Town. But at the back of Will's mind, was always the worry as to what was going to happen to his brain-child. A week went past, and he presumed he had better go back to his ship. No instructions had arrived, and the Admiralty knew he was in town.

He had a long talk with Isabella and they decided that as winter was settling in, it would be best if she travelled to Devon before the roads got too bad. She was now seven and a half months pregnant, and although she was in good health, it was felt that too strenuous a journey could affect the baby.

Whilst preparations were made for her journey, Will went to the Admiralty to inform them that he was returning to Portsmouth. He was just leaving the building, having sent a note to Sir Evan Nepean, when a servant came rushing out to ask him to return. Evan Nepean looked tired as Will was shown into his office.

"Ah, Sir William, glad we caught you. I am afraid politics is rearing its ugly head. The First Lord is having a very rough time at the present. I have some news for you; you might take it either way, but you are being relieved of your command of the frigate *Optimist*. No, don't ask me why; just take it from me that it in no way reflects upon your service to the country. I suggest that you go to your place in Devon and await events."

Will was shocked. He felt completely let down. He did not know if Nepean knew of his meeting with the Duke of York and the others. He could not refer to it, so he just had to bight his tongue and accept the hammer blow.

"I see. What will happen to my crew?"

"They will stay with the ship. Of course you may take with you your servants and your coxswain."

"Right, I can't say that I am pleased with this, but I suppose looking on the bright side I might be around for the birth of my child."

"Oh! Well then perhaps it has its benefits after all. As I said, this is no reflection on you. Take it from me, you are still held in the highest esteem."

Will broke the news to Isabella, who could not hide her delight. She was bitterly disappointed for Will, but it did mean he was out of danger, and he might even be around at the birth of the child. Will sent messages to *Optimist* to have his personal belongings sent down to Devon by carter and to instruct Allwood to bring Millward to Devon with him. To Tarrant and to de Cornes, he wrote individual letters of regret, hoping that they would serve together in the future.

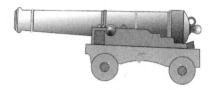

The roads to Devon were already getting very rutted and muddy as the convoy made its way westwards. They travelled relatively slowly, not only as a result of the roads, but also because Will did not want Isabella jolted about more than was absolutely necessary.

The baby arrived on the 19th of November, a fine little girl, with powerful lungs. She was christened in the Village Church, Mary Elizabeth. Christmas was celebrated in first-rate style, despite the heavy rain. All married servants, whose families lived elsewhere were sent home, and those who stayed were given a bounteous dinner. On Boxing Day the Kentons joined them, bringing with them their own servants to help out. New Year came, and went, but there was no news from the Admiralty.

Will thought he had been forgotten, and felt very betrayed. Obviously he had been too outspoken, at the meeting. He felt frustrated at his own stupidity, which was only partially relieved by the fact that he had Isabella and the new child to distract him. Isabella had fired the nurse the first day when the woman had insisted that they should get a wet nurse. Isabella had stated very firmly. "God gave me these breasts to feed my baby! I am certainly not going to allow another woman's milk to poison my child!" As a result their nights had been very disturbed, but Isabella's joy in her offspring was evident to all.

To take his mind of things, he concentrated on his estate. He was surprised to find that he was still being paid his full rate as a captain and appeared not to be on half pay, which would have been more usual.

After a few weeks Isabella was able to join him for short rides, but they always had to be back for feed time. The Gazette was always one or two days late, but was full of news of disagreements in parliament. Addington seemed to be having a rough time of it.

Will decided that if the Navy didn't require his services, he would look after his own future. He discussed his Ideas with Isabella and they were both in agreement. He should try to extend his area of useful contacts, and to do that he should for at least the Spring and some of the summer months be based in London. He managed to rent a suitable house Off Berkley Square. Both he and Isabella wanted their own base rather than being beholden to her parents when they were in London. As a result in March 1804 the Calvert convoy left Devon and travelled up to London to take temporary possession of the rented London house.

They had taken the house for a year, so as to give themselves the time to buy or build their own house. Lady Isabella had cards printed, which were then distributed to the wives of those they had already met in town. Lord Castlereagh was a great help and proposed him for membership of a number of London Clubs. Will decided it was best not to join a particular political party. He always asserted that he valued his independence in matters of thought and politics. This meant that after a few months he was made a member of both Whites and Brookes in St James Street. Will also decided to see if it would be possible to find a seat in Parliament as an Independent.

He was to find that it was almost impossible without a patron. He could perhaps buy himself a rotten borough, but that would have raised questions as to where he got his wealth. Politics he was learning was a very dirty business.

In late April a letter had arrived from Lord St. Vincent. Will had been extremely surprised because it was written in his own hand. In the letter he told Will to be patient, that his ideas had not been overlooked. It was taking time to get agreement, so they were waiting to see what happened. He said in the letter that if Addington was to resign, which seemed to be on the cards, he would be forced to resign, and that he would return to the sea. A little over a month later, Addington resigned as Prime Minister and on the 10th May 1804 William Pitt once again took the office. Will was well aware of what was going on. The clubs were buzzing with rumours. His contacts kept him well informed. Admiral the Lord St. Vincent did resign. However Lord Castlereagh became Secretary for War in Pitt's Cabinet, which meant that through their friendship, Will added a very firm supporter right at the top. Then one day the Prime Minister himself took Will aside and murmured that he had not been forgotten. It was more expedient to keep Will available than to send him off to sea from where it could take ages to recall him. At the Admiralty Lord Melville had taken over the reins, with Evan Nepean's replacement being his assistant William Marsden. All of these characters had passed through Will's orbit and were well known to him.

Slowly their ring of acquaintances began to spread out. Isabella was a gracious hostess, and became popular with many of the Ladies. 'Emily' Castlereagh took her under her wing and introduced her to another bank heiress Sarah Villiers who had just married the Earl of Jersey. Amelia was the same age as Isabella, but Sarah was younger. It was this pair that insisted the Calverts attend Almacks with them, and from there their circle of acquaintances expanded greatly. London fashionable society was based on privilege and money. The fact that Isabella was assumed to be an heiress and the title gave them the social standing necessary.

Will, on Isabella's advice refrained from pushing his case at the Admiralty. If they wanted him, let them come to him. He would seem more interesting she propounded. Not only had the prize money been paid for the Spanish frigate, but the bullion had been so valuable that with even a small percentage of the value as secret prize money, Will was now an extremely rich man.

They employed agents to look for likely houses or land that might come up for sale around the capital. Will seeing the gradual spread of the city, decided with all his money the best investment for his children's future would be land. When a farm came up for sale near the village of Highgate, Isabella pressed him to visit it. It proved to be moderate farming land, but some of the fields had wonderful views over the Capital. They decided that was where they should build their new London house. It was within easy reach of the centre, but outside the smoky atmosphere of the city. Their generous offer was agreed to immediately. Will gave the incumbent tenant farmer the right to continue to farm the land. He retained a modest plot of a couple of acres which had mature trees to one side protecting it from the prevailing winds, but an uninterrupted view to the south. He left the choice of Architect to Isabella, whilst he continued to look for more land both around London and in south Devon to purchase.

Will had never forgotten *Snipe* and thought back

to his father's merchant naval business. He considered long and hard over the relative benefits of a schooner over a normally rigged merchantman. After much thought, he wrote to the Master-Shipwright at Appledore to ask if it would be possible to build a similar vessel to *Snipe* but bigger. The reply was that in peacetime it might be possible, but with the continuing war against France there was not enough seasoned timber available. Will therefore wrote to the original builders in Nova Scotia asking the same question.

The Calverts time became taken up with attending the theatre (to be seen), soirées and balls.

Will became more and more aware of the effect his wife was having on the male members of their 'set'. The admiring glances, the mild flirtations. Yet Isabella seemed totally unaware of the effect she had on the opposite sex. Strangely the subject was raised by Isabella one night as they were preparing to go to bed.

"You are causing quite a stir with the Ladies. I shall have to watch you!" She said over her shoulder.

"Me? Why?"

"I heard one lady saying how dashing and dangerous you looked. It positively gave her the vapours just to look at you."

"Never!"

"True I heard it myself. She either didn't realise I was your wife, or didn't notice me. She said the broken nose and the black hair were irresistible!"

"Well you can't talk! I see the way men look at

you!"

"Ba! With so many beauties around, who is going notice little old me?"

"Rather too many to my liking!"

"Are you jealous husband?"

"Well I trust you, but I wouldn't trust the men!"

"Then you have nothing to worry about! I married you for love. Most of those people married for money or position. There is very little love about like ours. Emily is the only one I know who also married for love."

Two months after his letter to *Snipe's* builders a letter arrived confirming that the builders could very easily build the type of ship that Will had asked about, but suggested that if it was going to be that much bigger it should boast three masts. The cost would be less than Will had earned from capturing the French privateer frigate. He replied asking if it would be possible to build the vessel with a poop deck and a forecastle, without affecting the performance. He instructed the shipwrights to draw up plans for such a ship, with express instruction that it should be capable of mounting two long barrelled 18 pounders in the forecastle and two at the stern as stern chasers, to be able to fire through the aft cabin. Under the poop deck there was to be an owner's cabin. The forecastle needed to have enough space for two 12 pounders firing straight ahead in the same manner as the 18 pounders below. Provision for six 18 pounder carronades each side were to be made. He arranged through Childs Bank in the City for the necessary funds to be released at various confirmed stages of building. Childs Bank's chairman was the father of Sarah Villiers, so that word soon spread that Will himself was wealthy in his own right.

Isabella had found her young architect and was now to be found surrounded by plans and elevations. Like Will, she wanted the house to be family friendly and not too grand. In the end they decided to base their ideas on Kenton House as far as a basic plan was concerned.

The house would have a gracious hall lit from above by a glazed dome. There would be both large and intimate dining and sitting rooms, with a study for Will. Once the ground floor had been agreed the upstairs followed suit.

By Mid June, when most of Society was quitting London, the plans had been agreed and builders found and instructions given. The Calvert convoy retired back to the rural pleasures of South Devon.

Christmas passed with the usual frivolities on the estate in South Devon. With the New Year came the preparations for the Calverts to once again travel to London. How wrong could they be! A signal arrived informing him he was to travel to Portsmouth to take command of the frigate *Optimist*. Further orders would be sent to him when he had retaken command.

It was another Calvert convoy, this time without Isabella or the baby, to Portsmouth. Isabella would travel later when the roads were better to London and stay at the rented London House to arrange the finishing of their house in Highgate.

On arriving in Portsmouth he was relieved to find that his ship was expecting him. Directly his coach rolled onto the quay, a gig set off from behind another frigate and headed towards the steps. It was clear to see that this was *Optimist's* gig, because of the smart hats and the brightly coloured oars. Climbing through the entry port he was greeted by Lieutenant Cranfield, now First Lieutenant. There were cheers from the crew and smiles all round. His furniture was brought over and his quarters started to look like they had before.

Will asked Cranfield what had happened to the previous Captain.

"I have no idea Sir. We were back from patrolling with the Channel Squadron. He received a signal and left. That was it. No explanation, nothing."

"How peculiar!" Will shrugged at the strange ways of the Admiralty; and went to read himself in again.

Two days later a signal arrived from the Admiralty. *Optimist* was to rejoin the Channel squadron. After making sure the ship was properly victualled and armed, Will took his old charge back to sea and the Channel. For six months *Optimist* ploughed the seas off Brest under the ultimate command of Admiral Cornwallis. For three months she was with the inshore squadron, then the next three with the offshore squadron. She returned to Portsmouth to re-victual once in April.

Will was sure that his ideas had been forgotten,

turned down, or given to somebody else to organise. At least he still had the Surgeon de Cornes to talk with and his well trained crew. Because of the boredom of blockade work, the crew were not quite as happy as they had been when they had been on 'special' duty. The punishment book revealed the gradual grinding down of the crew. It was tiring for Will as he was constantly being called up on deck for one reason or another. The paperwork seemed to grow each day. He had little time to develop his ideas, which he still considered feasible, if only they got the support they needed from on high.

In the middle of June 1805 *Optimist* was back in Portsmouth for a dockyard inspection and to re-victual. The news that the French had escaped from Toulon, with some Spanish ships and had sailed for the West Indies was everywhere. The fact that the nation's favourite Lord Nelson was after them, was treated by the British as a sure sign that a great victory was in the offing.

Will took the opportunity of the ship being in dry dock to go to London to see Isabella and the baby. He received an ecstatic welcome and found both his wife and child in rude good health. He also learnt that he was to be a father again. He remained in London for just four days, before having to ride back to Portsmouth. He went with Isabella to look over the Highgate House which was nearing completion. Isabella and the Architect had done wonders. He did not bother to call at the Admiralty, as there seemed no point. He refused to call on Castlereagh as he didn't want to embarrass his friend. He knew that he could rely on Isabella to drop a word in the right place at the right time.

Back aboard *Optimist* expecting to sail back to the Channel Squadron, he found an urgent signal to detach to join Vice Admiral Calder's blockading squadron off Northern Spain, as news had been received that both the Ferrol and Rochefort French ships had orders to break out. It looked as if they might be aiming to join up with Admiral Villeneuve's combined fleet on its way back to the Channel.

The summer day helped lift the spirits of the crew as their frigate drove west under full sail.

Two days out, they sighted a British brig off the west coast of Ushant, which was hailed and informed them that it was carrying dispatches from Admiral Calder. This established the area that Calder had been sent to cover, which was just to the north of Cape Finisterre. Calder had been blockading both Rochefort and Ferrol. These two ports one French, and the other in northern Spain, meant that the Admiral's resources were stretched. He had fifteen ships of the line and two frigates. An extra frigate would be a Godsend. The information gave Will a rough course for the fleet. Two days later *Optimist* sighted sails on the horizon. As they gradually caught up they discovered that it was a convoy and not Calder's squadron. As *Optimist* drew level with the 'tail end Charlie', a brig; the brig altered course so that she could sail alongside *Optimist* and exchange news by speaking trumpet. It turned out that the convoy was bound for Gibraltar to replenish Admiralty stocks there. There were three brigs, two sloops and four Cutters[14] escorting the convoy that numbered twenty-three merchantmen.

Because the winds in the Bay of Biscay had been contrary, *Optimist* was a good fifty miles short of the area in which she expected to make contact with Calder's fleet. Will decided to sail with the convoy until they were off Finisterre, at which time they would start a box search for Calder. *Optimist* sailed through the convoy to reach the leading brig which flew a pennant to indicate its captain was in charge. Will being the senior officer and now having been a Captain for more than three years, and sporting two epaulettes, told the Lieutenant on the brig that *Optimist* would take station on the landward side of the convoy at the front. Later in the day as they neared the search zone to the north west of Cape Finisterre, the winds dropped. Extra lookouts were posted, but as evening drew in there was no sign of any masts on the horizon poking out above the rolling fog that started to form. At night it was going to be very difficult to maintain their position relative to the rest of the convoy. They took in sail, but maintained a round the clock lookout. As it was, at first light there was a thick fog all round them. There they sat, lookouts posted on all masts and at every quarter. It was possible to see the position of the nearest ships from the main topgallant mast as

---

[14] 68ft British designed schooners derived from Folkestone smuggler's vessels armed with 10 x18lb carronades.

their masts protruded above the low rolling cloud. The sun could be glimpsed on rare occasions, but the fog did not begin to clear until about 5 bells (1130) of the forenoon watch.

As the fog began to roll back slowly a gentle breeze stirred the sails. Gradually the convoy was on the move again. The progress was very slow. The wind came and went. Just as three bells of the first dog watch had been sounded there came the faint sound of cannon fire. It was difficult to sense the exact direction of the sound. With virtually every sail set, *Optimist* still hardly made any headway. More distant rumbles of firing could be heard, but it was intermittent. As the light began to fade so did the noise. Again the wind faded, and fog banks returned.

The following morning, *Optimist* cleared for action; found that the fog was still with them.

Slowly, very slowly the convoy continued to drift south. The fog stayed with them, sometimes wispy, sometimes dense. When it was dense it was difficult to place the nearest ships in the convoy, but then it would suddenly part and there would be a ship. This continued all day. There was no cannon fire to be heard. Darkness descended on the convoy, and lights were shown, to warn the other members of their position.

At first light, there were the first signs of a change in the weather. A gentle breeze began to roll back the fog and the sun shone through. Halfway through the Morning Watch, a look out called out that there were masts on the horizon. The wind grew stronger and then began to change direction. Two hours later the lookouts up the masts reported that there appeared to be two different fleets. They were about fifteen miles apart. An hour and a half later, they were identified as a British Fleet, and a Franco-Spanish Fleet, now beginning to work their way to the windward station. This meant the French and Spanish were in the best position to attack. As the fog cleared completely it was now possible to see the two opposing fleets. *Optimist* detached herself from the convoy and piled on all sail to join the impending battle.

Just when everybody on *Optimist* was certain that the Franco-Spanish fleet were about to attack the British line, the Franco-Spanish fleet seemed to start changing direction; instead of heading for the British, they were heading away to the south. It soon became obvious that the Franco-Spanish fleet were making for the ports of Spain. *Optimist* seemed to be in the best position to shadow them. The French frigates that accompanied their fleet did not seem interested in opposing the shadowing frigate.

For the whole day *Optimist* followed the enemy fleet, until it grew too dark to see what was happening. Will ordered a shortening of sail, but fearing they could change direction in the night, he still pressed on. They were rewarded at about midnight, by the moon, which came out and revealed the enemy fleet still on the same course, which now was obviously to Corunna. As dawn broke, the lookouts reported that the first ships, including the French flagship had entered port.

Who should Will inform? Admiral Calder's fleet was the nearest, so he turned *Optimist* out towards the north in search of Calder's ships.

A fruitless search of days, found no sign of Calder's fleet. It was a typical Biscay gale that meant the French coast was not a good place to be near. *Optimist* searching the north coast of Spain and had turned to search the area off Rochefort when the wind began to get up and the waves build. Both Will and Baldwin, the Master, agreed that it looked as if it was going to be a severe storm. Under reduced canvas, her upper yards taken down, *Optimist* clawed her way to the west. As the storm grew in intensity, the cloud coverage became total. Under leaden skies, with heavy showers of rain, the frigate set her bows to the oncoming waves. Both anchors had been given extra security lashings. The cutters were lashed twice over on their supports above the open area of the upperdeck. Life lines were fitted fore and aft. The helmsmen had to be lashed to the mizzen mast to make sure they were not washed overboard. The watch keeping officers had ropes tied round their waists which were then tied to a cross deck life-line just forward of the wheel. This meant they could move from side to side, but they still had to face the oncoming spray as the bows dipped into the white crested waves and scooped them up and threw them back across the quarterdeck. Down below the water seemed to penetrate everywhere. Clothing was damp; hammock mattresses and blankets seemed to absorb the damp air. Water spilling down onto the upper deck, would come rushing aft, no respecter of rank to wash across the deck of Will's cabins.

For four nerve shattering days *Optimist* fought a personal battle with the Bay. On the fifth, finally the sun was observed for a short time. Will and the officer of the watch grabbed the opportunity to take a sight, before the orb disappeared again. This meant some pretty fancy calculations to give them a very rough position. This turned out to be far further to the north than expected. With the wind veering to the south, it was going to take far too long to beat down to Ferrol. It would be quicker to make for Ushant to locate the Brest blockading squadron and learn of any news.

Two days later in the evening, just as it was getting dark, they spied a frigate, with a damaged top main gallant mast running north. The change in the weather had also meant that the night sky was clearly lit by a three quarter moon. *Optimist* caught up with the frigate at five bells of the morning watch (6.30am). As the sea was much calmer, it was possible to sail within hailing distance.

From the frigate they learnt that it was thought that some of the French ships had broken out of Rochefort to join the Franco-Spanish fleet. Later when they caught up with Cornwallis' Channel Fleet, Will was able to inform the Admiral that Villeneuve had retired to the Spanish ports. Cornwallis ordered *Optimist* to stay with his fleet until there was further news.

On the 15th August 1805, a splendid sight

emerged from the west. A British fleet joined Cornwallis' off Ushant. *HMS Victory* was easily identifiable by Will as he had served on her at the Battle of Cape St. Vincent. This meant that Admiral Nelson was in their midst. *Victory's* Admiral's barge was seen to cross to Cornwallis' flagship. Later it returned to *Victory* and she appeared to be getting under way. The Midshipman on duty read a flag signal from the *Ville de Paris* Cornwallis' flagship addressed to *Optimist*. Apparently *Optimist* was to accompany the *Victory* back to Portsmouth. Two other ships joined them, the *Belle Isle* and the *Superb* both 74s.

Back at Spithead *Optimist* was able to be re-victualled. It was also a chance to dry out everything from below decks. Immediately the anchor was adjudged as holding a naval cutter came alongside. A young midshipman climbed up the side and asked for Captain Calvert. There were two items in his bag. The first was an urgent signal for him to travel to London immediately. The second was a letter addressed to Sir William Calvert Bt. It gave no clue on the outside as to the sender. When Will opened it he looked at the signature first and discovered it was signed 'Castlereagh'. It asked Will to travel to London for a meeting. What the meeting might be about Will had no idea.

The appointment at the Palace of Westminster was to be as soon as convenient after he arrived in London, so Will went to the Admiralty to report. Here he found that there was a message for him to report back in two days. The next day Will, dressed in civilian clothes, was deposited outside the House of Lords entrance to the Palace of Westminster. The Porter who intercepted him at the castellated entrance, led him to a distinctly different type of building that stood adjacent to the Lords. It was built of brick, and looked in need of repair. There was no architectural merit about this building. He was shown up to a private room, furnished more as a sitting room than an office. The Porter announced him.

"Ah, Will; good of you to come so soon...and in one piece. How went it?" Castlereagh said as he advanced to shake Will's hand.

Will then related to his friend a brief description of what had happened off Finisterre.

"So near, so far. What do you think the Allied[15] fleet will do?"

"From what I saw of them I think a lot of them need the services of a dockyard. I imagine they must have had a pretty rough time of it in the Atlantic."

"Meanwhile Nelson is back. So we have adequate ships to stop them if they try to penetrate the Channel."

"Just so! And not the time of year to attempt to do so, or for that matter to invade England if they did."

"Thank God for that. Now, I must apologise for the delay that you have suffered. Politics can be a dirty business. I sometimes wonder if we are

---

[15] Allied was the word used for the Franco-Spanish enemy.

fighting this war against the French or vested interests! The Prime Minister admired your report. Excellent and very clearly thought out, I must say. The Duke of York is adamant that your ideas should be put into practice. Only last week he summoned Lord Keith and read him the riot act. Nominally you will appear to be under his command, but he has been told not to interfere and to give you every support he can. He was of the opinion that his fleet could keep the French invasion at bay. It was only when we were able to give him first hand intelligence that the French have chains across their harbours, and that the blockading gunboats now have chain moorings, that he was forced to admit that cutting out was out of the question.

So, despite others trying to get their oar in, you have been given command of this project. Hiley Addington will be in touch about the royalist recruits. We have had an enthusiastic response from the Duke de Bourbon. He has promised at least seventy royalists for us to choose from. He promises they are all fit and well educated. Hiley Addington, who I understand you have met, will be in contact very shortly about where and when the selection process should take place. Colonel Smith has volunteered to supply instructors, what of, I am not sure, but he too will be in touch. It might surprise you to know that Prime Minister has arranged for you to have the ships you need for this 'little adventure' as he refers to it."

Lord Castlereagh, still talking rose from his desk and opened a side door. He stopped speaking to

Will and asked a question to somebody the other side of the door that Will was not able to hear. He shut the door and started speaking as he regained his desk.

"The present First Lord, Lord Barham, is being kept informed as to details, as are the whole Board of Admiralty. All have been sworn to secrecy. Lord Keith has a strange aversion to espionage. He has some old fashioned idea that it is not quite the thing! The Duke had to explain that this was not espionage, this was a special mission. So, Lord Keith is nominally your Admiral, but you report direct to Lord Melville or the Prime Minister. If you need anything nautical, ask Marsden, if you need anything military, ask Colonel Smith."

There was a knock on the communicating door.

"Come!" Shouted his Lordship.

The door opened and a head popped round it to nod and disappear.

"Good timing, the Prime Minister wants to see you, come with me." So saying his Lordship got up and walked to the door of his office and walked through leaving Will to trail behind him. They crossed to a high ceilinged room that Lord Castlereagh informed him was called the Painted Chamber. There were people milling about and at the far end stood the Prime Minister talking with Hiley Addington and Colonel Smith. The Prime Minister raised a hand in greeting. As they walked toward the small group, Lord Castlereagh nodded and smiled at various people, but had time to inform Will that the Commons chamber was in St.

Stephens Chapel next door.

"Commodore Calvert, welcome. Of course you know these two don't you?" The Prime Minister's greeting was warm.

Lord Castlereagh said something Will did not catch to Hiley Addington. The Colonel greeted Will with a vigorous shake of the hands. Will was puzzled over the 'Commodore' title he had been given. Obviously the Prime Minister had made a mistake.

"Castlereagh filled you in, what? Good! Just wanted you to know you are to brook no interference from anybody in achieving this project. If anybody tries to play games, let me know immediately. Marsden is arranging for you to keep your old ship....*Optimist* isn't it... thought so. He will also make available any other craft you need. Hiley here will be providing you with as up-to-date intelligence as possible. Charles here will help you with non naval armament and any instructors you need." He paused for a moment and then went on after looking down at his notes.

"Not quite sure where you get your poachers from; I suppose the goals. Anyway, good luck and keep us informed as to progress. Lord Keith wants to meet you, bye the bye. Tell him as little as possible, and that goes for everybody. This must be kept a strict secret if it is going to succeed. Any questions gentlemen?"

Hiley Addington turned to Will and asked. "How do I get in touch?"

"I shall be at the Berkeley Square House, I shall

write down the address for you."

"Where are you going to train these Royalists?" Asked the Colonel.

Will was not sure if this was a trick question or not, but he could see no guile in the man's countenance. He replied. "I shall train them in Devon on my estate down there. It is sufficiently remote to make sure no questions are asked, whilst the terrain provides very similar cliffs and sandbanks to practice landings. However, I propose that we cut the number down by a series of tests, the first being physical stamina, before we embark the selected. I shall anchor the ships above Dittisham, if you know the Dart. The Royalist will live aboard, but be trained partly ashore."

"Like to come and visit you when it is up and running." Commented the Colonel; with a broad smile.

Will nodded his acceptance as the Prime Minister was speaking again. "Good luck Commodore." He shook Will's hand.

"Prime Minister, I think there is some mistake, I am only a Captain." Said Will.

"I don't make mistakes like that Sir William. Lord Barham made you a Commodore as soon as I approved the operation."

"Thank you My Lord, I apologise for questioning you on the matter."

"Bah! You had every right."

Will left with Hiley Addington and the Colonel, who suggested they should repair to their club,

Brooks, to celebrate Will's promotion. Will pointed out that a Commodore was only a temporary rank, and that he would revert very quickly. Will being a member of that illustrious club was not surprised by the noisy enthusiasm he found inside. There were gentlemen standing about talking animatedly, some lounging at tables with wine goblets, others seen through an open door gambling, even at that time of day. There were friendly nods of recognition as Addington and Colonel Smith led the way through the main salon, a large room with a vaulted ceiling and a splendid chandelier with tables to one side. Then it was up stairs to a quiet room, where they were served drinks, and then the door shut. The Colonel got up and turned the key in the lock.

It was normally bad form to talk business, but they had a very short discussion about communication, before generally discussing life in general and London Society. There were a few eye openers for Will, which he memorised for Isabella.

The pair also revealed that the Prime Minister wanted Will's ideas to be put into action immediately and an attack made as soon as feasible.

Back at Berkeley Square, a flushed Will took out his uniforms that had been hanging in the wardrobe and decided to have two; one dress, the other undress converted. He called Allwood and asked him to have them taken to his London Naval tailors to be changed. Allwood looked almost as pleased as Will felt.

The early next day, a message arrived asking Will to report to the Admiralty. Luckily he still had a Captain's dress uniform hanging in the wardrobe. He kept one there for his visits to London as travelling played havoc on clothes. Dressed as a Captain, he took a chair to the Admiralty and after a short wait was shown up to Sir Evan Nepean's old office. He found that it was William Marsden, Sir Evan's number two, who now held the office.

"Sir William, good of you to come at such short notice. Good thing Lord Jervis isn't here, he would be berating you for being improperly dressed." Marsden smiled conspiratorially. "Now in your report you stated, if I am correct, that you thought you needed a couple of sloops and three schooner rigged cutters. Lord Jervis crossed that out and made a note. I quote 'No Commodore can be expected to operate from a sloop!' Lord Barham agreed so you are to keep *Optimist*. Now the sloops, I know that Lord Keith doesn't want to lose any of his. We are rather short of this class, quarterdeck or flat decked. I can offer you a Confounder class brig and two Astute class gunboats, if that would help. I know you have strong opinions as to schooners, so I thought I should wait and see what type you thought best. However I do have two brand new schooners, should be arriving at any time from Bermuda."

"They wouldn't be Ballahoos, would they?"

"Yes I believe they are." Marsden looked surprised.

"Then no thank you. I hear they are pigs to sail! What about Archer gunboats or Coursers?"

"I'll see what I can do. You need shallow draft don't you?" Marsden looked at his notes as Will said.

"Exactly!"

"Then of course there is the question of commanders for these vessels. I suspect that they need to be experienced in shallow water work?"

Will nodded.

"Anybody you particularly would like to have with you?"

"Is Commander Derwent available?"

"Ah, if I remember he was your First when you were in the Caribbean. I shall check."

"Is Lieutenant Craddock still around?"

"Again I shall have to check. Craddock would be a good choice, because he was with you in *Snipe* wasn't he? So he knows the coast well."

Will nodded again, not wanting to halt Marsden's flow.

"Any others?" Asked Marsden

"I am sure you are in a better position to choose. You know of many more suitable Commanders and Lieutenants, than I. All I ask is that they are battle proven, and used to inshore work."

"On another subject." Marsden dropped his voice. "Can you be available to meet a gentleman of French origin the day after tomorrow?"

"Certainly, but where?"

"That will be up to him."

"Might I suggest Kenton House, my father-in-law's house. I have taken a house near Berkeley Square, but I think Kenton House would be better. He could well be going to see a Banker, I imagine."

"What a capital idea. I shall put it to him. What

257

time?"

"Anytime after nine o'clock."

"One more thing Sir William; it is of great benefit that this operation is so secret. I have to advise you that Admirals like Lord Keith do not approve of such operations. They believe the Navy should fight battles like Cape St Vincent, ships-of-the-line against ships-of-the-line. Earl St Vincent tended to keep your exploits quiet as much to protect you as to maintain secrecy! He didn't want you to be side lined."

"I understand, thank you."

Marsden was then called away, but made his apologies, and stated that Will could call on him at any time. Will in the afternoon paid a visit to his London Bank. His share of the prize money from the Caribbean adventure was revealed. It had not gone through a Prize Agent, due to the strict secrecy of the operation. It had instead been paid directly into his London Bank. Will found it difficult to appreciate just how wealthy he had become.

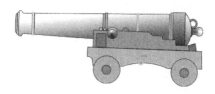

Back at Berkeley Square, Will was informed that there was a gentleman waiting to see him, by the name of Addington. Hiley was standing in the sitting room looking out over the garden.

"This is a pleasant surprise." Said Will; as he crossed to shake hands with Hiley Addington.

"Thought I should drop by. Understand that a Monsieur Lefarge wants to see you. He is the Duke of Bourbon's man. Where do you suggest?"

"I have just been asked that question by Marsden."

"Oh! Where did you suggest?"

"Kenton House after nine o'clock – day after tomorrow. I suggest that you attend to help me."

"Doubt you need much help, Calvert; you seem to have everything sewn up tight."

"Well thank you for the vote of confidence!"

"You were talking about sorting the Frenchmen out. What were you proposing exactly?"

"I thought I would take about five at a time for a run round Hyde Park to test them for stamina. We don't want more than that number or questions would start to be asked. The ones who passed would be invited back for the next test."

"And what might that be?"

"I need to know that they are genuine, we can't risk having a double agent in our midst. I had hoped you would undertake that part of the selection process for me."

"Delighted! But I want you to meet somebody who knows rather more than I on that particular subject. You met him a few months back, William Wickham!"

"The quiet gentleman who never said a word; yes I remember him, but not well."

"You will find him at the House, House of

Commons, he is a Member. Give him a list of names, he will do the rest. So; the ones who have passed the tests; what then?"

"Once that has been achieved, I would have them taken down to Portsmouth to be put aboard *Optimist*. We would then take then to the Dart to start their training."

"If you don't mind my asking; what sort of training would that be?"

"To start with they would need to train to a high level of physical fitness, way beyond just being about to run about five miles in a given time. They need to learn to navigate on land by compass, using a map, both by day and by night. They need to be able to land without making a noise on a beach and then be able to carry heavy loads up cliffs. Beyond that there is the use of close quarter fighting, explosives; and so it goes on."

Addington looked impressed. "You are forming a completely new type of corps, aren't you?"

"Yes, I hope if they are successful, we could use them for more operations."

"And where exactly is your estate in Devon?"

"Up the Dart from Dartmouth, on the way to Totnes. Do you know that area of the country?"

"Can't say I do, no. Like to come and have a look at you in action, so to speak."

"You shall be our guest."

Late in the day a coach rolled up at the front of the Berkeley Square House. To Will's surprise his father-in-law got out and entered the house. Will, who was about to go out, met him in the hall

"Will? What are you doing here? I thought you were still at sea. "

"I was summoned to London. What can I do for you?

"Isabella sent word that she had ordered some things to be delivered here, but she did not know if you would be returning to Devon soon, so asked me to pick them up."

"Ah, I'll have to ask the housekeeper. Can you rest awhile – have drink?"

"That would suit me. I am here for a few days: hope we can see something of each other. Isabella and the baby are doing very well. She misses you very greatly. Let us hope we can manage to topple the Corsican very soon."

"I have a favour to ask of you."

"Oh! What's that?"

"I have to interview a foreign gentleman in secret. I have asked him to go to Kenton House. It might then be assumed he had gone there to see you. I hope that is alright by you?"

"Certainly – but intriguing!"

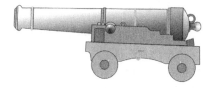

Monsieur Lefarge was a short swarthy fellow, dressed very much in the French pre-revolutionary mode. He spoke English with a heavy accent, but was obviously intelligent. Will led him into the small library which doubled as Mr. Kenton's office when he was in town.

After the usual social politeness, and Hiley had joined them, they settled down to discuss the real reason for the gentleman's presence.

It was arranged that starting in a week's time, six of the Royalists would report at the south eastern corner of Hyde Park at eight o'clock each morning. Will hoped that not many of the upper classes would be about at that time, especially in the late summer. They were to wear suitable clothing and to come in boots. Will had found that shoes came off too easily when running. He had already started his own training so that he could accompany the group each morning. He had found at first, he was very out of breath when he completed the run, although he considered himself fit. He hoped that in a week's time he would be able to match anybody.

It was quite a shock when Mr. Kenton, happened to meet Hiley in the Hall of Kenton House, just as

Hiley was leaving. That evening when Kenton called at Berkeley Square, he asked why a Privy Councillor was visiting Will. Will was at a loss for a moment to think who it could be and then remembered the early visit.

"I did not know he was a Privy Councillor!" Remarked Will.

"For God's sake you must have known that he is the Paymaster-General!"

Will just sat back and roared with laughter. Hiley had become a friend, but never mentioned anything about his position in society or government. Later Will realised that he was moving in very influential circles now. He made a point of not talking politics, as he had realised with Lord Jervis leaving office, that to take sides could well jeopardise his career in the Navy.

The morning runs had set Will up, and from the first of the test runs, he was able to keep up with the leaders. Those that were far too slow had their names noted. Halfway through the series of tests Will got a note from Hiley.

Please could you write to Isabella telling her you have met a Frenchman whilst running and this fellow asked you if you would help pace some of his fellow countrymen. Say that you were given no reason; also tell her you are frustrated waiting for a posting. We shall make sure the letter passes through the wrong hands.

It brought home to Will very forcibly, that there must be spies everywhere. He wrote the letter to Isabella, adding that the running incident had been very bizarre, but had stretched him. He also added that he had been to the Palace of Westminster to see how to become an MP as that might give him more influence. He added that he was sure that he would lose his command because it was the only frigate not assigned, so somebody would soon put pressure on some member of the Admiralty.

By the end of the ten days, the list of Royalists was whittled down from sixty-four to thirty- eight. Will sent the list over to Hiley.

Soon afterwards, Colonel Charles Smith called on Will to find out what type of instructors Will needed in Devon. They discussed at great length what the requirements might be, and the Colonel left with a list of the required expertise. He admitted he had no certain knowledge of any poachers.

Will, worried about *Optimist* sent word to Cranfield, to say that he was delayed in London. He instructed him to keep exercising the guns each day and to allow the Commissioned and Warrant Officers short periods of leave.

At the Admiralty Marsden was at last able to confirm that Will's little flotilla would have two flat decked brigs, and three gunboats; one a Courser with a Schank[16] lifting keel and two Archer class. These would await orders as to where they should rendezvous. Will asked Marsden if the other craft

---

[16] A lifting dagger plate

could make their way on separate dates to Dartmouth. He also confirmed that extra ship's cutters would be available for landing purposes.

Allwood had proved invaluable. He ran errands for Will and acted as Will's door keeper. Banker Kenton had left for Devon the day after meeting Hiley Addington in the Hall of his own house; with him he carried more of Will's letters to Isabella. The previous letter had been sent by the mail.

Now a newcomer came within Will's orbit. His name was Gavin Bracken, and he arrived through the servant's entrance, to ask to be taken up to Will. Allwood had not been at all sure about this man, so accompanied him when he was shown up. It turned out that he had been sent by Hiley, and was very doubtful if Allwood should be there when he spoke to Will. Once assured that Will trusted Allwood with his life, and had good reason to say so, Bracken it turned out was a fixer. He was quite obviously very intelligent, though he looked like a broken down bare fist bruiser. He wore shabby clothes, and shuffled everywhere. The strange thing was that directly he was in the house, his posture changed entirely and he stood ramrod straight.

It was a cover; it meant that he could go about his business un-noticed. He spoke fluent French, with a flair for the various accents. From what he was able to tell Will, it was obvious that he spent a lot of time behind the French lines in Northern France. He was able to show on a map, where the various military camps were set up, and where there was a military presence.

Another caller at the house was the best dressed gentleman Will had ever seen. He seemed to mince about a lot in company, but once he was alone with Will, his whole persona changed. He knew everybody who was anybody in London. Will recognised him, but had never spoken to him. His name was Granville Horan, and Will found that he was very good company. Horan revealed that he had been sent by Mr. Wickham, who had not always been 'just' an MP. Will gathered from what little Horan told him, that Horan was one of Wickham's 'people'. He could furnish Will with the essential intelligence that he needed if the operation was to be successful. To be seen with Horan meant that Will was able to meet people like the Prime Minister at social functions, and have brief conversations, without it being apparent that they were doing business. He made sure that Will was seen in all the best clubs, and soirees in town. It meant that Will began to get to know the influential politicians and people of influence. The private joke that became their secret code was, 'How's your search for the poachers coming along?' Both the Prime Minister and Lord Castlereagh used this as a method of engaging Will in conversation, which others would not understand. In fact Will's search for a poacher was a serious concern; the ones in prison were not good enough for Will, he wanted those who evaded capture all the time. He wrote to Simpson, his steward to get him to put the word out to find the very best poacher in the district.

Will was missing Isabella, but he was so busy he

did not think it would be fair to drag her back to town just as Winter was beginning to show itself.

Finally everything was set, and Will, accompanied by Allwood and Millward, made the journey to Portsmouth. He wore a Captain's uniform, so as not draw attention to himself. Cranfield was overjoyed to see Will climbing back up the side of the frigate, and even encouraged the cheer that went up when Will crossed the threshold of the entry port.

Once he had settled in he discovered that due to his absence none of the Midshipmen had been able to take the Lieutenants exam. This was because they had to be proposed by their captain. One of Will's first acts was therefore to send a note to the Port Admiral, explaining that he had been called to London, and asking that three of his Midshipmen might take the next Wednesday exam. Really what he wanted were potential skippers for his gunboats, if necessary. The request was agreed to, so three days after Will had returned to *Optimist* Hinton, Harris and Tucker all were rowed across to the flagship and interviewed by a board made up of the Admiral, Will himself, and a senior captain from one of the ships in the dockyard. All their journals showed just what experience they had, although Will expressly forbade them taking their journals from the period they were in the Caribbean. This caused a sharp question from the Senior Captain, Will was able to counter this, by just stating that Lord St. Vincent had ordered that those Journals should be lodged with the Admiralty, so they were not available. Will did not reveal to the Captain or the Port Admiral that he out ranked the Senior Captain. Will knew well the trick questions asked by boards for Lieutenant and had repeatedly gone over the answers to these tricky questions. Hinton, although the most experienced was very bad at such examinations and had failed more than once before. This time, with Will on the Board, he gave a creditable performance and scraped through. Tucker was outstanding, answering all the questions with assurance. Harris completely lost his nerve at first, but recovered to scrape through.

To pass the exam did not mean they became Lieutenants immediately; they had to wait until they were sent to a ship as a Lieutenant. From Will's point of view it meant he had extra watch-keeping officers for the Brigs and gunboats.

So as to make sure a crowd of French Royalists were not observed moving on mass, the hopefuls were sent at various times to the ports where the rest of the little flotilla were berthed. When *Optimist* sailed she had ten extra crew onboard; all Royalists. They had been brought out by various means. Three had come with a victualling barge; two had come via the dockyard as seamen, whilst the rest appeared to any onlooker to have been rounded up by a Press gang led by Mr. Tarrant. For all the Royalists it was the first time they had been aboard a Royal Navy ship, and they reacted in various ways, closely observed by Tarrant and the commissioned officers, who were now partly in the know. What nobody knew was that their Captain was in reality a Commodore. It had come as a complete shock therefore when the night before they sailed a waterman arrived alongside and when challenged replied by calling out '*Optimist*' this got a cheeky reply from the sidesman. The passenger though on closer inspection was indeed a Captain. The waterman rowed his skiff alongside and the Captain climbed up the steps and came aboard. Warned that a strange Captain was coming aboard, Lieutenant Cranfield met the Captain at the entry port.

The young, single epaulette, Captain, announced that he had come aboard to take command. Cranfield told him that there must be some mistake; *Optimist's* Captain was still aboard.

"Well, those are my orders, and you are?" The young Captain asked.

"Cranfield, First Lieutenant."

"Captain Miller, pleased to make your acquaintance, Cranfield. Perhaps you could introduce me to the Commodore."

"Commodore?" Queried Cranfield.

"Yes Commodore Calvert."

Cranfield shook his head as if to try to get his brain into gear. He was sufficiently on the ball, to just ask the newcomer if he would like to follow, and led him to Calvert's quarters. The Marine came smartly to the 'Port' and Cranfield gave the newcomers name.

"Number one and Captain Miller!" Announced the Marine.

Cranfield opened the door for Captain Miller,

and let him pass through first. Will in shirt-sleeves rose from the table in the stern cabin to greet the newcomer.

"Captain Miller, Sir William, come aboard to take command."

Will blinked, looked enquiringly at Cranfield, who standing slightly back shook his head to indicate he had no idea either.

Will took the papers from Miller's outstretched hand and indicated he should sit. He briefly read the orders. "Well, Captain Miller these seem to be in order. ...Millward some refreshment for Captain Miller and Number One. Cranfield take a pew. One moment gentlemen."

Will went into his sleeping cabin and put on the Commodore's coat, to re-emerge to a startled Cranfield. The First Lieutenant, looked extremely surprised, but did not say a word. Millward entered with the refreshment, but he had already discovered the uniform and had been sworn to secrecy.

"So is this your first command?" Asked Will.

"No Sir, I had command of a sloop for the last year. This is my first command as a Post Captain." Will thought this young man must have influence.

"Seen much action?" Will asked.

"Not really Sir. Before I got the sloop, I was on a second rate in the Channel Fleet. We did a lot of sitting about at anchor, or if it was fine, cruising off Ushant. The French did not seem keen to come out, so it got a bit monotonous. I remember admiring *Optimist* from afar. She always seemed so smart and well handled."

"Well let us get on with it, shall we?" So saying Will stood up. Millward appeared with his hat and sword.

"Number One; if you would do the honours and call the crew?"

Cranfield darted out, and soon the ship vibrated to feet mounting the ladderways. Miller took his commission out of his pocket and looked nervously at Will.

"I'll be right behind you." Said Will; gesturing for Miller to lead the way.

Out on deck the crew were gathered forward of the wheel, eager to hear what was about to happen. They all looked extremely surprised when a young Captain appeared and took out what was obvious to everyone, a commission. Whispers started and Tarrant had to shout for silence. Then Will appeared, and a roar of approval was so great, that all on the nearby ships turned to try to see what was happening. Tarrant looked overcome, but recovered sufficiently to bellow for silence. A shaken Miller read his commission to a silent audience. Then he turned to Will.

Will stepped forward and said. "It is alright boys; it is only a temporary elevation. I shall probably be back down again as fast as I have come up, but that's the Navy for you!" There were cheers and cat calls. Miller looked completely bewildered, but soon realised that the crew were laughing and making ribald comments, which the Commodore seemed to take in his stride, grinning hugely.

Early next morning, *Optimist* was towed out into

the Solent, with three extra Lieutenants in waiting aboard. Miller took the ship to sea; Will remaining in his quarters until they were well past Bembridge Ledge and turning south to head round St. Catherine's Point for Dartmouth. He came up for air in his old sailing coat without any insignia, which caused Miller to take a second glance, when he saw him appear out of the corner of his eye. Will smelt the air and walked over to the Master, Baldwin.

"Well we have the tide, but not the wind, Master!"

"Aye Sir." He dropped his voice. "I asked Captain Miller what he wanted, and he just said he would leave it up to me, Dartmouth was the destination; do my best."

Will nodded as if responding to an observation, because he did not want to upset the new Captain. At least the young man wasn't throwing his weight around trying to impress his Commodore or the crew. Will walked over to Miller.

"I love this time of year. All those golden leaves; has a certain glow about it; when it's not raining that is; don't you think?"

Miller still hadn't got a handle on his Commodore. He had dined with him the night before, but then so had the First Lieutenant and Surgeon.

"Aye Sir. Very pleasant, though I am sure you would prefer an Easterly to speed our progress to your home."

"That would have been a bonus, but we must be content with our luck. At least it isn't raining! Mr.

Tarrant, she still looks well set up."

"Thank you Sir!" Tarrant came up to join them.

Since Tarrant was with them, Will asked how the Royalists were settling down on the upper deck.

"Finding it a bit strange, Sir. They had trouble with their hammocks the first few nights. I think they have got the hang of them now. I suppose you will want them to exercise on deck, will you Sir." Tarrant had turned to Miller with the question, which Will thought showed an admirable understanding of sensibilities.

"What do they normally do?" Asked Miller.

"Well they run round the deck, generally led by the Commodore, but he seems a little shy this morning!" Tarrant gave a big wink. Miller was rather startled by the familiarity of the Boatswain to his Commodore.

"Got me there Tarrant! Must keep them fit. Up to you Miller when you think it would be the best time."

Miller thought for a moment, then said. "I think the Boatswain is probably the best judge of that Sir, it is his deck after all."

Tarrant had not expected that, nor had Will, but he appreciated the wisdom of the decision. Perhaps this young Captain would fit in after all.

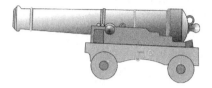

Will had the night before gone through the strengths and weaknesses within the crew for the benefit of the new Captain. The appointment must have been Lord Barham's idea. Will supposed it made sense to give him more time to concentrate on the forthcoming training and operations. Once he had got over the surprise at the arrival of Miller, he had also realised he would be able to spend more time with Isabella. At least the new Captain seemed good-natured, and appeared to appreciate any help if offered; not that it had been necessary so far. *Optimist* was a well oiled machine. Although the wind was fresh, it was not cold, and the sea was showing few white horses.

Will had given over his dining cabin to the new Captain. The first night, the young Captain had to sleep in a sailors hammock slung above the 18 pounder. The Carpenter and his mates soon had a cot made for him by the second night. Will had a canvas screen erected across his sleeping cabin, making a corridor to the great cabin. It meant that anybody coming to see him did not have to cross the new Captain's cabin. Whilst they were in harbour, the two 18 pounders that were normally positioned where the dining and sleeping cabin gun ports were positioned, were moved out onto the upperdeck to give more space. They were back in their correct positions now, as there was always the off chance of meeting a French Privateer.

It was late in the afternoon when *Optimist* glided in past the castles on either side of the entrance to the Dart. The wind had dropped slightly because of the land, but it was still from the West, though the hills made it fluky. In front of Captain Miller, Baldwin had asked Will if he could advise him on navigating the river. So now Will pointed out the marks, and where the winds were likely to catch them out. As they passed Baynard's Cove, they could see people gathering on the quays to watch as the frigate sailed majestically past to head up river. The harbour Master came rowing out and Will leaned over the side.

"Evening Constant, just going to see the wife. We shall be anchoring up past Dittisham."

"Very good Sir William!" Shouted the Harbour Master; with a broad grin on his face. The whole of Dartmouth would be laughing at the antics of the Baronet that evening. Miller stood beside Will as they coasted up river, Will pointing out Old Mill Creek, the Anchor Stone and other landmarks on the way. Finally the few cottages that formed the hamlet of Dittisham appeared on the left bank, and the anchor was lowered to hang just touching the water, the cable flaked out ready for letting go.

"Stand by to let go the anchor," Tarrant's voice could be heard on the quarterdeck. Miller looked at Will. Will did nothing. The Master sidled away from both of them, seeming intent on the starboard shore. Will moved his hand to Starboard without saying a word and the quartermaster turned the wheel until the hand stopped. Miller could not see this and was getting jittery. "Let go!" Came from the bows and they all heard the splash and the roar of the anchor warp running out.

"Back the sails" The Master ordered. *Optimist* ran on slowing down, then on a word from Tarrant up in the bows, a snuffer was tightened on the cable and the ship seemed to jerk to a halt, before beginning to swing round to the anchor. Miller was blinking hard. Up on the yards the sails were being furled without a word. No boatswain's mates were shouting or waving starters.

Will smiled at Miller. "Well this is the Dart, what do you think?"

"Err... very beautiful Sir. Might I ask; is that the way it is always done on this ship?"

"Yes, Justin, the crew all know their jobs and their stations. They have been doing it long enough. No need for useless shouting, it only distracts them."

It was the first time Will had used the Captain's christian name, and the friendly tone did much to reassure the young man. He had never seen anything like it before. As he turned to survey the position and the shoreline, he caught sight of the Surgeon smiling at the back of the quarterdeck. Miller had dined with him the night before with the Commodore. He walked over to him.

"Takes some getting used to doesn't it?" Said de Cornes with a smile.

"Yes. It is a bit tricky. I am not sure quite how much the Commodore still wants to be Captain!"

"Don't worry! He knows this river like the back of his hand. We used it as our base when we were on *Snipe*. *Snipe* was our pride and joy. Fastest ship you could ever imagine. Schooner, built in America. Mr. Tarrant was the Boatswain then, and he knows the river bottom better than most. "

"It's just that there are so few commands! How did the quartermaster know when to turn? Why was the Boatswain in charge of anchoring, not the Master or even myself...not that I know this river."

De Cornes laughed. "The Captain's...sorry the Commodore's little game. He used to do that a lot. The quartermasters look at Calvert's hand, which is generally by his side. He will turn his hand a little for a small change of direction, or more for a larger. Then it is back to fore and aft for centre the wheel. If you watch carefully, you will see that. All the captains of the various parts, will be watching carefully too. A nod; or a shake of the head. It is like a conductor with an orchestra playing a well rehearsed melody. Don't be down hearted, remember he let you take the ship out of Portsmouth and to be in charge all the way to the Dart. He wasn't interfering, the Master has never navigated the Dart; he asked the Cap...Commodore. We always anchor at this spot. We know there is enough depth, at all states of the tide."

"Thank you." Said Miller, and it sounded as if he meant it. He realised now why Sir William was a Commodore at such a young age. It had nothing to do with influence; he really did know his seamanship.

It was getting dark, but Tarrant had all the ship's boats hoisted out and put in the water, to 'take up'

The Captain's gig was manned and Commodore Calvert was rowed up river to the small quay at the bottom of the lands belonging to Calvert House. Will walked up the greensward slope to his house. He was not observed, until he entered through the Kitchen entrance, when there little screams of recognition from the maids. He silenced them and then went through to the main part of the house. He stopped to listen, and then he heard the sound of voices coming from the sitting room. He crossed the hall and stood outside the partially open door. Behind him he heard a sharp intake of breath and whirled round, finger to mouth to find his butler Clarkson.

He used a finger to indicate to Clarkson to come to him with his tray. Then he whispered that he would take the tray. It contained a jug of coffee, two cups and saucers, with the sugar bowl and milk jug with a side plate of small sweet biscuits. Nodding his thanks, Will turned and walked straight into the room without looking at the two occupants. Out of the corner of his eye, he could see that Isabella was leaning forward rocking a wicker basket on a stand. His mother-in-law was sitting with her back to the door. Because Isabella was so concentrating on the child, she did not look up at the sound of what was obviously the butler entering. She looked up to smile her thanks, and then screamed with joy. She leapt up, nearly falling over the wicker basket as she rushed to embrace Will. A startled Mrs Kenton was half standing as Isabella wrapped her arms around her husband and kissed him fondly on the mouth.

"How did you get here? She asked as she stepped back, and then realising that her chin had been scratched slightly she looked bemused for a second or two. "Why the cuffs, surely they are an Admiral's?"

Will laughed in delight as he led his wife back to her seat, and managed to say. "Good Morning, Mother-in-Law!" He then bent over his daughter, who gurgled at him. She had dark hair like her mother, but had inherited Will's piercing blue eyes. She seemed contented and kicked her tiny feet a lot, dislodging her blanket.

"How long are you staying?" Was Isabella's question; as he bent over his daughter.

"About a month at the very least. I shall have to go to sea for short periods, but otherwise I shall sleep here. *Optimist* is anchored just above Dittisham."

"What's with the uniform?" Asked his mother-in-Law.

"Oh I am a Commodore for the moment, before I revert to a lowly Captain again."

"But why are you here on the Dart?" Asked Isabella, still holding Will's hand tightly.

"Oh! Well I am in charge of a new unit. Very hush, hush! So once again I am not at liberty to tell even you, my love."

"It's not dangerous is it?" Isabella's eyes were

279

filling with tears.

"No, as I said I am in charge, others risk their lives!"

"Thank God!"

Mrs Kenton stood up. "Well I shall leave you two, to it." She bent over the baby to blow her a kiss and then with a smile swept towards the door waving Isabella back to her seat.

The next morning Will called a meeting of his officers. The most junior Midshipman found himself acting as Officer of the Watch, proudly pacing the quarterdeck. Below in his day cabin Will revealed for the first time the whole reason for their being in the Dart. Miller sat entranced as the whole objective was outlined. The Jolly boat was manned and Tucker was sent off up the Dart to find an old man who constructed coracles. Tarrant had the Royalists, as they were termed for a collective word, given instruction in rowing a cutter. This was just the start, once they could row properly, they would be taught to row silently with the thole pins or the crutches well greased to prevent any squeaks. Later the Royalists would be taken out to sea and have to practise rowing silently in wavelets, then waves. What they were not told was that when they really did land on the French coast, it would be the sailors from the various ships that transported them ashore. This exercise was in case they had to steal boats to extract themselves.

Each officer had a special responsibility. Jackson the Marine, would be training his men in the art of securing a landing zone. An art perfected by the Marines from *Snipe*. Cranfield had enough to do just being the First Lieutenant; whilst Miller was in charge of making sure everything was carried out to Will's strict requirements. Formby, with Midshipmen Harris and Hinton would go with Will to set out the training ground ashore on the Calvert estate. Mr. Noble the Gunner was responsible for training the Royalists in swordsmanship and how to load and fire pistols in the dark. Tucker acted as the Commodore's Aide.

Once everybody knew and understood what was required of them, Will had Allwood take him in the Gig up river to the Calvert jetty. When they landed, Harris and Hinton went off to map the lie of the land, whilst Will went back to his wife and new family.

Two days later, the first of the Brig-Sloops arrived, commanded, to Will's delight by Commander Craddock. Will was up at Calvert House, so Craddock had himself rowed up and joined Will and Isabella for dinner. His ship, the *Tara*, carried ten of the Royalists who had been transported all the way to Plymouth by coach, only to be shipped back to the Dart. The following evening the *Augusta*, another new Brig-Sloop arrived commanded by Commander Derwent with another twelve Royalists from Chatham. Within the week the three gunboats had arrived each on a different tide. At last the whole training programme could start in earnest.

Of the thirty six Royalists who had passed the physical, de Cornes had told Will that he doubted two had the real desire to strike a blow for their cause. Very quietly they had been taken by cart to a cottage near Kenton House, and then put on a stage to London, under the guard of the Sergeant of Marines. Now there were three teams of ten, and four 'idlers' as the crew termed them. This did not mean that they stood about doing nothing, on the contrary they partook in all the training classes, but they were not assigned to one particular team.

Simpson had managed to trace a brilliant poacher who had never been caught. He had to be forcibly kidnapped, for Will to be able to meet him. He had been drinking in a small hostelry when sailors from *Optimist* had burst in, tied him up and carried him away. He had been justifiably angry, for he thought he had been 'pressed'. When Will had explained they wanted his expertise only and that he would be well paid, did he relent. He started timidly with Will and de Cornes as his first students. As he gained confidence he got better at explaining himself.

Once he had found he could show by example, as well as by description, he was given a group of ten Royalists at a time to train. He taught them how to disappear, to hide and to transform themselves into everyday objects of the countryside. They were made aware of the wind and that their scent could spook animals and give their presence away to an enemy. He also taught them how to catch game; to skin them or pluck them and how to cook in the open without too much smoke. He showed them which plants and berries were good for eating.

Once each team could row, they practised landing silently from the cutters. Then they repeated the exercise in the dark, at the beaches beside the river, where officers from *Optimist* and the sloops waited to find out if they could hear or see anything from a distance of about a cable. The Master, Baldwin taught them how to use a compass, and then they were taught to read maps, starting in the day and then by night, using shuttered lanterns, so that they could navigate between places marked on the map.

Colonel Smith arrived with a couple of piratical looking characters who stayed and taught the teams how to kill silently. As the teams got better, the gunboats, all rigged as schooners, took the teams out into Lyme Bay, and then landed them on beaches; again starting by day and then with less and less light. Then it was to the cliffs and the defiles.

From *Optimist's* own crew the best young top-men at climbing, were chosen and taught separately to climb cliffs, first by day and then by night. They carried ropes with them, so that when they made it to the top they could throw down the rope to help others follow. Gradually the skills were brought together, so that the whole flotilla would sail out of Dartmouth in the evening, and then practise a run in to a dark shore. The Marines would be landed to secure the area and the sides of a defile or beach. Then, the ships' cutters would be rowed close inshore and the Royalists landed. They had to work as a team to make their way inland, and to remain unseen for the rest of the following day. The various officers from the ships took it in turns to be ashore to try and catch them.

At last Tucker's coracle maker delivered what he had fabricated to Will's design. These were constructed of light ash frames with tarred canvas skins, but were more like fowling punts than coracles. They were very light to carry, and had a freeboard of only inches. The Royalists who could swim were taught to paddle these strange craft, lying on their stomachs, so they appeared to be more like floating tree trunks than anything else.

Then came the final series of courses. These were about the use of explosives and how to employ them. It was also necessary to devise methods of transporting the explosives, without drawing attention. The gunpowder was put in flat sacks that could be carried beneath clothing. The length of fuse was carefully worked out and knocked into the brain of every Royalist. Stone jars, arrived by barge from Plymouth. There were two types. One had smooth sides, the other rough sides. The ones with rough sides contained Acid, the others Oil.

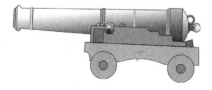

Lord Castlereagh arrived to inspect what was going on, first hand. He brought with him Mr. Wickham, who this time was prepared to speak. They stayed as the guests of the Calverts, and took a shine to Isabella. Both Castlereagh and Wickham were most impressed when they were taken across three of the Calvert fields and did not notice any one of the twenty Royalists hidden around him. Halfway across the last field, Will gave an order in French and five cows stood up and revealed themselves as humans. Castlereagh was so startled, he physically jumped. Wickham thought it a great joke. Then Will pointed out others, some behind hay as if blown against a hedge, others just lying low in a depression beside a hedge, but wearing mud coloured clothes with bits of twig caught up in them. They were shown the 'punts', but since they were not staying long, they did not really get a true impression of their worth.

Wickham took Will aside and revealed that Fulton had now produced his torpedoes which were made of copper and had clockwork fuses. He wondered if they might be of any use to Will's expedition. Will asked if he might be sent one to scrutinise. Wickham rubbed the side of his nose.

285

Bracken appeared without warning, just as Will felt the Royalists were about as ready as they could get. He came with detailed hand drawn maps of both the Boulogne Area and the area around Ètaples. They were copies of maps that the First Consul had ordered. They showed roads, conspicuous landmarks, as well as a crude form of lineal delineation. Obviously somebody had been to a lot of trouble. There were added small farms with notes as to their livestock and their wagons. What interested Will most were the rivers, which were drawn in far more detail than any map he had previously seen. Even the types of banks were indicated.

Will had decided which teams he would send into which area. The first attempt would be made during a quarter moon. Two teams would go in, one to head for Boulogne, the other for the River Bresle. The later augmented by the idlers team, for unloading.

Towards the last part of the training Will was unexpectedly called to London. He instructed that the training should continue during his absence. When he got to Kenton House in London there was a note awaiting his arrival. He was to send a note to the House of Commons to say he was in town. The next day another note was delivered asking him to take a hackney dressed in civilian clothes to an address in Southwark. On arriving he was shown up to a room above the hostelry, where Colonel Smith met him.

"Good man, Sir William. Let us go!"

"Where?" Asked Will.

"Walmer Castle. Cousin Sydney is arranging a demonstration of Fulton's new torpedoes in action. You know Sir Sydney Smith."

They rode in a plain black carriage, which went rather faster than expected, drawn by four very varied looking horses.

"Walmer Castle is the home of our distinguished Prime Minister. He hopes to be there, but it all depends on the demands put upon him, poor fellow. I expect you will meet cousin Sydney, if you do, please don't reveal who you are or anything to do with our little project. He is a dashing fellow, very full of himself, but is not the most discreet of characters. Very vain in fact. Tends to wear exotic Eastern clothes. He has a chip on his shoulder; his knighthood is foreign, even though he out-smarted Napoleon at Acre. How he came to be part of our family, I shall never understand. By the way, he knows nothing about what I do, when not on military duty, if you take my drift!"

"Heard of him, of course, but never had the pleasure!"

"He'll tell you all about his heroics at Acre, and how he was really the cause of Napoleon's loss of Egypt, rather than Nelson's exploits at the Nile. Mark you there is some truth in it, but it rankles that he is not as lorded as the Admiral. Oh and if he starts talking about being a prisoner in Paris – that is true."

"Tell me about this fellow, the American Fulton." Said Will.

"Strange fellow, very sure of himself. Boasts that he constructed an underwater weapon he called a submarine. Says he actually dived in it in the Brest Basin. How much of it is true, or self promotion, I have no idea. Now he has come up with these torpedo thingies. They are copper balls filled with explosive and have clockwork fuses inside. You tie two together apparently and then float them down stream so that they go either side of a ship's mooring line and then pushed by the tide drift alongside the target and sit there until they explode, hopefully sinking the ship."

"How big are they?"

"Have no idea. That is why we have brought you along so you can see for yourself. You will be introduced as an advisor to the Admiralty Board, but no names given. If pushed call yourself 'Blessed' that is your code name."

"Good God, do I really have a code name?"

"Absolutely. Means we can talk about you in public, without anybody knowing who we are talking about. Neat, eh?"

Will shook his head in bewilderment. He was a plain sailor, not a secret agent.

When they arrived at Walmer Castle, they were given refreshment, and joined by a number of other gentlemen, only a few of whom Will knew by name. He had expected to see Lord Keith there, but he was nowhere to be seen.

Walmer Castle had a round central keep with four round lower gun terraces at each corner, joined together. The terrace, with its imposing cannons that faced the sea, could only have been about a hundred yards from the sea, so provided an ideal vantage point to witness the trials.

What looked like a shallow draft brig was anchored opposite the castle. Apparently the castle was the residence of the Admiral of the Cinque Ports, which at the time happened to be William Pitt the Prime Minister.

Once the party was assembled, a thin middle aged fellow with a high forehead and receding hair, which was brushed forwards to conceal the fact, came out of the castle. He was wearing a Captain's uniform. He had a long nose and arched eyebrows, which seemed to Will, to give him a mildly supercilious expression.

"Gentlemen, I am Sir Sydney Smith. What you are about to witness, is a new advance in naval warfare. The cutter you see up tide of the brig will release Mr. Francis' new weapon, which will float down with the tide and sink the brig. This weapon will destroy the French fleets in their secure harbours. Let battle commence!"

Sir Sydney was handed a large flag on a pole which he then waved vigorously from side to side.

Out on the water the cutter responded and was seen to start to row and then to be allowed to drift with the tide towards the brig. Will did not have a telescope with him, so was unable to see in detail what happened next. All he saw was a splash, followed a little later by a second splash, and then nothing. The cutter pulled hard to get away from the brig. Then there was a long pause followed by an

289

explosion. The brig lifted and then settled serenely back in the water where she had been before. There was complete silence. Nobody appeared to be brave enough to speak.

Then there were a few coughs, and the visitors began to drift away. Colonel Smith took Will by the arm and led him around the side of the castle, before bursting into muffled laughter.

"Well that went well, didn't it!" He gasped; collapsing in paroxysms of stifled laughter.

"Well the mines were interesting, even if they did not succeed in their purpose. I should be interested to see the workings of the clockwork fuse." Stated Will; hardly daring to look at the Colonel.

"See what I can do. Stay there, back soon." And he was off, the way they had come.

A couple of minutes later he returned. "I found out where Ful...Mr. Francis makes the things. I have arranged for us to visit tomorrow. Told the fellow that there might still be interest, if he was to show his weapons to an advisor to the Admiralty. It worked; he could not contain himself, after his disappointment. Sir Sydney was spouting that they needed more practise."

The next day the Colonel took Will to visit the Inventor, where Fulton proudly showed them how his torpedoes were constructed. Will considered they were merely mines, but the technique involved in their manufacture interested him greatly. The light copper construction coupled with the clockwork fuse was just what he needed. The problem appeared to be the time it took Fulton to construct the casings. Will examined the clockwork fuse mechanism with great interest whilst the Colonel engaged Fulton in a conversation about submarines, which was Fulton's pet project.

When they left the Colonel asked if the visit had been of any interest. Will replied.

"How sensitive are we to borrowing other people's ideas?"

"How do you mean?"

"Well, we could do with those clockwork fuses to ignite our bombs. Even better we could use smaller versions of those mines of Fulton's because they would be less bulky to carry and weigh less than our wooden barrels."

"So?"

"Does the Admiralty employ Fulton to make such items for us; because I rather feel that he would try and muscle in on the project. He is American; can we trust him with our secrets?"

"I doubt it!" Replied the Colonel.

"Then the Admiralty will have to find others who can construct such mines and others to make the clockwork fuses. That is if the Admiralty will agree to the idea."

"Why involve the Admiralty at all. Leave it with me, I shall have a word in the right quarters for you... and it won't be with Lord Keith!" And he chuckled to himself. Will felt that there was no love lost there.

Will hired a chaise and returned as fast as he could to Devon. Then word was brought by sloop from Portsmouth. The copper mines were being constructed in the middle of nowhere, and three clock makers in various parts of the country outside London had been commissioned to make the clockwork fuses. Who was designing the mines and the fitting of the fuses was not mentioned in the secret dispatch.

To pass the time and to make sure everybody was up to scratch, Will decided to have a dummy run on the river estuary of Salcombe, just around the coast from Dartmouth. The Midshipmen from all the ships involved were sent overland to the estuary. They were given précis instructions as to where they should position themselves. *Optimist's* crew were given the task of making hazel wood frames whilst the sailmakers covered them with canvas, then tarred them ashore. These were then taken around by one of the gunboats under the command of its Lieutenant with 'Lieutenant' Tucker as his number one, with the responsibility of anchoring these Targets. The Targets would act as the Chaloupes and Caiques to be found in the French harbours.

There were two sets of Targets. One in the part of the estuary that led up to Kingsbridge and the other in the eastern part that finally ended at South Pool. Just as in the planned raid on France, the Royalists would be put ashore by narrow defiles to the east of the estuary mouth and they would have to make their way to the Targets. It would be tougher landing on rocks and then having to scale cliffs. The cliff climbers, one to each boat, would be the first ashore followed by the marines to secure the landing area.

The group attacking the Kingsbridge branch of the estuary had to carry their coracles or punts, because they would have to cross the river to get to their targets.

The Midshipmen had been posted ashore to positions where they might hear or see something of the raid. If they did they were to report what they saw when it was all over so the culprits could be identified and warned.

Late in the evening, the little flotilla set sail from Dartmouth and made it round Start Point to lay off the mouth of the Salcombe Estuary, as darkness fell. The gunboats set down the cutters in a moderate sea, with a light swell breaking against the rocks. Once on dry land, the climbers would hopefully be able to scale the low cliffs and drop down their ropes to aid the rest of their teams. The marines then signalled that they had secured the landing site. The royalists dropped down into the cutters and were rowed across to the rocky ledges. Standing on the quarterdeck of *Optimist* rather closer in than they would be off the French coast, Will and his officers strained to see or hear the landing parties. The sound of the sea made it impossible. Mr. Baldwin, the Master was particularly worried as they were so close in and if the wind changed they could end up on the self same rocks. As a result they turned and headed out to sea. Salcombe has a bar, which made it impossible for *Optimist* to even consider going up the estuary at night. The gunboats did not have the same problem, so Will hailed one and was taken up the river to try and see what happened.

The Kingsbridge group had just over a mile to cover overland to the estuary beyond. The South Pool group had about a mile and a half to a small sandy bay. The canvas targets on the South Pool side had been moored to the shore. The Kingsbridge targets were in the middle of the river.

Very cautiously the gunboat *Gloria* made her way up river under sail and oar. Will strained to see if he could recognise any movement ahead of them. When they recognised Snape Point to larboard, the oarsmen rested on their oars and they waited in the eerie silence.

And there they sat, nothing moved, a few fish broke the surface, but otherwise all was quiet. Will had no timepiece so he had no idea of the hour. It just seemed to drag on. Just as he was going to order the *Gloria* to put about there was a muffled explosion and then fire erupted in the middle of the river leading up to Kingsbridge. There was a small cheer from the crew of the gunboat. Still there was no sign of any action on the South Pool Reach. The targets there were easier to get to, surely? They would have to come back in daylight to find out what had gone wrong. The gunboat turned and was rowed down past the fishing village of Salcombe. Just as they were opposite North Sands, they all heard it, a series of dull explosions up river.

To make the rehearsal authentic, the groups had to wait holed up by day and then make their way back to the landing sites by night. The Flotilla cruised off the coast, much to the alarm of some fishermen in their little craft. The next night they closed the shore, *Optimist* standing off with the brig-sloops to cover the gunboats which closed the shore. Even from *Optimist* it was possible to see the shielded lanterns that signalled the groups' positions on the rocks. The sea had more of a swell, the hangover of a storm in the Atlantic, which would make recovery more difficult.

Finally a rocket signalled that the groups had been recovered and they put out to sea, to wait for first light.

Back at anchor above Dittisham, Will held a debriefing. The Midshipmen each made their reports first. Some said they had heard noises, but could not confirm what exactly they had been. Two from the South Pool side said they had seen activity, but they had realised when the cloud broke, that they were watching salmon poachers. Then it was the turn of the leaders of the groups. It transpired that there had been poachers after salmon in the South Pool reach, so the group had waited until the poachers had given up and gone home before placing their charges. The new copper mines, of which they had only two had proved easier to transport than the wooden barrels. The Kingsbridge group had found navigating in their coracles at night very difficult when there had been complete cloud coverage. That was why it had taken them so long to lay their charges. Once they had found the targets, the difficulty had been extracting the corks protecting the clockwork fuses, setting the clock going and then re-fixing the corks in the dark by feel. The one copper mine they had to practice with had made quite a bit of noise when rolled into the target. The wooden mines had been very difficult to lift into the targets from the coracles, without upending their boat. So difficult in fact, that the leader of the group had instructed that the barrels be tied to the sides of the targets. The Caiques would be a lot more difficult to mine because they had much higher sides. It was agreed by all that the exercise had been well worth the effort.

Will sent off a missive to Wickham, detailing what had happened. He decided that more practice was needed, especially with the new clockwork fuses, which were fiddly to set in the dark, and therefore could easily misfire too early and endanger the setter. The rub was that they had no clockwork fuses to practise on. Urgent appeals were posted to Wickham, who was now Will's contact. After four days a messenger arrived with one fuse. A mock up of the copper mine was made using hazel and canvas, so that the minelayers could practice at night setting the clock. It was Mr. Tarrant who taking the fuse from one of the Royalists turned it over in his hands and examined it closely. He gave it back and then went off to return with a short piece of fine whipping cord. He retrieved the fuse and tied a knot around the trigger and a mini Turks-head at the other end of the short piece of line. Stuffing this down the tube, replacing the cork, he then got the Royalist to hold the dummy mine. Tarrant shut his eyes, felt for the cork and pulled it out with his teeth. Then, still with eyes shut, he hooked his baby finger into the tube retrieving the Turks-head knot and was able to pull the line so setting the fuse. The problem he then found was he could not replace the cork with his eyes shut. More thinking and then he wound the line round the trigger quite a few times, stuffed it down the tube and replaced the cork. Again, eyes shut he took out the cork with his teeth, felt around with his baby finger and then pulled the line hard. The trigger snapped into place setting the clock going, but the line came away in his hand. Everybody thought that was it; but no, Tarrant then tried again but this time he left the end of the cord hanging out of the hole before replacing the cork. He then, with eyes shut, felt for the cork, pressing down firmly on it he then located the cord and pulled it. A click was heard from inside. On closer inspection the trigger had worked, but the cork remained in place. Tarrant, triumphantly stalked away, job done.

A message came from Wickham to say that Sir Sydney Smith had tried to sink some of the gunboats guarding Boulogne on the night of the 1st October, but it had been a failure.

Now it is up to you!

Ended the message.

Two days later a couple of wagons arrived loaded with copper mines and the all important clockwork fuses.

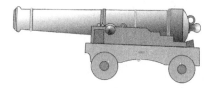

Optimist raised her anchor and led the small flotilla down the Dart and out to sea on a clear fresh morning. The winds strengthened as they cleared the protection of Start Point. Two landing points had been identified. Will had hoped to land both teams at the first place, but because of the size of the French Army camp on the East side of Ètaples, this would no longer be possible. He would have to divide his forces. *Tara* and one of the gunboats would land one team two miles from Hardelot Castle. There was a shallow defile in the sand dunes where a stream met the sea, and a large wooded area beyond, ideal for hiding such a small team.

Augusta with another gunboat would land the second team on a beach with sand dunes behind, further down the coast the other side of the river mouth of the River Bresle. This had a scrubby area backing the dunes, where the second team could easily disappear. Both teams would strike on the same night. Both teams would try to meet up at the Hardelot beach to be taken off, as there were more places to hide around there. *Optimist* and the remaining gunboat would cruise offshore, ready to intercept any French ships that came to investigate. Will had thought of leading one team himself, but had thought better of it once training was halfway through. The leaders of all three teams had emerged as resourceful and dedicated. What helped was that in the second team was a man from near Ėtaples, who knew the countryside, and especially the farm that they intended to 'take over' so as to borrow their wagon. The Hardelot team would carry their coracles and their explosives. Because there was no useful farm and it was only two and a half miles from the landing, the idlers had been added to this team. Each team would hit the river upstream of their targets, and then work their way down to the area where the landing craft were moored or drawn up on the banks.

Will had gone through each team's plans in detail with them before they had embarked on the Gunboats. The First team would be landed just after midnight. They would then make their way inland as far as they could the first night. They would then lie low, to start off again the next evening. They would only have one and a half miles to cover before they reached the river between the village of St. Leonard's and Boulogne. Here they knew there were small boats, used by the locals for fishing. They would try to steal the boats and use them to transport themselves and their hardware down to within a mile of the harbour. They would then use the coracles to unwind a thin line behind them to the first of the landing craft, which were known to be Caiques. They would cut a Caique adrift and use it to take them down river, the fishing craft following behind. Acid would be poured into as many of the boats they passed as possible. The crews of the coracles would try to fix explosive packets to the side of the larger vessels, which according to intelligence were berthed nearest the sea, using lanyards and river mud to hold the charges in place. All charges were to be placed on the seaward side of the vessels. One charge had a very short timed fuse, and the coracle was to lie by it until they heard the signal. The signal to operate the first fuse was the sound of a carronade firing out to sea. Once they had operated the short fuse they were to paddle as quickly as possible to the other side of the target vessel to protect themselves from the blast. They would then set or light the rest of the fuses. The oil would be used on any open boats, so fuses could be thrown in on their way back up river. The coracles fine line would be used to haul a stronger line down to the team, so they could use it to get back upstream where the four 'idlers' would stay to haul them.. On the upstream trip they would try to appear as if they were French soldiers or sailors trying to put the fires out. They would shout a lot in French to try to cause as much confusion as possible. Will had explained at length that a boat damaged by explosive would only take a short time to repair. A burnt or acid eaten boat would be useless from then on. The explosive charges were designed to try and sink the larger ships, so blocking the harbour.

The River Bresle team, had rather further to travel, but would be aided by the fact they would have transport. Marines would secure the landing zone, dressed in black uniforms, instead of their customary red coats, white breeches and piping. A group of Marines under Lieutenant Jackson would then press on with the Royalists to the earmarked farm, to hold the owners and workers as prisoners. Then a wagon would be used to transport the whole of the Royalist team's utensils to the river bank. The Farm was only one and a half miles inland. The Royalist team and the Marines together could carry the jars of oil between them to the farm. The third Royalist team would be used as 'porters, to carry the rest of the oil once it had been unloaded. Since the farm was so near, it was hoped that at least one wagon could be persuaded to get within easy reach of the sand dunes. Originally it had been planned that once the oil had been stored at the farm the support team would get back to their ship. Will had decided after carefully surveying the maps that it would be better if two teams carried out the attack, one working downstream of the other.

There were a series of lanes that rang in a zigzag pattern from the farm to the river bank half a mile upstream of Ėtaples, drawn in by the man from Ėtaples . The distance as the crow flies was only a mile or so, but by the lanes at least two and a half. Only part of the teams would travel with the wagon, the rest would act as scouts, until they hit the river bank. They would work their way north towards the sea and operate from the bank, or from their punts, pouring oil into each boat from the shore where possible. There was a punt/coracle for every two men. Any guards would have to be dealt with silently, though it was hoped that the guards would only be near the mouth of the river, where cutting out parties could be expected. They carried extra long fuses, which could be used between craft, if they were not right next to each other. Subsidiary fuses being tied to the long ones. A few of the upstream boats would be left to the last as they would be filled with oil and explosives and cut lose to float down the river, hopefully setting light to more vessels. Two marines guarding the farmer would make sure he returned to the farm with the wagon. Once the team had done its work, if anybody appeared they would pretend to try and help put out the flames, only to cause more havoc. What they did not have was up-to-date intelligence of the position of the larger craft. For this reason, one of the ship's cutters from *Augusta* had been painted black, and her mast and sail plan altered to match more closely the rig of the local French fishing boats. De Cornes would take a crew of four with him in on the first night to pretend to be a local boat. It was hoped that he would then be able to come out in the afternoon, to liaise with *Augusta* and *Tara*. The cue for the Bresle group to light their fuses was again dictated by the ships offshore, but this time it would be a series of Congreve's rockets fired high into the air. The idea was that the French should think that the British had a new form of rocket that could be fired at a great distance accurately.

After the second night's operations, both teams would retire to a holding point inland. This was the forest between Tingry and Lacre. They would wait two days before returning to Hardelot beach. To confuse the French military, the marines after they had made sure the teams were safely ashore, would retire making sure that their footprints would be clearly visible next morning and all point to the team having been taken off already. Two of the Gunboats would approach the Hardelot beach each night and wait for a signal. It was hoped that all twenty-four Royalists could be extracted at that point.

Lord Keith had been sent a signal to make sure no British ships were in the area between Boulogne and St Valery-sur-Somme on the nights in question. It would have been disastrous if there had been a battle between British ships and their own.

A week before the landings were due to take place Craddock took one of the Gunboats over to the French coast and laid lobster pot type buoys either side of each beach to help guide the gunboats and their cutters into the designated beaches. This had been an operational procedure when *Snipe* was landing agents on these coasts.

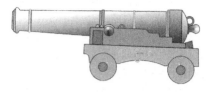

On the night of the landings, the sea was rather rougher than Will would have liked, but they had practised landing off the Devon coast in all types of sea state. With a quarter moon, and mostly cloudy, the gunboats sailed to within the two fathom mark. Here the cutters were manned and the Marines taken ashore, then when the signal was received that the beach was secure, the Royalists were rowed in. This time the 'climbers' would not be needed. The Brig-Sloops lay about a mile off the River Bresle landing to give cover if necessary to the gunboats. Both gunboats used for the landing had been schooner rigged, as it meant they could manoeuvre better in all winds. The great advantage of the gunboats when landing men was that they could be rowed. This meant that the final approach could be made without fear of being blown in on their sides. It was for this reason, that only very strong seaman had been sent to crew the three gunboats in Will's little flotilla. The gunboats towed the cutters behind them and then transferred the crew and Royalists.

However well the operations went, it was known to all that they must never breathe a word. Everybody had been sworn to secrecy. To achieve this all the crews had been told by Will that they belonged to the elite in the British Navy. They were the best of the best!

Optimist waited just over the horizon from Boulogne. The timing was essential. She, like the two Brig-Sloops, would approach the French coast to arrive at four bells of the Middle watch (2AM) on the second night. At that time they would start to fire their carronades or rockets. The carronades would have no shot loaded; just double charges, to make a bigger bang. *Optimist's* was the most dangerous position, as it was well known that the French had gunboats out at sea patrolling the coast. She would come straight in, turn and fire, keeping a barrage up of twice the number of shots as the charges the shore party had with them.

On the second night the gunboats lay near the ships to add fire power to repel any opposing force. The moon kept appearing and disappearing as the hour for starting the runs loomed. Will was praying for complete cloud coverage to disguise their approach. Baldwin, Miller and Will had all calculated the time that they needed to start the run, separately and then compared notes. They were within minutes of each other.

"Starting the run-in now" Said Captain Miller. The helm was put over, the guys and sheets taken in and sailing almost as close to the wind as was possible with the main coursers still set, *Optimist* surged in towards the French coast. Ahead of them the port entrance was clearly lit, by the camp fires on either bank. Extra lookouts had been posted all round the ship. The most experienced leadsmen were in the chains on either side, passing their findings by messenger to the quarterdeck. The courses were furled as they closed the shore. As the readings came down to six fathoms, *Optimist* turned to present a broadside to the Port of Boulogne, but beyond the known range of the anchored French gunboats guarding the port. No bells were sounded as this would give away their position in the dark. As the sandglass ran out for four bells, the first carronade was fired, followed a minute later by the next. Between the camp fires the first flash of an explosion was seen, just as a French gunboat opened up on *Optimist.* There was a crash as the ball hit the upperdeck between two gun ports. Immediately an 18 pounder, using the flash as a sighting point returned the fire with grape shot already loaded. A ball might sink the French gunboat, but grapeshot was certain to inflict a greater number of casualties, with a greater percentage of chance of hitting the target. Almost immediately another 18 pounder fired a ball at the Gunboat. Whether it hit or not, nobody knew as it was too dark to see. Another French gunboat must have got within range, because a crashing sound, closely followed by a bang, took the steering wheel away, killing both helmsmen, badly injuring Miller. Will felt a sharp pain in his right leg as he found himself dropping to the deck. Cranfield ran towards him.

"You alright Sir?" He asked anxiously, as more carronades and 18 pounders opened up making conversation impossible. Will looked around to find Miller groaning nearby. Tarrant's loud voice, calm but authoritative, was ordering hands to the steering lines.

"Get Captain Miller to the Surgeon!" Ordered Will; before he passed out with the pain in his leg.

Will awoke wondering where he was in the semi-darkness. He could hear groaning from nearby, and it brought it all back to him. A shadow fell across him and somebody took his hand to feel his pulse.

"What's happening?" Whispered Will.

"Oh you're back with us are you? Fine mess you made of things, getting felled just at the wrong time!" de Cornes familiar and reassuring voice came from above him.

"What happened? Is the ship alright?" Will whispered.

"Well, sorry to say we lost three hands. Captain Miller will live...just, he has a bad wound in the abdomen, but they got him down here quick enough for me to be able to patch him up. Five wounded in various places, not including a certain Commodore! Cranfield has assumed command. He will be down soon I should think. We are if I am informed correctly about to rejoin *Augusta* and *Tara*."

Will relaxed slightly and wondered why he did not feel worse.

"You Commodore Calvert have a flesh wound to the leg. How you achieved that I hate to think, but I have cleaned it up and sewn it up. You will walk again! You might have a slight limp to go with the pugilist's nose, so you will frighten even more ladies, and put the fear of God up the French once more." de Cornes sounded jovial.

Will lay listening to the familiar sounds of the ship. He could not hear any pumps, so that meant that the hull could not be damaged below the water line. He felt slightly light headed and realised he had felt this way before, when he had been given Laudanum. Down here, besides the groans of the wounded, the song of the ship was very different from his cabin on the upper deck. He must have drifted off, because he woke to find Cranfield speaking to him.

"What? I am sorry I must have dozed off, what did you say?"

"We have completed our first part of the operation successfully. We are sailing in line with the others of the flotilla. You know about Captain Miller and the others I am sure. Otherwise everything is fine, so don't worry."

Then Cranfield was gone, and Will dozed off again, to wake to the sound of the ship making an alteration of course. He could hear stamping feet right above his head, and wondered what could possibly cause men to march up and down in clogs on the deck above. Then as his faculties came back he realised it must be the steering party working the lines on the mess deck above. He must be in the Orlop. Then he heard de Cornes' voice.

"Very gently lads, mind his right leg. Don't you dare let it strike anything, or I shall have to do some more needle point."

Then hands gently pushed something under his

308

back. Other hands were at the other side, and then he was floating on canvas. He realised he was being moved. Tarrant's voice was giving orders somewhere near his head. He looked up and saw that the ladderway was appearing, then he was gently elevated from the head to a semi vertical position and passed up the ladderway to other waiting hands. Then it was round in an arc, still in the same position and up another ladderway where there was much more light. He realised he was on the upper deck, the cannons neatly lashed to the cross beams above the gun ports. Then he was carried through to his sleeping cabin and gently lowered into his cot. Smiling faces came and went as the canvas they had carried him in, was slid from around him. Tarrant loomed over him.

"Alright Skipper?" He asked.

"Thank you my friend, Yes!"

Then it was de Cornes. "Another twelve hours before you need to worry about anything. Cranfield has the whole thing under control."

"How did the operation go?" Asked Will, now propped up against pillows, and feeling more in control of his own destiny. Tarrant answered.

"You mean the attack, not your operation? Well Boulogne was lit up like a birthday cake. Explosions everywhere in the Port. I bet the French are asking themselves right at this moment, how come the English have such long range guns!"

"And the ship?"

"We are in the process of mounting a steering tiller and lines on the quarterdeck. The Carpenter has drilled two holes in the quarterdeck, so we can pass the cable up through blocks to the tiller. Using a spare yard attached to the mizzen. The length of the yard should give adequate leverage for the helmsmen."

"What about the others?"

"They signalled as soon as it was light, that they were alright. We haven't found out how it went for them, but I assume it was good, because Derwent had a smile on his chops. I took a look through your scope. Sorry but it was handy."

"Where are we?"

"Middle of the Channel, stalking up and down. Winds got up a bit, so the sea is a bit on the turbulent side for landing. Expect it will drop as it gets dark." Tarrant's name was called and he excused himself and was gone.

Will forced himself to try and relax. Millward came over with a drink, which helped a lot. Will then dropped off to sleep, to be woken by Millward with food. Through the open door to his day cabin, he could see that it was beginning to get dark. An hour or so later de Cornes came to ask if he felt he could stand on his good leg.

"I can try!" Replied Will. So with Millward on one side, and de Cornes on the other he managed to put his left leg on the deck whilst still leaning on his cot, which was now at an angle to the deck. Using his two aids, he found he could move putting his weight solely on his left leg and hopping.

"Feel like going up on deck?" Asked de Cornes.

"I doubt if I could stand for long." Replied Will.

"No need, we've put one of your easy-chairs up there. You can sit and give orders to your heart's content."

"The men at the wheel?"

"Killed outright. Wouldn't have felt a thing!" Said de Cornes.

"Oh God , Allwood!"

"Allwood wasn't at the wheel. Remember?"

"Oh yes! Sorry!"

Hopping as he went, he managed to get forward to the ladderway to the quarterdeck. Here they allowed him to rest, before he attempted the climb. He was touched to realise that seamen had come forward to give assistance. With the rolling motion of the ship, he would not have made it, if it hadn't been for the extra hands. It was quite a sight. Where the wheel had stood, protected by Will's patent screens, there was now a hole in the deck. Seamen stood either side of the horizontal yard that was secured to the mizzen mast about three feet from the deck. Lines from blocks on either side ran across the deck to the yard. Will was lifted bodily over the steering lines and placed in a seat lashed to the larboard side of the mizzen mast. From here he could see exactly what was happening. Cranfield came up with a smile and just stood a few feet away, quietly giving orders when necessary. Elliot Crosby, the new third officer had the watch. He was a very quiet man of about thirty, of stocky build he was a competent sea officer, if not very charismatic.

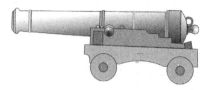

Optimist and the two Brig-Sloops would be about five miles off the coast guarding the three gunboats, which would be rowed into try and retrieve the landing parties. It was a very dark night, and the sea state meant that it was not going to be easy for the cutters towed by the gunboats to get to the beach. One ship's cutter had a detachment of black coated marines ready to give covering fire. The other three would be ready for the Royalists if they appeared. The cutters would only go in if the correct signal was given from the land. From where Will sat he could only occasionally see the dim outline of the French coast, when *Optimist* rolled that way. In the half-light Will made out the shape of Thomas Tucker standing nearby, a scope hanging by his side.

"Thomas? How goes it?"

"I can just make out one of the gunboats, but it is too dark to see the others."

"Any sign of any French craft?"

"Not at the moment. Luckily the moon has decided to stay in bed tonight."

The waiting went on, and on. They all realised that there was not going to be a retrieval that night.

Cranfield came over and asked permission to recall the gunboats. Will refused, pointing out that any signal would alert the French onshore. The skippers of the Gunboats, should realise, if they had studied their orders closely enough, that Will had laid down a retirement at the change to the morning watch.

It was a cold dispirited Will who was helped back to his cot. He feared that the Royalists had been caught. His idea, his responsibility! However well the operation had gone, and there was no knowing; if the Royalist were taken, it was on his shoulders that the blame would lie.

The pain in the leg returned as the Laudanum wore off. De Cornes did not want to give him too much, as Will was still in command. As long as *Optimist* cruised in the Channel, the flotilla would stay together awaiting his orders. The day dragged by, until once again as it grew dark Will was helped up on deck. From his chair he read the burial service whilst there was still enough light, and the poor fellows who had given their lives for their country were committed to the deep. Miller was conscious, just, but would have to be dropped off at Haslar for the Naval Hospital when they finally returned to England. At midnight the flotilla returned to the French coast. Once again *Optimist* and the two Brig-sloops kept guard, whilst the gunboats approached the shore. Tucker had appointed himself, Will's eyes for the night and reported when he could see anything. The wind had dropped a bit and the sea was calmer with the occasional white cap to remind them it was in charge, as always.

"Light on the coast!" Tucker sang out. Then: "Yes it is the signal!" There was another agonising wait, as it was too dark to make out what was happening at that distance. Then after another hour and a half of lying wallowing, sails backed, there was a report from a gun, followed by another and then a third. That was the signal that all three gunboats were back at sea. It did not mean that they had been successful; it just meant they had left the coast. Another hour passed and then three shots came out of the dark, closely followed by another three. That was the signal that the Royalists had been taken off.

Cranfield had obviously studied the orders, because he gave the order to get under way. A lantern was brought aft to be hung from the stern of *Optimist* to give a guiding light to the other members of the flotilla. Once again Will was helped below to lie wondering, always wondering how many had survived.

At first light the shadow of land appeared on the starboard bow. Slowly as the sun rose behind them they were able to make out the familiar low cliffs of Bembridge on the Isle of Wight, with the windmill behind. Will was brought up and ordered a signal to be flown for the rest of the Flotilla to anchor in St Helen's Row off Bembridge Village. Once all the ships were safely anchored, the hoist for Captains to repair aboard was made. *Augusta* was first off the mark with Craddock arriving and being piped aboard. The Derwent from *Tara* was next. The three Lieutenants in command of the gunboats had to use their cutters, so took slightly longer to make it. Will, sitting in an Easy-chair in his day cabin welcomed them as they entered together. Millward carried a tray of drinks around, before disappearing.

"Right, reports please!"

Craddock was the senior commander, but he turned to Derwent who in turn put out his hand indicating that Lieutenant James of the Gunboat *Seahorse* should speak first.

"I have to report Commodore that we successfully landed the marines to cover the retirement of our French colleagues." Then Lieutenant Elder of the gunboat *Hercules* spoke.

"I have to report that we took seventeen of the Frenchmen off the beach." He turned to his fellow Lieutenant standing slightly back.

"I have to report that we took seven off, but one died last night." That was Lieutenant Forrester of gunboat *Miranda*.

Will regarded them for a moment, letting them consider what their replies might be to any questions he was likely to ask.

"So twenty-four made it back alive. Do we know what happened to the others?"

"Sir, I took off the Boulogne party. Two were killed; I am not sure how, and four are missing. Those four failed to turn up at the rendezvous." Lieutenant Elder stated.

"Two of the Bresle party are missing, reason not known. They failed to arrive at the rendezvous as well. One died apparently mortally wounded by a musket shot."

"Have we any idea as to what they achieved?" Asked Will. Both Lieutenants Elder and Forrester took papers from their inside pockets and handed them to Will.

"Excuse me Commodore, but what happened to you?" Asked Lieutenant James.

"Just a leg wound! Not sure how it happened, but they got Captain Miller. He is seriously wounded and we shall be taking him to Haslar. We lost our wheel and with it two very fine quartermasters." Will pursed his lips. He then opened each piece of paper in turn. Here written in French was the report of what the team leaders felt they had achieved.

The first was from the Boulogne team. They had successfully managed to get down the river to the port where they had set the charges from the coracles. They had then managed to get back up the river setting charges and delivering the acid, finally using the oil and fuses. By this time the first fuse had been primed and then the subsequent ones on the larger vessels. There had been wild scenes with troops and sailors rushing about wondering how the English could shoot so far. Then three of the team had been seen in a stolen boat. They had been challenged, but had convinced those on shore they were trying to cut out the Gunboats to save them. One of the stolen boats had capsized, but it was not known what had happened to those on board. The team leader was certain that the explosive charges set on the larger vessels had gone off, but what damaged had occurred was not known, because of the risk of being caught.

A very similar report was penned by the leader of the Bresle team. Their oil attack had gone well. They had managed to pour a lot into a number of the Caiques. Their charge laying had not been so successful as unlike Boulogne, the vessels were manned. However a number had burned and the fires had spread to those alongside. What had happened was that those onboard the Caiques had tried to push them off the mud, and where successful, there were not enough crew to control them, so they had floated down stream setting fire to others. Again numbers damaged or destroyed were not known. Trying to get away, a group of eight had been fired at and the fellow who had subsequently died had been hit in the shoulder. When they tried to rendezvous, two failed to appear. They had no idea what had happened to them.

Optimist left the rest of the flotilla and sailed into Portsmouth Harbour, to drop off Captain Miller. He was rowed in Will's gig and then carried to the new hospital, with de Cornes in attendance. Later *Optimist* returned to St. Helen's Row, with de Cornes back on board. Then in the late afternoon they upped anchor and sailed West for Dartmouth. Once again the winds were not kind. A westerly meant that they had to make broad tacks to reach their destination, although the use of the tides did help. Obviously their progress was slowed by the slowest vessel which was the Schank fitted gunboat. The difference in speed was somewhat levelled by the fact that the gunboats were schooner rigged and therefore able to sail closer to the wind.

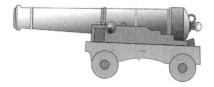

Isabella was appalled to find that her husband had been injured again. De Cornes assured her that Will would be able to walk and ride again within a month or so, but this did little to placate her. The one consolation she had was that she could look after him in their own home.

Will had written a full report to Wickham, and received a terse 'thank you' note. Will was certain that he would lose command of *Optimist*, now that the enterprise was over. He waited for letters from the Admiralty Board, but nothing came. Now that Captain Miller was no longer aboard *Optimist*, Will decided he had probably reverted to plain Captain.

No reports of the expedition had appeared in the Gazette. There was a complete silence from the British Government over the whole affair. Three weeks later whilst Will convalesced at home Wickham sent a secret report. In it he revealed that the expedition had been a partial success in putting out of action twenty or so Caiques, and disabling a couple of Prames, and other vessels, although none had sunk as had been planned. What had been achieved though was the belief on the French side of the Channel, that the British had new long range cannons and rockets. The feeling amongst the

French Military in charge of Napoleon's invasion fleet was that Boulogne was now not considered to be as safe a harbour as before. If the British could fire at that range into their harbour unchallenged, what could they do at sea to an invasion fleet making its way across the Channel? Apparently Sir Sydney Smith was still pressing to use 'Mr. Francis' torpedoes in an attack on the guard ships outside the port.

Then Will read that Sir Sydney Smith had attacked the gunboats off Boulogne using a new secret weapon. It looked as if Will's ideas were no longer flavour of the month. Then another secret missive arrived from Wickham exploding the myth put about by Sir Sydney; his attack had been a failure. Lord Barham, as First Lord at the Admiralty, had demanded to see the secret intelligence about Will's expedition. He now wanted to know if such an attack could be mounted on Brest Harbour to sink the French Fleet. Wickham through intermediaries had let it be known that there was not enough intelligence. Agents would have to be injected into the harbour to report the situation.

Still Will waited. Now able to walk again, he took *Optimist* and its flotilla to sea, to keep the crews up to the mark. The Royalists were still aboard and getting used to life in the Navy. Reports filtered back to Will that the food was the best they had eaten since leaving France. Certainly it helped that they were being provisioned from Dartmouth so fresh meat and vegetables were the order of the day. The French also started to acquire a liking for the beer drunk by the sailors aboard. Since no news or orders had filtered down to them and the weather was getting decidedly wintery, Will took *Optimist* back to Portsmouth Harbour, leaving Craddock in command of the rest of the flotilla. From here he hired a chaise to take him to London and the Admiralty. Still a Commodore, he was not kept waiting around as long as some. He was seen almost immediately after arriving. A harassed William Marsden greeted him.

"We are still considering a raid on Brest, but await more information." Marsden rubbed his head distractedly. "I fear we might be at the mercy of the French. What if their rush westwards was a feint. They could be heading back to join up with the Brest fleet. Stay in London tonight, I shall try to have a word with the First Lord tomorrow. Come back in the afternoon."

Will spent the night at Kenton House, before returning the next afternoon.

Finally the long awaited order arrived. *Optimist* was to join Lord Nelson's fleet. It was an emergency; they needed as many frigates as possible to scour the area for the French. The problem was that nobody knew where the fleet might be. Nelson's fleet had disappeared along with the French Fleet from Toulon. The latest information was that they had sailed west. Will was told to collect his commission first thing the next day.

Early next morning Will had himself carried by

chair to the Admiralty. However he was not the first caller. Rumours were flying around of a great victory at sea, but also the death of Lord Nelson.

Will had to wait along with a growing number of officers. Finally he was the first to be called to see Marsden.

"Very sad news I am afraid. Admiral Nelson is dead. He died as his fleet won a crushing victory over the Allied fleet off Cape Trafalgar. The battle took place on the 21st October. We have only just received the intelligence. Lieutenant Lapenotaire of the sloop *Pickle* brought the news. Apparently there were severe gales immediately after the victory, so all communication was delayed. I am afraid I must let you go. Come back tomorrow. Just remember we have lost our Admiral, but he has destroyed all chance of the French being able to invade our shores!"

The next day there was still no news or orders for Will or *Optimist*. Will left word that he would return to his base on the Dart and continue to train the Royalists in case they were needed for an expedition against the French mainland.

Will returned to Portsmouth and *Optimist* to sail back to the Dart to await further orders. Their joining of the Mediterranean fleet had been revoked. Obviously any attempt on Brest was now doubtful.

One advantage as far as Will was concerned was that he could return to Isabella who was now beginning to show a small bump. November turned into December and the flotilla arranged their own

Christmas celebrations. On Christmas day Will took a service aboard *Optimist* and Isabella joined the officers for Christmas lunch aboard. The table was extended to accommodate all the officers from the ships in the flotilla. Will's own chef prepared as French inspired meal as possible to Henri de Cornes instructions and this was served for the Royalists on Boxing Day in the Dining Room of Calvert House. New Year came and passed with an invitation for Commodore Calvert to attend the funeral of the late lamented Admiral Nelson.

Isabella insisted that she would like to go to London with Will to at least witness the procession. The Kentons demurred from joining them. On the day after New Year, the Calvert convoy started out for a slow trip to Kenton House in London. Millward and Allwood went in the second coach along with Isabella's maid and the nurse with baby Mary

Once in London they found an invitation for Isabella to witness the procession from the windows of a house on the Strand, thanks to the Castlereaghs. Will was surprised to find that he was expected to walk with other senior Naval Officers behind the funeral carriage. There were five days free before the coffin would be brought up the Thames to lie at the Admiralty for the night before the actual funeral. Isabella insisted that the Castlereaghs should go with them to see the new house in Highgate. The Salon was part furnished, but the private Sitting Room was complete, so the servants lit a fire there. They had taken a picnic with them and dined at the new table in the formal Dining Room, with a blazing fire in the hearth. The Castlereaghs were much taken with the house and were particularly taken with the view across London, when the rain lifted and all was revealed.

They joined their friends to watch the water borne procession pass up to the Westminster Steps. Isabella much moved by the Royal Barge draped in black which carried the coffin of the hero. The day of the funeral was a nightmare. Because the procession was to leave the Admiralty, the crowds had arrived to line the streets early. It was difficult for the Calvert coach to force a passage to the house, from which Isabella would be watching the procession. It was even worse trying to get to the Admiralty, so Will instructed it to drop him off beside St. James Park, so that he could walk the short distance to the back of that building. Once inside he found himself surrounded by Admirals of every hue; Blue, White and Red. He was by far the youngest and the lowest in that Rank, but looking about he realised that there seemed over a hundred Captains. Admiral the Lord St. Vincent spied him and came across to speak to him, which immediately showed that he was well regarded. After that various Admirals he had served under had a few words as they waited to leave. Captain Crick came over and congratulated Will on his rank.

Finally the coffin was taken out and placed by members of *Victory's* crew aboard the carriage which apparently was supposed to represent the ship herself. Will thought that it would have been more tasteful for it to have been a plain gun carriage. Then the coffin's carriage moved off drawn by six horses, followed by the Military and their bands. Once the coffin was on its way the Admirals filed out into the courtyard; followed by the Captains. Will made sure he was at the head of the later group, as he didn't want to upset those above him in the pecking order. As it was he need not have worried, the groups tended to intermingle as people drifted towards those they knew best. Captain Crick was now a relatively senior Captain and he joined Will at the beginning as they set off.

"Always knew you would do well for yourself, but I never expected you to advance quite so quickly. What have you been up to?" He asked.

"I am afraid that some of what I have been engaged in is highly secret, so I am not at liberty to discuss it. Otherwise I have had the honour to Captain the frigate *Optimist*."

"So I heard. Saw your ship off Ushant. You escorted *Victory* back to England. Did you get to meet him?"

"I had that honour a number of times. I served under his command in the Med, but as an independent."

"Never got to meet him. Was he as charismatic as everybody seems to be saying?"

"I found that he had a very quick brain. You only had to suggest something once and he would give you a reasoned argument whatever he thought about it."

"So you liked him?"

"What little I had to do with him, yes."

"And I gather that you are 'Sir William'. How did that come about?"

"His Majesty was kind enough to allow me to inherit an old title. It is a Baronetcy."

"Oh! Well that can't be sneezed at can it? Must help in your dealings with the Admiralty."

"Well when you don't have any influence at Court or in either House, it probably does open a few doors."

At that moment an Admiral drifted across to join them. He had a long face with a high forehead and hooded eyes.

"You Calvert?" He asked bluntly.

"Yes my Lord!" Will thought it prudent to add the 'My Lord' as most Admirals were made Barons.

"At last we meet Sir William. I am Keith."

"I would normally say a pleasure to meet you, but I am not sure quite what one should say at such a time."

"I appreciate your tact. I have heard a lot about you. I was even instructed to keep my ships away from Boulogne in October last year. Only found out later it was at the express demand of the Duke of York. Then I finally discovered it was so your band of cut-throats could attack the Port. Nobody seems to say much about it, so I gather it must have been a similar damp squid to that of Smith."

"I am restrained by a vow of secrecy to talk about it, My Lord. I must say I am extremely surprised that you as Commander-in-Chief of the Area have not been informed as to exactly what occurred. If I was in your position I would be very angry."

Keith looked surprised. He was now walking beside Will, with his eyes to the front as they passed by a very subdued crowd lining the street on either side.

"I am warming to you Calvert. I appreciate your forthrightness. I did tackle Barham, but he said virtually the same thing. May I ask, without compromising you, were you successful?"

Will paused to think about his answer. "I think the French might be forgiven for thinking that the British Armament on their ships has been greatly upgraded. "

Keith took a sideways glance at Will.

"Oh! So it was more successful than Smith's?"

Will was about to say that intelligence suggested so, when he stopped himself, because he knew Lord Keith despised 'Intelligence'. Instead he said. "Well we managed to sink quite a number of their landing craft and support vessels, well beyond their line of defence."

"You staying in London?"

"Yes My Lord."

"Good, where?"

"Kenton House My Lord."

"So a note would find you?"

"Certainly My Lord."

Keith nodded and drifted off to join other Admirals. Crick returned to his position beside Will.

"Doesn't sound as if he is a friend of yours!"

"First time I have met him!"

"Ah! Didn't like to eavesdrop too much. So you parted on amicable terms?"

"Frankly I haven't a clue. He did ask where I was staying."

"Sounds much more promising!"

The long walk began to have its effect on Will. His recent injury began to pain greatly. He was grateful when at last the procession delivered them up to St. Pauls. His seat was in a terrible position, so he could not see a thing that was going on. Another Admiral was heard to voice his complaint rather loudly. For Will he was just grateful to have a seat, especially as the service went on and on.

Five hours after it had begun, the service drew to a close. Will waited until most of the Congregation had left before attempting to leave. Various Captains he had met came within his orbit and had a word or two, but it was such a scrum, it was difficult to have a reasonable conversation. Once out of the Cathedral and into the winter sunlight, Will was faced with how to get back to where Isabella was being entertained by the Castlereaghs. He decided to walk, but struck south to the river to try and avoid the crowds. The two mile walk after the one in the morning, brought back the pain in his leg, so when he finally arrived he was limping. He tried to disguise the fact, but Castlereagh was too sharp-eyed.

"Why Will, your limping. Wound giving you trouble?"

"Just not used to walking quite so far."

After a late supper with the Castlereaghs, Will and Isabella returned to Kenton House exhausted.

Isabella thought her husband had looked very smart as he marched past.

The next day they spent their time at the new Calvert London House. It was decided to move their servants the next day and then follow the day after, so the servants could get used to their new surroundings. Will suddenly remembered to make sure that any missives were to be sent round to the new address immediately. Allwood would make the trip each afternoon after dinner to make sure nothing was missed. Will himself went to the Admiralty to inform them of his new address, but did not bother to try and see Marsden.

The move to their new house in London went fairly smoothly, as there was no furniture to move. They spent a fortnight at the new house, Will waiting for news from the Admiralty. They invited their friends to a series of dinners to repay them for past courtesies. Then came the news that the Prime Minister, William Pitt had died, two weeks after Nelson's funeral As a result Lord Grenville became Prime Minister. With the change there was change at the Admiralty. There were nearly three weeks of confusion and then George Grenville formed a Ministry of all the talents. Charles Grey, Viscount Howick was named as First Lord of the Admiralty. With still nothing from the Admiralty Will realised he had to return to *Optimist*. As a result the Calvert convoy would once again make the trip to Devon, so that Will could return to the little flotilla.

During the political vacuum Castlereagh managed to meet up with Will.

"Will did you hear about the question in the house?"

Will shook his head.

"Well one of the Members asked a question as to why a junior Captain was made a Commodore when there were plenty of more senior Captains on the Navy List."

"And?"

"Well as you know the new First Lord; Viscount Howick has only just taken up his post. He said that if the Honourable Member gave him chapter and verse he would look into it. He took it to Earl St Vincent. That noble Earl was furious. He demanded to know who the member was who asked the question. When told he realised it was Captain Lamphrey's brother in law. Lamphrey is in command of a third rate with the Channel Squadron. He was hauled before the Admiral and given a dressing down for questioning the wisdom of their Lords of the Admiralty. He was told in no uncertain manner that it was a black mark against him for raising such a question."

"Oh God, a new enemy. There are enough jealous Captains as it is!" Groaned Will.

"Ah, but that's not all. Apparently he was told that since the country was at war, they needed the most brilliant minds in command. From now on talent would take precedence over age and it was no longer a question of patronage!"

329

"I doubt that the Navy can change!"

The Admiral added that Commodore was a temporary rank normally. The Admiralty used it to make sure that Senior Captains didn't interfere with their orders. He ended by suggesting that Lamphrey might look to his own record as he had never commanded in battle!"

"Really?"

"Absolutely. Thought you'd be pleased! Oh, by the way what did you mean 'more enemies'?"

"Well I noticed the looks I got when we were following the coffin. Talk about daggers!"

"But there weren't that many Captains in the precession!"

"But there were a lot on the route!"

Back in Devon there was a letter from Nova Scotia, saying that the schooner was well under way and plans for the owners suite under the poop deck would be appreciated. Will was undecided as to the feasibility of the whole venture, now that Napoleon was threatening Portugal, which would have been the schooners natural trading area. There was no way he could cancel the construction as it was too far advanced. A week after they had returned a letter arrived forwarded from Calvert House London. It was from Lord Keith, who expressed the wish to meet Will properly when he was next in London with any time to spare. He, Lord Keith was headquartered at Walmer.

Finally an Admiralty messenger arrived at the

Devon House. The flotilla was to be broken up. The various vessels and their crews assigned to different commands. Will was to take command of an 84 gun ship of the line, the HMS *Imperial*. He was to take command of the ship which was refitting at Chatham. Will immediately replied to the order, but added a letter asking permission to take with him the Surgeon as well as his usual Coxswain, servant and clerk.

As soon as the crew got wind of the loss of their captain the requests came thick and fast. Heading the list was Boatswain Tarrant, who asked if he could join Will in any capacity. It was normal for the Boatswain to remain with the ship. A Boatswain was a 'Standing Officer' which meant he was a Warrant Officer assigned to the ship. The list of men requesting a transfer was so great that Number One decided to forward the list to the Admiralty under his own name, as if he passed it on to Will it might embarrass him. Nobody knew what was going to happen to *Optimist*, as no order had arrived. Will had his furniture packed up and shipped ashore to Calvert House for onward transmission to his new command. He was no longer a Commodore, just a plain captain.

Since it was now the end of February, Will would travel without Isabella. She would remain in Devon until such time as Will knew where his new ship was to be stationed. After a farewell dinner given by the Officers of all ships in the flotilla, Will was rowed ashore to cheers from his crew.

The trip to Chatham was tedious in the extreme.

The coaches got bogged down in the deeply rutted turnpikes, and it took time to pull them free. Luckily because they were travelling in convoy, they were able to un-hitch horses from the other coaches to add to the team pulling the bogged down coach. They stopped at the new London Calvert House for the second night, the first having been spent in a hostelry on route. The next day Will travelled through London to the South and on to Chatham Naval Dockyard.

Imperial was not a new ship. She had just been warped out of dry-dock and now sat in the basin. There was only a skeleton crew, most 'lent' from other ships so that she could be taken out of the dock. To Will's surprise the only Warrant officers aboard were the Sailmaker, the Carpenter, the Master and Gunner. The First Lieutenant, who met him on the quay, was an aged fellow with a stoop, premature grey hair, and a limp from an old wound. He did not instantly inspire confidence.

Viewing *Imperial* from the quayside Will was aware of her portly lines. She would be a slow sailor! Once aboard, after having been shown around by Lieutenant Kendal the aged First, he felt very depressed. The ship was not really fit for sea. She had a decided twist in her keel; added to that some of her 'knees' appeared to be rotten. She would have to be warped back into dry-dock to have the rotten timbers removed and replaced. How she had been passed fit for sea duty was an outrage that would have to be taken up with the Admiralty.

Having made a detailed list of the faults, he

tackled the Superintendent of the dockyard. This man was truculent. He suggested that if Will was to pay himself, things might proceed a good deal faster. It had been Lord Jervis, when First Lord, who had stirred up a hornet's nest by implying that the dockyards were a disgrace. This was proof, if ever there was any, that it still prevailed. Will immediately called for a coach and had himself taken back to London, and next day the Admiralty. He had a long wait. He was no longer a Commodore, so his seniority reverted to his position on the Navy List. Late in the afternoon he was at long last shown into Marsden's office.

"I thought you would be in Chatham taking up your command!" Marsden said as Will walked in. The man looked tired out.

"I am very sorry that I have to trouble you again, I know you have much to deal with, but I should like to leave you this list of defects to consider, as well as informing you that the Superintendent suggested that if I was to pay him, the defects could be rectified very quickly!"

Will presented his list of defects.

"Sir William, do sit down, let me quickly scan your list."

Marsden untied the file and started to read. Every now and then he would look up and tut, before returning to the list.

"And you consider the *Imperial* unfit for sea?"

"I understand she has been used as a hulk, before being brought back. No maintenance has been carried out obviously. Frankly, and the Gunner agrees with me; the first time we fire a broadside, we will blow out our own sides!"

"Let me take this up with the Board. As you are probably aware there have been changes here at the Admiralty. I shall take this up with a Naval Member of the Board, and see if we can progress from there."

"Thank you Sir. I shall remain in London, staying at my London address."

"Not to the ship?"

"No I have not read myself in. Frankly I shall refuse to take the ship to sea, even if ordered. I shall not risk the lives of over seven hundred men!"

"I take your point. I shall raise the matter with the Board tomorrow

Will sent a message to Lieutenant Kendal, informing him of the position.

Will did not hear a thing for two weeks. He realised it was going to take some time to resolve, so sent for Isabella and the family to join him. After all it would soon be the Season again, and Isabella would enjoy seeing their friends again.

No sooner had Isabella settled into the London House, than a message arrived summoning Will to the Admiralty to see the First Lord.

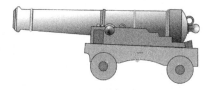

Charles Grey, Viscount Howick, was seated behind his huge desk in the First Lord's Office when Will was shown in. He recognised the gentleman as having been pointed out to him by Castlereagh. The Viscount had slanting eyes over a long nose, but the expression seemed friendly.

"Sir William, I am delighted to meet you. Though I feel we have met somewhere – one of the clubs I expect. Do take a seat. Now I understand that you were given command of the err...*Imperial* a second rate 80 gunner. I gather you consider she is not fit to go to sea, let alone fight."

Will nodded to confirm Howicks's summary.

"Marsden informs me that you are a very distinguished officer, with an unblemished record. Added to that, I had the pleasure of dining with the noble Earl St. Vincent the other night, and your name came up. As you know or may not know, I am presenting before the House a motion to thank Lord St Vincent for his endeavours in trying to eliminate corruption in the Naval Yards. He gave me a brief background summary on your secret service to the Nation. He said most emphatically that if you declared the ship to be unseaworthy, it would be unseaworthy! So just to let you know, I have rescinded your commission to *Imperial*."

"Thank you Sir!"

"I gather that you are personal friend of Castlereagh. He told me that you have ordered a schooner for trading with Portugal. Is that correct?"

"Yes Sir. I have approved the plans. She is being built in America, by the same yard that constructed the schooner *Snipe* that I had the pleasure to command."

"The one that was wrecked on the French coast when you were landing agents?"

"Exactly."

"You do realise that Napoleon has his eyes on Portugal. In fact we have just instructed Sir Sydney Smith to sail to Portugal to arrange for the safe transfer of the Royal Family to Brazil. We are informed that Napoleon might even consider invading that country to deny us their support. What Spain will make of that I have no idea! When will this schooner of yours be finished?"

"It will take about two more months. I shall dispatch a crew to bring her back to England when she has completed her trails." Will wondered where this was leading.

"You have distinguished yourself in a number of secret projects for the Nation, and they have remained secret which speaks volumes for the loyalty your crews seem to show to you. I gather that the complete complement of your last crew have petitioned the Admiralty to be allowed to serve on your new command."

"Really Sir! I had no idea"

"If Napoleon does set his sights on Portugal, we are going to have considerable problems. I doubt that we can stop him invading, but by Jove we can make it more difficult. What say you to the idea of chartering your schooner to the Navy?"

"Might I ask for what purpose?"

"The Board knows of your success in landing agents in the Channel. We shall have need of doing the same and some type of irregular forces into Northern Spain and Portugal. St. Vincent told me it was a brutal area for ships. Admiral Gambier is always complaining of the gales and winds whilst he tries to blockade Rochelle and Ferrol. I am not a Navy man, but Wickham and his friends were telling me how successful your raid on Boulogne had been. If we chartered your new ship, we should of course have to arm her..."

"Of course."

"Well what we thought was if we were to charter her and you were commissioned as her Captain, you would make the ideal team. You would of course be able to choose your crew!"

"I should like to consider this, if I might. I know this might sound strange, but I just wonder how this would affect my progress as far as promotion prospects."

You were a Commodore, were you not?"

"Yes I was."

"So if we reinstate you to that rank, that would place you in line for promotion to Rear Admiral, would it not?"

"Only if the rank was made permanent; which

337

would be most unusual."

"These are unusual times. We need the best, and you are considered to be one of the best!"

"Thank you Sir!"

"Gambier won't be pleased."

"Admiral Gambier? Sir!"

"Yes, he wrote that he was looking forward to have you as one of his officers. This new venture, would not come within his command. You would be on your own, once again. Answerable to the Board of Admiralty direct."

"I see."

"The Aliens Office is very worried. It is one thing to have plenty of 'agents' in Paris. It is totally another to have no agents in Northern Spain to get us intelligence. We desperately need to try and recruit agents in that area. I am informed however, that the area is divided into different regions that hardly talk to each other, let alone Madrid. Why they even speak different languages."

Will nodded so as to not interrupt the flow.

"So what they want – the Aliens Office – is to get you... they asked for you by name.... to call at the various ports along that coast and to try and make contact with gentlemen of influence, to recruit them as agents for the British Government."

"Can we wait for the schooner to be built?"

"It will take at least three months for us to get together interpreters for the various languages that can be trusted. Napoleon is otherwise engaged at the moment, so I doubt if he will make a move for another year or so." Lord Howick rested back

338

against the chair and considered Will carefully.

Will considered for a moment. Digesting what he had just heard.

"I should be allowed to choose my own crew?"

"Absolutely!"

"How soon do you want an answer?"

"As soon as possible, Commodore!"

Will gave a wry smile. "I take it that was a titbit to encourage me?"

Howick laughed. "Yes!"

§

William Calvert is back in Secret Assignment

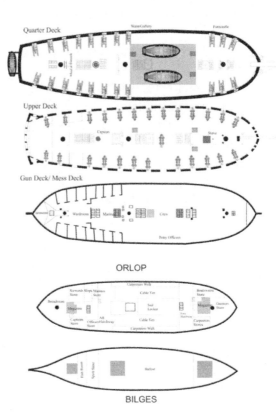

FRIGATE PLANS

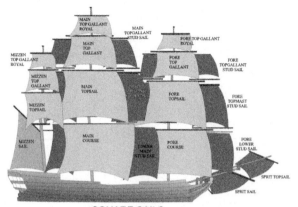

SQUARE SAILS

FORE AND AFT SAILS

Other works by Leighton Harding.
Calvert Series
When Duty Calls
Secret Assignment
Calvert's War of 1812

Havoc
Beyond Honour
Tirpitz Nemesis
Hunt the Bear
The Red Dressing Gown
Murder on TV

For more details including Naval terms etc go to:
www.leightonharding .com

Printed in Great Britain
by Amazon

51478443R00195